MURDER at FIRST PRINCIPLES

A novel by
BEN WIENER

Praise for *Murder at First Principles*

"A well-designed thriller that I didn't want to put down! Ben Wiener's incisive, fast-paced novel balances plot and well-developed characters with strategy lessons drawn from Hamilton Helmers' renowned *7 Powers*."

NICOLAS COLIN
Cofounder of The Family
Writer at *European Straits*
Author of *Hedge: A Greater Safety Net for the Entrepreneurial Age*

"Ben Wiener has a gift for weaving together clever, captivating narrative and essential startup principles. If you haven't yet read Ben's writing, *Murder at First Principles* is the place to start."

IAN HATHAWAY
Co-Author of *The Startup Community Way*

"An educating, entertaining, and captivating book for novices and executives alike. Ben Wiener makes important business strategy concepts accessible via an intriguing whodunit that perfectly captures the San Francisco Bay Area vibe. A fun read!"

JOSEPH LIPUMA
Senior Lecturer and Global Entrepreneurship Faculty
Boston University Questrom School of Business

"This page turner of a mystery book is an engaging way to dig deep into successful business strategies. I liked this book so much I read it a second time to get the business concepts that Wiener does such a good job of integrating into the mystery."

KERRY PLEMMONS
Professor of Practice
Daniels College of Business
University of Denver

Cover design by Tom Howey

ISBN: 979-8731225663

a PennedSource Production

To Shafrira

CHAPTER 1

ROCKY VIOLETTO WAS THE FIRST to die. I was there, the night he fell from his eighth-floor balcony at Bayside Towers in San Rafael. I cannot pretend that I foresaw the ensuing chain of events. I could not have dreamed how Rocky's death and the deaths that followed would thrust me, Addison Morita, the girl the world had left behind, into the action's vortex. How I would be catapulted from my dismal existence as a frustrated computer crime researcher into the heart of one of the most baffling homicide investigations in California history.

Rocky's body hit the pavement below Bayside Towers just before 10:00 p.m. on Thursday, the ninth of May. That night, and for most of the next week, nobody guessed Rocky's death was the first in a string of murders. Nobody even guessed Rocky had not jumped to his death, until the mysterious murderer told us so.

I was in North Tower, just one floor below Rocky who lived in 8A, visiting Elyse Bluth in 7B. I had paired up with Elyse for my first "Throwback Thursday" in weeks, maybe months. When the auto-email arrived on Monday morning, as always, with the subject "Business Strategy Seminar - Alumni TBT," I had decided to click the link to the shared document and tag Elyse for a TBT.

Two years since Professor Mallory's seminar and our subsequent graduation from First Principles College, even those of us who still lived in and around San Rafael hardly saw each other anymore. So I had gotten together with Elyse for a TBT because LinkedIn said she had been promoted *again* at Carrie's Cosmetics. Was this her third promotion in two years? Professor Mallory had helped her get the job, of course, through his Hollywood connections, but Elyse had done the rest, moving straight up the ladder on her merits. I had brought a bottle of Elyse's favorite Pinot Noir to celebrate her latest elevation in status.

I had come up from my apartment in South Tower around six o'clock, after riding home from the D.A.'s office, and it was now close to ten. We had been chatting and watching TV for hours. Elyse had dozed off after downing most of the wine while we talked. My own light-headedness was possibly a harbinger of the drama to come.

"Elyse, do you hear that? There are a lot of sirens outside." I jostled Elyse's leg. We both rested on her couch, across from the softly babbling TV, with the empty wine bottle on the coffee table before us.

"You go check it out," Elyse muttered with a passing wave, only partially alert.

As I rose from the couch, my legs Charley-horsed. I wobbled toward Elyse's porch and slid open the screen door. Flashing lights cascaded across the building's facade. At least four Sheriff's cruisers had arrived at the base of North Tower.

"There are a bunch of police cars down there. I'm going to see what's happening," I called out to Elyse, as I ducked back inside the apartment. Elyse mumbled something incoherent as I hastened into the hallway toward the elevator.

Despite my curiosity about the commotion downstairs, I rode the elevator to the lobby without undue agitation. Bayside Towers generally enjoyed quiet and tranquility, with very little crime or police activity. Though college students populated most of the complex's apartments, First Principles students generally behaved peaceably.

The elevator doors glided open at the ground floor, and two square-jawed officers faced me, their burly chests and arms bursting out of light tan uniforms and large revolvers protruding from their waistbands. They pushed brusquely past me into the elevator without a glance.

My reflection in the lobby mirror confronted me. Was the pony-tailed young woman facing me that shabby-looking after four hours of after-work wine with Elyse? My half-Japanese, half-German look, my lean and athletic figure, could usually turn a guy's head. But none of that had attracted either of those two cops' attention, even for one second.

Police cars blocked the entire traffic circle in front of Bayside Towers' two tall apartment buildings. The clamor of police radios and deputies yelling at people to stand clear shocked me as I exited the lobby doors. A crowd gathered behind a hastily erected yellow tape barrier. Patrons streamed out of Christie's, the sports bar just beyond the Bayside Towers parking lot, toward the tumult.

I shielded my eyes in the darkness from the blinding, flashing lights. Two more of my former Mallory seminar-mates who lived at Bayside, Tiffany Chen and Brian Monroe, stood together off to the side of the yellow barrier.

"What's going on?" I called out, trotting toward them. Brian, in slippers, a muscle shirt and sweatpants, held his mouth agape, and Tiffany had both palms pressed to her cheeks in horror, her straight, jet-black hair in sharp contrast to her blood-drained complexion.

"Crazy," said Brian, shaking his head. "I think it's Rocky." He pointed up at the North Tower. A number of policemen jostled on a balcony at the top of the building. *One, two, three*...I counted eight floors. Elyse's porch, where I had been standing moments before, was just below and to the right of the officers. Elyse was now outside on her porch. She gawked down and then diagonally up at the commotion.

I put my hand to my mouth and gasped. "He jumped?" I asked. Tiffany remained unresponsive.

Brian shrugged sadly. "That's what it looks like," he said. "It's crazy, man. Crazy, crazy, crazy."

"Was anything going on with him?" I asked. Tiffany faintly shook her head, still transfixed, catatonically staring straight ahead. A detective crouched on the sidewalk, covering a large, limp body with a blue plastic tarp. I averted my eyes, unable to bear the sight of blood. "Wait...Didn't Rocky have a TBT tonight with Peter?" I asked.

Tiffany broke her stare and faced me. "You're right...I saw that on the sign-up sheet," she said, her shaky voice just above a whisper. "So bizarre...Wonder if something happened between him and Peter..."

"It's crazy," repeated Brian, his eyes still wide. We stood, an island of stunned silence in the midst of the cacophony and chaos.

After a long pause between us, Brian pronounced, "I don't think we're going to find out anything tonight." Shaking his head again, Brian left us and shuffled his slippers on the pavement as he plodded back toward the entrance to North Tower.

I clutched Tiffany around her shoulder, embracing her tightly. Her palms were back on her cheeks as she watched the policemen and medical personnel moving between their cars, Rocky's body, and an ambulance that was now on the scene.

"I wasn't even so friendly with him," Tiffany said softly. "He was just...in our class, you know? I hadn't even seen him in months. Where did he work?" She glanced at me for help in placing Rocky.

"He is—was—at Netflix, I think. Him and Cindy, from our class."

"Right," Tiffany said, shifting her confounded gaze back toward Rocky's lifeless form, now fully covered in blue plastic. As if continuing to stare at Rocky could make him rise again.

"I wonder if he left a note..." Her voice tailed off.

Rocky Violetto had not left a note, because he had not jumped. The only communication relating to the cause of Rocky's death would be an anonymous email. Sent by Rocky's killer, a week after his death. Addressed to me.

CHAPTER 2

ANDY FREEL, WELCOMING REMARKS, FIRST Principles College Freshman Orientation

"*Hey, everybody, I am incredibly excited to welcome you, as the initial class of First Principles College. You are all awesome.*

"*For those of you who don't know me, or haven't played any of my video games, I'm Andy Freel, founder of Endscape Labs, and the founder of First Principles College. I created this school, because my friends and I in the world of technology innovation can't find enough qualified, young and diverse entrepreneurs and business leaders for our companies. So we're going to produce them, here at First Principles College. Together with my good friend and partner, Doug Mallory, Founding Dean, we have put together a fantastic curriculum that will immerse you in scientific method as it applies to innovative thinking.*

"Our mission statement is 'Truth is as diverse as the colors of the rainbow.' You will pursue fundamental truths in every aspect of your studies, the way great leaders from Rene Descartes to Elon Musk have used first principles methodology as their philosophical guide. You will distill every topic, every issue, every subject, into its foundational elements. This skill, honed over time, will give you special superpowers as you enter the world of disruptive technology.

"You guys are the best and brightest, and I strongly believe that in a couple of years, you will be at the forefront of the next generation of leaders, moving our greatest companies toward, and past, society's boundaries and frontiers."

$$\Omega$$

Thwack. Thwack. Thwack.

No matter how tight I pulled its elastic strings, the small nylon rucksack wedged between my shoulder blades always had just enough slack to smack against my back as I jogged.

Thwack. Thwack. Thwack.

My Saturday morning run was my weekly religious rite, my church, my two hours of Zen. Perhaps the rucksack smacking me was part of the ritual, some subconscious purifying self-flagellation.

Thwack. Thwack. Thwack.

The rucksack held, as always, a bottle of G Zero Berry, some energy gels, and my wallet and phone, just in case. I ran without music, instead soaking in the serene surroundings of San Francisco Bay, and the sights and sounds of the gliding, swooping oystercatchers and egrets.

My Saturday long run, often as far as ten miles round trip, out to the bay along Point San Pedro Road and back to Bayside Towers, was my time to contemplate, reflect and plan.

This week, thoughts of Rocky's death dominated my run. The tragedy had already galvanized the rusting social wiring of our Mallory alumni group. After two years, few of us kept up the TBTs anymore. Based on my review of the TBT sign-up sheet Saturday morning, other than me and Elyse, and Peter with Rocky, nobody else had paired up on Thursday.

But in the past two days the email group had crackled to life with a flurry of "reply-alls." Condolences, and also questions. Why would Rocky jump? What motivates someone to do the unthinkable? For the first few days, when everyone still thought Rocky had taken his own life, the questions about motivation revolved around Rocky, and suicide.

Completing my run, I jogged into the traffic circle at the entrance to Bayside Towers. As I approached, the glass doors to the South Tower lobby parted, and Tiffany emerged. I waved to her and we met on the sidewalk.

Tiffany's quiescence on Thursday night had been uncharacteristic. Tiffany was the earpiece, and the mouthpiece, of our alumni group. If anyone had gathered any gossip by now about Rocky, it would be Tiffany Chen.

"Hey," I said, catching my breath. "Have you heard anything more about Rocky?"

Tiffany shook her head. "No word about any troubles, that's for sure. Anyone who saw him this week said he seemed OK, normal. And you were right—Peter had been at Rocky's for a TBT."

"Did you speak to Cindy?" I asked.

"I did. She told me that Peter went to Rocky's Thursday evening to hang out for a while, and then Peter went down the block to Christie's.

"In fact," Tiffany continued, "A bunch of the guys from our class ran up from Christie's when they saw the police cars Thursday night. I don't know if you noticed, but they were standing on the other side of the circle, across from where we were."

Later on, I would question Tiffany about exactly who she had seen among that Christie's group.

"Did Cindy say anything about Rocky and Peter having a fight?" I asked.

"No, not at all. In fact," Tiffany lowered her tone, "well, you know there's a history there?"

"Right, I remember now. Before Cindy and Peter got engaged, she had dated Rocky. "

Nobody could remember precisely when Cindy Caldwell had shifted her affections from Rocky to Peter Greene. Red-haired and intense, Peter was the alpha male of our class, the kind of student Mallory described to future employers as "exhibiting leadership tendencies." But Rocky Violetto was Peter's close second, with his booming voice and imposing frame. During our freshman and sophomore years, Cindy had dated Rocky on and off. But Peter had gradually encroached, and by senior year had swept her away, no doubt aided by access to his parents' Aspen condo, country club credentials and limitless credit cards. Immediately after graduation, Peter proposed.

"That's also why it's so ironic that both Cindy and Rocky went to work at Netflix," Tiffany continued. "Mallory wanted me to go to Netflix too, by the way."

At least you didn't betray him by ditching tech and going into public service, like me, I thought.

"So they all get—*got*—along now?" I asked.

Tiffany nodded enthusiastically. "Yes, Cindy was insistent. She says Peter and Rocky were cool. But you know," Tiffany continued, leaning in to me, as if there was anyone else within earshot who could potentially hear, "Peter and Cindy have pushed off their engagement *again.* Nobody knows why, and Cindy didn't want to talk about that. But I have my theories."

"Like?" I prodded.

"Well, I recall Cindy once mentioning...I mean, she kind of slipped, I don't think she meant to tell me, that she had some amazing job offer from a company in New York City. She didn't say anything more and she dropped it quickly. I wonder if Peter doesn't want to leave Twitter and the West Coast, and they're fighting about where they'll live, or if they can split the coasts."

"How would *that* work?" I muttered.

"It wouldn't," Tiffany said. "The only other thing Cindy told me is that Peter's going to host a memorial for Rocky, at his place. Probably this Thursday, as a kind of group TBT. I guess that's as good a sign as any that Peter and Rocky were on good terms."

Or the perfect cover if they weren't, a distant voice whispered, from deep within my stirring investigative machine.

"Keep me posted," I said, and I continued on into South Tower, thinking again about what motivates people to do the unthinkable.

Ω

From Monday to Thursday of the week following Rocky's death, and for the last time in my young career at The Northern California

Computer Crimes Task Force, work progressed as usual. "As usual" meant riding my Mantis scooter each morning the five minutes from Bayside Towers to the Marin County District Attorney's office, swiping in at around 9:00 a.m., climbing a flight of stairs to the open-space configuration of desks and cubicles on the second floor, taking my seat at the furthest desk in the southwest corner, and doing whatever Marvin Hoag told me to do, until 5:30 p.m.

Senior Investigator Marvin Hoag of the NC3TF was a short, greasy, obsessive creature resembling the male human species. He controlled every aspect of my work like a one-way valve, preventing any direct contact between me and superiors within the NC3TF or the District Attorney's office. In close to two years on the second floor, I had never spoken with or even met the floor-master, District Attorney Ronald Schmidt.

Marvin was one of the two Senior Investigators stationed in the open space, then there was the NC3TF Director, Irene Gonzalez, in her enclosed office to our left. Gonzalez reported to the District Attorney, himself barricaded behind an impenetrable phalanx of underlings in a gaudy corner office at the opposite end of the floor.

On Thursday morning, May 16th, Marvin approached my desk just after I had settled into my squeaky office chair. He executed his signature move, raising one butt-cheek just high enough to plant it on a stack of papers on the edge of my desk, and shifted the weight of his formless mass onto said butt-cheek while folding his arms.

"Passed you on your two-wheeler this morning, Morita. When are you gonna buy yourself a car?"

"I can't afford a car, Marvin. Maybe when I win the lottery. Or publish my memoirs. *My Years With Marvin.* I'm sure it will be a best-seller. In the *Horror* genre."

"*Ha-ha*. Listen, I'm gonna need that memo comparing the San Francisco Trust and CreditEgg data breaches." When Marvin spoke, it was a scene straight out of *Office Space*. He glanced over his shoulder. "My money says it was the Chinese. But Gonzalez is working a lead on a fifteen-year-old hacker from Florida."

"I'm almost done with the report, Marvin. You should have it today."

"Great. And go easy on the dramatic composition. Just the facts. Remember, this isn't Creative Writing 101."

"I'll keep it simple for you, Marvin. Wouldn't want to tax your brain cells." As Marvin left I flipped over the stack of papers he had smothered.

For the last hour of my professional life as I knew it, I tapped away at my desktop keyboard. The NC3TF was too cheap to issue laptops to junior investigators. They also did not want us to check personal email on our work computers, and so it was that I checked my iPhone at around ten o'clock for any new messages.

There was an email from Peter Greene to the TBT group, confirming that the memorial gathering for Rocky would take place at Peter's villa on North San Pedro, at eight o'clock that evening. "BYOB," the message instructed.

And there was another email, addressed to me, from an account I did not recognize:

> *From:* unluckysevenfp@gmail.com
> *To:* Addison Morita
> *Subject:* Investigate this
> Rocky didn't fall from his balcony
> Someone put the "throw" back into TBT

The TBT group members had exchanged plenty of chatter and conjecture over the past few days. Most comments had been serious, but some were misguided attempts at lighthearted humor which were in poor taste. I ignored the dubious message, unsure what if anything I should or could do. My uncertainty did not last long.

At around 3:30 p.m., our former classmate Vanessa LeBleu, who worked at Amazon in Seattle, posted the following email to the group:

From: Vanessa LeBleu
To: TBT Group
Subject: Sad News
Hi guys from rainy Seattle - so terrible about Rocky, and unfortunately I have more sad news. Apparently I was listed as Indigo Murray's emergency contact at Intuit, where he worked. I just heard from someone at Intuit. Indigo had been AWOL and the police apparently found him yesterday at home. Seems he had been dead for a day or two - they think it's drug-related, an overdose or some-thing. Again so sorry to pass on bad news. And sorry I can't be down there for Rocky's memorial.
Regards,
Vanessa

I immediately dialed Tiffany.

"I just saw it," she answered gravely. "Drugs, makes sense. Indigo was a total pothead."

"Where did he live?" I asked.

"He had a place out near the Bay, I think," Tiffany said. "He was such a weird guy. Always kept to himself, remember? I think he just liked to kayak and smoke weed out there."

"Didn't he post something to the group earlier this week?" I asked.

"You're right...here it is," said Tiffany. "From Indigo Murray. 'Hey guys, Indigo here. Sorry about Rocky. Taking two days off Monday/Tuesday to be a loner and a stoner. Anyone welcome to stop by. BYOW.' Here's his address, on Marine Drive."

"*BYOW?*" I asked, then immediately answered my own question. "Oh, *bring your own weed.* I wonder if anyone took him up on it."

"Doubtful," said Tiffany. "Weird. Weird guy, weird times. Everything's so weird. Listen, I'm at work, I gotta go. See you tonight at Peter's?"

"Sure," I said. "Hey, can I catch a ride with you from Bayside?"

"Meet me downstairs at ten to," Tiffany said, and we said goodbye.

Fifteen minutes later, I received another email:

From: *unluckysevenfp@gmail.com*
To: *Addison Morita*
Subject: *Re: Investigate this*
One at the Bay's side, one at Bayside Towers
Can you match these two to Helmer's Powers?

I gasped audibly, then coughed loudly. jolting a few occupants of nearby cubicles.

Helmer's Powers...Hamilton Helmer's book, *7 Powers?* The business strategy book that Mallory taught in his seminar? That had to be the reference. But what did that book have to do with Indigo's death? And Rocky's?

No time to try to decipher the emails. I needed to tell someone with authority about the two messages, immediately.

CHAPTER 3

DOUG MALLORY, BUSINESS STRATEGY SEMINAR, Lecture 1 — The Seven Powers

"Failure. The greatest fear of every business leader. We all dream of success. We relentlessly pursue success. Yet, most businesses fail. Over ninety percent of startups fail. Almost fifty percent of the companies that make the Fortune 500 are gone from that list a decade later. We desperately seek to avoid failure, to identify its causes and prevent them.

"What if I told you, dear students, that there was a secret? A proven, time-tested, method for achieving long-term growth, value, and success? Could it be? Is it possible that such a strategy, such a Holy Grail of business strategy, exists?

"My friends, such a Holy Grail does in fact exist. Not one Holy Grail actually, or one strategy, but rather, seven strategies. Seven business powers, that have been proven to generate long-term, competition-crushing success.

"This book in my hand, ladies and gentlemen, is the Bible of prolonged value creation. Reed Hastings, the founder of Netflix, says, if you don't read this book, your business is going to die a lot sooner. A famous investor, Patrick O'Shaughnessy, calls it one of the best business books in history. Many venture capitalists I know give a copy of this book to the CEO of every new startup they invest in. This is 7 Powers, *by Hamilton Helmer.*

"In this book, Helmer describes how, after literally decades of research and investment, and hundreds and hundreds of case studies, he has determined that there are precisely seven strategies a business can pursue in order to achieve extended profitability and growth. These seven strategies, or powers as he calls them, are: Cornered Resource, Counter-positioning, Network Economies, Scale Economies, Switching Costs, Process Power, and Branding.

"We are going to study each of these powers in depth this semester. Then, for the rest of your careers, you will harness these superpowers, to wreak havoc on the markets of your choosing..."

Ω

For a change, I was standing alongside Marvin's desk.

"Hey, Marvin," I whispered.

"What?" He did not look up.

"When you speak to the D.A., how do you address him? Is it 'Mr. District Attorney,' or 'Mr. Schmidt,' or what?"

"I don't speak with the D.A.. I just speak with Gonzalez. Why?"

"I need to tell him something,"

"You can't just go and speak to the D.A.," Marvin growled at me from his chair, his face buried in his desktop screen. "If it's about one of our cases, you need to speak to me, and only to me."

"It's not about one of our cases. It's about something else. Something bad. Some information has come into my possession and I think the D.A. should know about it."

"Something bad?" repeated Marvin.

"Pretty bad. Worse than computer crime."

Marvin squeezed his eyeballs cross-eyed. "Traffic violation?"

"Thanks for your help, Marvin," I snapped, and strode down the corridor toward Schmidt's office.

I barreled straight past three startled secretaries before they had a chance to react. I knocked on Schmidt's door and immediately opened it, planting myself firmly in the doorway of his spacious office. "Mr. Schmidt, sir?"

Marin County District Attorney Ronald Schmidt was seated, hunched over his desk, shirt sleeves rolled up to his elbows, scowling through his reading glasses at a document that, it seemed, he was trying to fry with excessive concentration. "What is it?" he barked, without lifting his head.

"Mr. Schmidt, I'm Addison Morita, from computer crimes—"

"Excuse me, you can't go in there," a voice called from behind me. I slid further into Schmidt's doorway.

"I'm busy. Take it up with Gonzalez," he ordered, still leering downward at his papers. A secretary grabbed my shoulder.

"Mr. Schmidt, it's urgent," I blurted out, shaking off my accoster. "I have some information. Not about a computer crime. I believe there's been a homicide. Two, actually. I think the person—the killer, I mean—I think he just contacted me," I insisted.

Schmidt's head shot up, and his gaze investigated me over his reading glasses. He motioned for his assistant to back down.

"Start again. You're the gal from Gonzalez's group, you say?"

"Addison Morita, sir. Junior Investigator."

"Morita. Is that Mexican?"

"My dad's Japanese, sir."

"And you say you have possible information about a...a homicide?"

"Yes, sir. Two homicides. I think, sir."

Schmidt removed his reading glasses and slowly placed them on his desk. "OK, I'm listening. Make it quick. And stop calling me 'sir.' I hate that."

"OK, sir—Mr. Schmidt," I said, still standing in the doorway. He signaled to me to sit in one of the chairs facing his desk.

Talking quickly as I grabbed a seat, I recounted the events of last Thursday night at Bayside Towers, the news of Indigo's overdose, and the two emails I had received. I handed Schmidt a printout of the two emails, which he placed on his desk.

"I live at Bayside Towers myself. I knew both Rocky and Indigo," I added. "We were all the same year at First Principles College. We were all in Professor Mallory's course. I think the person who sent the emails knows that we were all in the seminar together, or perhaps was with us in the class."

Schmidt's focus remained riveted on me, unwavering. "Explain," he said.

"The head of the college, Doug Mallory—"

"Mallory. That hot-shot guy they brought in from New York, right? Some kind of tech guru?" asked Schmidt.

"Yes. He teaches an exclusive senior seminar in Business Strategy each Spring. He handpicks the top twenty-five students. I was in that seminar, with Rocky and Indigo, two years ago." I felt my cheeks flush, realizing that I had just referred to myself as "top" and "exclusive."

I continued. "The second email—where he writes about 'Helmer's Powers'—I believe that's a reference to Hamilton Helmer's book, *7 Powers*. It's a business strategy book, and Mallory swears by it. It's the core of the course. Helmer describes seven types of competitive advantage, that he calls 'powers.' I'm sorry if I'm boring you with this," I tapered off.

"I'm listening closely," said Schmidt, rubbing his balding scalp. "So, you think that the killer, for some reason, chose these two victims, because they somehow relate to two of those seven—whatever you call them—business powers?"

"Maybe. Yes. I don't know," I stammered. "I'm just saying that this person, he emailed me, and seems to know I'm an investigator, and referenced the book, and we were all in that seminar. There are dots to connect, but I just felt someone in charge needed to know."

Schmidt's hand was already in motion toward his large telephone console. He pressed a speed-dial button and lifted the receiver.

"Frank, it's Ron. Yeah, I'm good. Listen, you had two fatalities in the past week. One at Bayside last week..." he glanced up at me and I whispered *Violetto,* "...a Violetto, and an overdose near the bay a couple days ago?" He paused. "Right, Murray. Your guys turn up anything on either of those?" Schmidt grabbed a pen in his other hand and he scrawled notes on a pad, as he muttered *uh-huh*s and *yup*s.

"OK, so no evidence of foul play with the first one, and toxicology showed fentanyl on the overdose. Who do you have on the overdose?" More *uh-huh*s. "Listen, I've got a junior investigator over here, says she knew both casualties, former classmates, and may have some relevant information for your guy. Send him over here tomorrow?" A pause. "OK, great. Thanks, Frank." Schmidt hung up the receiver, put on his glasses and quickly reviewed his notes. Then he looked back up at me.

"OK. That was the Sheriff. No sign of foul play on Violetto. Says he fell from his balcony, looks like an accident or a suicide. Had some alcohol in his blood. On the second one, Murray, they have a detective looking into the overdose, which is standard procedure when drugs are involved. Seems he had five times the lethal amount of Fentanyl in him, and they found lots of marijuana lying around. The detective's name is Mike Bromley. He'll be over here to talk with you tomorrow. Tell him everything you told me."

"OK, thank you, I'll do that," I said.

"This could be a joke, you know," said Schmidt, tapping the paper with the printed emails that I had handed to him. Neither of us spoke for a moment. "By the way—did you say you received both emails at the same time, today?" he suddenly asked.

My stomach fluttered. "The truth is," I said, "I received the first email this morning, and yes, I was concerned it might be some sort of bad joke, so I didn't do anything about it right away. I apologize for that."

Schmidt waved his hand dismissively as if to parry my apology, and I continued. "When I got the second email in the afternoon, after I'd heard about Indigo, that's when I felt I needed to tell someone. I hope I haven't wasted your time."

"Let's see what happens. Talk with this guy Bromley tomorrow, and see if they're interested. The investigation is up to them. Nice to meet you," he said. Schmidt was back to burning laser holes in his paperwork, and I was dismissed.

Ω

"Great spot." Tiffany congratulated herself as she eased her Corolla alongside the curb directly in front of Peter's house just after eight o'clock. Hitching a ride from Bayside with Tiffany had ensured I would arrive at Peter's on time. Tiffany would not want to miss any gossip, and I did not want to miss any potential clues.

"A lot of people RSVP'd," Tiffany confided as we exited her car. "Except for the two in Seattle and Jason in New York, Cindy told me almost everyone else should be here. She said even Mallory may stop by."

"I can't wait to see everyone," I said. *I can't wait to observe everyone*, I thought.

Tiffany rang Peter's doorbell. She held a wine bottle, decorated with a ribbon. My bottle was in a cheesy plastic bag.

"Heeeeeeyyyyy," Peter greeted us, with his pretentious, SoCal affect. "Tiffany, Addie! Great to *SEE* you!" Peter always sounded like he was running for public office.

Tiffany handed me her bottle while she cheerfully chatted with Peter at the doorway, and I proceeded past them into the kitchen.

Peter's ranch-style rental was a posh bachelor's pad. Down the short hallway from the front door were two bedrooms, one of which he had converted into a music studio. The open living and dining area had a corner dedicated to a huge TV screen and video game console with two top-of-the-line gaming chairs facing the screen. Based on how tidy the place was, I guessed that between work downtown at Twitter and Cindy's more luxurious house ten minutes away on Point San Pedro, Peter did not spend much time here.

I rejoined the small group in Peter's living room. Aside from Tiffany and me, Perry Greenberg and Victor Rojas had also arrived.

Perry and Victor both worked at local startups, and both also still resided at Bayside Towers.

"So the Baysiders got here first, of course," Peter crowed. Turning to me and Tiffany, he said, "Cindy should be here soon. She got stuck late at work."

More people arrived, and animated huddles formed. Deep *ha-hah-ha*s and *huh-huh-huh*s from the men, and *tee-hee-hee*s and *oh-my-god*s from the women. More *amazing*s and *incredible*s than a Steve Jobs keynote. In only two years, everyone had dutifully adopted the Silicon Valley cocktail party parlance.

A day earlier, I might have been self-conscious, eager to be found in the center of the *ha-ha-ha* and *tee-hee-hee* circles. But now, an investigative spirit compelled me to remain on the periphery, listening and observing.

Peter had set some wine bottles and glasses on the buffet in the dining area. I detached from a scintillating discourse by Bill Yelovich on the benefits of Product-Led Growth, and poured myself half a glass of chardonnay. Arranged on the buffet were framed portraits of Peter, posing with various celebrities—movie stars, Los Angeles Laker players, and popular singers.

"Little Petey looks so natural in those pictures, like he actually belongs there," sneered a voice to my left. It belonged to Tyler Lukela, standing next to Jimmy Tresko.

"*Ha-ha*," laughed Jimmy encouragingly. "Peter's all like, 'Look at me, my dad's a hotshot Hollywood entertainment lawyer, *ef* you.'" Jimmy and Tyler snickered and bumped their shoulders, jostling their beers.

Not satisfied with taking down Peter, Tyler teased me. "How are you doing, Morita? You still a policewoman, or whatever?"

Still a jerk? I considered responding.

"Still investigating computer crimes," I said. "How about you guys? What have you been up to lately?" I asked, seeking to shake out a relevant lead.

"Still trading stocks," said Jimmy. "I'm on this platform, TradePeek. People can follow my portfolio and mirror my trades. So when I trade well, I make money, and make even more money off my followers."

Jimmy frowned, seemingly disappointed that I did not shower him with the approbation he expected for his money-making scheme. Instead, I faced Tyler.

"Me? Free agent," he said. "Soon to be a second-time founder."

"Meaning, his startup just went bankrupt," Jimmy added, smacking Tyler on the shoulder and laughing. Tyler gave Jimmy the finger. I excused myself and wandered away in search of more interesting company.

I continued to drift in and out of conversations. Virtually all of the chattering concerned work. This startup, that company, the next venture capital round. Almost no mention of Rocky, or Indigo. I brushed past Tiffany who was making a beeline for a wine refill.

"Is this a memorial, or a party?" I whispered to her.

"Oh, don't be so stiff," she chided. "Do you see how many people are wearing Allbirds? I have to get a pair tomorrow."

Almost everyone wore jeans, and footwear so shoddy or offbeat that they had to be the latest expensive styles. Many sported company T-shirts, their personal identities already having morphed into those of their employers.

Cindy had finally arrived, striking a sharp contrast to the other casually attired women with her navy-blue business casual Kate Middleton ensemble. Cindy absentmindedly tucked her straight blond hair behind her ears as she chitchatted with Caroline Wei and

Janet Hudson, who both worked at Facebook and were roommates in Union City. Had I seen Cindy next to Peter at any time this evening? It was already close to ten o'clock. Tiffany's remark about Peter and Cindy's postponed engagement resurfaced in my mind.

Jimmy and Tyler had remained glued together all evening, and they veered away any time either Peter or Cindy came close. I filed that observation as well.

I brought up Rocky in conversation, particularly with those who still lived at Bayside Towers and might have some further insight. Perry Greenberg, Brian Monroe and Warren Zhang were all Baysiders, and I approached them as they stood together near Peter's video game alcove, nursing beers.

"...so then he says to me, 'Come on, Brian, I know why you came in late today. You were up all night again playing Endscape.' I mean, the guy had me nailed," Brian told Warren as Perry listened.

"They gonna fire you?" asked Warren.

"*Nah.* Hope not, anyway. Hey, Addie," said Brian, noticing me.

"So crazy about Rocky," I said, shaking my head. "And Indigo too."

All I got back were some mumbled *yeah*s, *crazy*s, and *too bad*s. My mention of such needlessly negative topics apparently was intruding on their cheerier confab.

I hovered next to Chris Butler and Marcus Newman, hoping that they might have recently had contact with Indigo. Chris was telling Marcus about his employer, an organic foods manufacturer in Novato. They welcomed me into their colloquy and I asked Marcus about his work with the California Housing Partnership.

"Addie, you and I are the only two people here pursuing justice for this world," Marcus responded, raising his drink to toast me.

"To justice," I said, raising my wine glass, and I changed the topic. "Crazy to lose Rocky and Indigo in the same week," I said, as Chris and Marcus responded with solemn nods. "Had either of you guys been in touch with Indigo lately?"

"Nope," said Chris. "I was just telling Marcus, I hadn't seen that dude in a real long time. Guess he just got some bad shit from someone. I mean, everybody knew he was into weed."

"Not that you know anything about that kind of thing yourself, Chris," said Marcus, and they both burst out laughing.

The noise level in the room dipped temporarily, and we instinctively shifted our attention toward the house's front hallway. Doug Mallory had entered. Mallory appeared, as always, suave and debonair. He wore a thin red cashmere sweater over a white oxford, black jeans, and loafers. His wavy brown hair was perfectly combed, and his permanent smile radiated confidence.

After the momentary pause, chatter picked up again quickly. These people were all professionals now. Colleagues, even. They weren't going to gawk at Mallory anymore.

Cindy approached Mallory and whispered something in his ear. Mallory bent lower without making eye contact with her and muttered something in return. Almost immediately, Peter climbed up onto a chair, clinking on a wine glass with a piece of tableware.

"Can I have everyone's attention? Cindy?" Peter glared at Cindy, momentarily, and motioned briefly but insistently for her to join him at his side. She obediently detached from Mallory and stepped closer to Peter.

"I see that Doug's here, so let's get started," Peter said. *Doug?* Not even *Professor Mallory* anymore.

"I don't have a big speech or anything prepared, don't worry," continued Peter. "I just thought it would be the right thing for us to remember Rocky, and it would give us a good excuse to get everyone back together again. As some of you know, Rocky and I didn't get along at first, but we actually became close friends." He glanced at Cindy. "I was with Rocky the night he died. It's still a huge shock to me, as I'm sure it was to all of you. We never know what's really going on in someone's head, I guess. But I know Rocky would have wanted us to all move on with our lives. So let's all raise a glass to Rocky, and go out there and be successful, for Rocky's sake." He raised his glass, and there were murmurs of *to Rocky* from around the room.

I covered my mouth to hide a grimace of disgust at the content of Peter's remarks, and at his failure to mention Indigo.

The displeasing event broke up shortly after Peter's speech. Tiffany wobbled over to me, dangling her car keys.

"Did you drink, Addie? Would you mind driving home? We're giving Victor a ride too."

We bid goodbye to Peter and Cindy, who stood in the doorway waving as we walked to Tiffany's car.

That was the last time I saw Peter Greene.

CHAPTER 4

"ARE YOU ADDISON MORITA?"

Someone cleared his throat alongside my desk. It was around eleven o'clock Friday morning, and I had been at my desk, filling in a chart I had scratched out in pen on a yellow legal pad. At the top I had written "Mallory Business Strategy Seminar Class List" and the left-hand column already listed all twenty-four students' names, other than my own.

At my shoulder stood a wiry man, probably just a few years older than me, with shoulder-length brown hair parted in the middle, a goatee and hazel eyes. His rust-colored, fitted polo shirt with "Marin County Sheriff" emblazoned on the chest was tucked into his tan chinos.

"Detective Mike Bromley, Investigations Division. Sheriff Davis sent me over."

I rose and we cordially shook hands, attracting attention from the junior staff nearby, who had never seen me interact with anyone other than Marvin.

Detective Bromley surveyed the open space desks. "Is there someplace quiet we can talk?"

There were two small conference rooms on the second floor, but I had never been inside either of them.

"We can check out the picnic tables outside, on the ground floor. It's usually quiet out there," I suggested.

"Lead the way," he said.

Outside the rear door on the building's first floor, a covered patio sheltered three picnic tables. On nice days you might find staffers at the tables eating their brown-bagged lunches; fortunately, today the patio was unoccupied.

The late-morning sun blazed overhead, but the patio's canopy provided comfortable shade. A lone woodpecker sounded nearby, and chickadees called their *chickadee-dee-dee-dee* alarm as we intruded on their solitude.

Mike Bromley settled onto a bench opposite me at one of the tables, clasping his hands together with fingers intertwined.

"So you're with the computer crimes group? Not what I expected," he said.

I wrinkled my nose. "Coming from someone who looks more like a washed-up child TV star than a detective," I retorted.

"Touché," he laughed, raising his palms toward me in surrender. "Left my fedora and trench coat at home today, *shweethaht.*" He grinned.

"What type of cases do you usually work on?" I asked. "I don't know much about the Investigations Division."

"We provide support to the different police departments with their investigations. I'm junior on the staff, so most of my day-to-day is juvenile stuff. Crimes by juveniles, I mean," he clarified with another smile.

"Any homicides?" I asked.

"Here and there. Not many so far. The more experienced guys typically get the homicides. You like homicides?"

I blinked. "I...I don't *like* homicides. I'd like to catch people who commit them, if that's what you mean."

He smacked the table and pointed at me. "See, that's the thing. Prosecution, prosecution, prosecution. Computer crimes, huh? You've never had to handcuff a punk kid against the back wall of a pawn shop for dealing hard drugs, send him away for eighteen months, he comes back a murderer."

He snapped his fingers repeatedly. "What's that fancy word, for people who leave jail and return to crime?"

"Recidivism?" I said.

"Exactly. I see it every day. Prosecute 'em, send 'em away, they come back worse."

"Sounds strange coming from a detective," I commented.

"Not for long." He waved his hand. "Been chasing delinquents for four years. I'm done. Applied to social work school. Gonna leave this beat, become a guidance counselor. Yes, sir. Get to these kids before they're too far gone. Prevention, not prosecution."

"That's very noble, Detective Bromley. I mean that sincerely."

"*Ah*, call me Mike," he said. "But you like homicide, huh? Sheriff Davis says you think you might have one for us."

"It's not a sales pitch," I said. "Two of my former classmates died in the past week. The D.A. told me that your office found no sign of foul play. But I've received two emails from someone claiming to be responsible. Or hinting at it, at least. I think it warrants investigation. And, you can call me Addie."

"OK, Addie. Why don't you start from the beginning, and tell me about these emails?"

I recounted everything I had told District Attorney Schmidt the day before. As I spoke, Mike produced a small pad and made notes.

When I finished, Mike reviewed his scribbles, and scratched his goatee. I expected him to ask me some prodding follow-up questions. Who might have wanted to kill former First Principles students, who had some possible vendetta or motive? What makes someone do the unthinkable?

Mike tapped his pad with his pen. "So far, as the Sheriff told your D.A., we've found no suspicious evidence of any kind, at either fatality. Nada."

I pressed him. "I think the emails suggest that the deaths are related to a book we studied in the seminar at First Principles. A book called *7 Powers*. Do you want me to tell you about it?"

"*Noooo*, no." Mike laughed, pretending to hold me off as if I was an onrushing attacker. "I didn't come here to hear a lecture. Failed Econ in high school. I don't think we need to dive into that just yet, solely based on these anonymous emails."

"I think the book could be important—"

Mike interrupted me. "And these emails are all you've got? Has anyone else that you know heard or seen anything that would suggest murder? Two murders? And there's no way to tell who's behind that email address, or is there?"

"Could be anyone. Anyone who was in the seminar with me and Rocky and Indigo knows I work in law enforcement, and would have my personal email."

"You recognize this could just be a joke," said Mike, cutting me off again. "Or an attempt at a joke, at least. It's pretty distasteful, I know, for someone to do that. But we have no indication, other than these two emails, that the deaths were homicides. No evidence at either scene." He shook his head.

Mike closed his notebook, and tucked his pen inside. Standing up from the picnic table, he reached into his pocket and handed me a business card.

"Listen, I don't mean to discount your story. I'm just saying, it's not enough for us to go on right now, in the absence of any other evidence. You have my number. If you see, or hear, anything more, of course I'll be all ears. But right now, like I said, there's not enough to go on. It's probably just some twisted joke, some kind of prank or something."

Mike stepped off the patio toward the building's entrance. "Can I let myself out this way?"

"Through the gate," I said, still seated at the picnic table.

The chickadees above the patio resumed their *chickadee-dee-dees*, and somewhere in the distance the woodpecker continued to hammer his head against a tree.

Ω

Thwack, thwack, thwack.

Before anybody takes the anonymous emails seriously, before the murder investigation, before the arrival of Special Agent Hope Pearson, I am on my sacred Saturday morning run.

Panoramic vistas unfold of Nature in her full glory. Willowy marshes at the bay's edge. Herons dipping their beaks into the water and then popping up again, startled as my slender shadow carves its route along the ribbon of road.

I crest a rolling ridge, trying to cleanse, to purge the jumbled reflections ping-ponging in my head.

The D.A.'s just doing his job. Why should he take me seriously? Some junior investigator he's never met, barges into his office ranting about an Economics book...and anonymous emails?

Mike seems like a nice enough guy. Cute even, if things were different. If I wasn't so focused on calling attention to those emails. Can't really blame him either, for blowing me off.

I glide past patches of coastal sagebrush. Feeling the breeze on my face, I close my eyes momentarily as I run into the wind.

I'm back in Fresno, running through a field. I'm about six or seven years old. Mom and Father are still together. Mom has set out a picnic lunch and I'm running, making wide circles, the tall grass swishing against my shins. I'm holding the string of a kite. Father is sternly calling in Japanese, "Faster, faster!"

Thwack, thwack...buzzzz.

Buzzzzzzzzz.

I open my eyes and reach backward, drawing the rucksack forward over my shoulder to fish out my phone as I break stride.

"Hello?"

"Morita." It's a male voice, insistent, vaguely familiar.

"Yes?"

The harsh voice grunts, "Ron Schmidt. Where are you?"

The D.A.? "Who—Mr. Schmidt?"

"Yes. Where are you right now?"

"I...I'm on a run, near the bay," I stutter. "What's...Is everything OK?"

"Peter Greene, one of your former classmates. Have you heard anything?"

"Heard anything? We were all just at his place on Thursday night, for a memorial. Why?"

"He's dead, Morita. We're in the office. Get over here as fast as you can."

CHAPTER 5

*DOUG MALLORY, BUSINESS STRATEGY SEMINAR, Lecture 6 —
Network Economies*

*"...So now that we've discussed Network Economies, I'm going
to unveil a practical experiment, a kind of proof to you, that networks
are inherently valuable.*

*"As the best and brightest of First Principles College, you are all
destined for great careers. You will develop fantastic individual
capabilities. But one of your greatest assets—in fact, arguably your
greatest asset—will be your network of connections to other people
with similarly fantastic capabilities and connections. A kind of mesh
matrix.*

"Now, as Helmer and others before him point out, your network grows in value with its size. You need to keep your network strong, and healthy. You need to exercise it, keep it fit, like a muscle. So thanks to your fearless T.A., Danny Armstrong, we've created a program called 'Throwback Thursday' or TBT. Immediately following graduation, every Monday an automated email will go out to each of you pointing you to a shared document. You'll be invited to tag another former classmate for a TBT. You'll get together, one-on-one, preferably on Thursdays or on another day you choose, to keep up and stay in contact. This way, if you're diligent, you can meet up with each of your former classmates twice a year which will be good enough to keep your networks vibrant. You won't always feel like it, but trust me, it will pay dividends. The more you invest in your network, the more valuable it will be and the more return on investment you'll receive back..."

Ω

The eerie quiet of the District Attorney's office on Saturday was a stark contrast to its usual hustle and bustle. I located the small group assembled in the conference room at the far end of the second floor near my desk. The conference room door *clicked* as I opened it, and the three men inside lifted their heads.

Mike Bromley and an older man with neat, gray hair sat at the conference table. Schmidt was standing in front of a whiteboard, wearing a golf shirt and blue cargo shorts. He appeared harried and incredibly displeased.

My hair was still damp from my quick shower after my sprint home. I had thrown on a pair of jeans and the first clean T-shirt that emerged from my drawer, and raced to the office on my scooter. It had only been about thirty minutes since Schmidt's call.

Schmidt said, "OK, Morita's here. You already know Detective Bromley, and this is Sheriff Frank Davis." The Sheriff bent his head politely but sternly. Mike rocked slowly in his swivel chair.

"Frank, Morita is the one I told you about. She's in our computer crimes group, and she's received some communications from someone claiming to be involved in these first two deaths."

Turning to me expectantly, the District Attorney inquired, "Have you heard anything new?"

"No, sir," I responded, then bit my lower lip as Schmidt frowned at the word *sir*.

"Well, then. We're just waiting for one more person to join, and we'll get started. She'll be here any moment, she just called me from the exit off Highway 101."

Schmidt glanced at his watch, and then at Sheriff Davis. "My daughter's pitching in the regional finals today. If I miss it for this bullshit, there's going to be another homicide investigation for you." The Sheriff chuckled nervously.

The door to the conference room *clicked* open. Countless times later, I would mentally replay the moment I first met Hope Pearson.

"Good morning," said the casually elegant black woman who glided into the room. I recognized her immediately from her book jacket photo, and I stared, starstruck. Hope Pearson was taller than I had expected, with short, afro curls, and creamy cinnamon brown skin that made it impossible to guess her age. Given her professional status and accomplishments, she was probably close to forty, though she could easily pass for a decade younger. She wore loose black slacks, and a thin black cardigan over a peach-colored linen top that hugged her figure and perfectly matched her manicured nails. And her eyes—those amber eyes. Alert, and probing, yet impenetrable. I would discover that, if the eyes are truly the window to the soul, Pearson's were one-way glass.

"OK, introductions." Schmidt pointed toward Davis and Bromley as Pearson coolly settled into a chair and leaned forward. "Sheriff Frank Davis and Detective Mike Bromley of our local department. Addison Morita, a junior investigator in our Computer Crimes Task Force. And I'm pleased to have Special Agent Hope Pearson, of the California Department of Justice, joining us. Agent Pearson, your reputation precedes you, and I've personally thanked the Attorney General for making you available to us." Pearson dipped her head in acknowledgement.

Pearson's eyes flickered toward me. "Computer Crimes?" she asked.

"I'll explain," said Schmidt. "We've had three fatalities in the past ten days, and all three, along with Ms. Morita, were former classmates at a local school, First Principles College. We believe the person responsible may have contacted Ms. Morita, by email." Pearson's gaze lingered on me for an extended moment.

Schmidt addressed the Sheriff and Mike. "Agent Pearson handles special assignments for the D.O.J., specializing in complex homicides and serial murders. She has an unparalleled record and we are fortunate to have her involved. As of this moment, she will be leading this investigation."

Sheriff Davis murmured in protest, and Schmidt immediately silenced him.

"Now Frank, with all due respect, we have an unusual situation here. As soon as I heard about this third fatality, I contacted the A.G. It's his call." Schmidt swatted with his hand, dismissing any further objection. "Agent Pearson's record speaks for itself. There's no discussion."

The Sheriff leaned back in his chair in resignation. Schmidt planted himself into a chair and raised his eyes toward Pearson, cueing her to preside.

We had now entered her church, with Hope Pearson, High Priestess of Homicide, officiating. Pearson spoke in a smoky, solemn, attention-commanding tone.

"Thank you for your kind words, Mr. Schmidt. Mr. Davis, you have nothing to fear. I am sure we will get along perfectly well." Her voice visibly disarmed the sheriff and his cheeks flushed momentarily.

"I know very little about the case, so perhaps give me the relevant details so far?" Pearson purposefully addressed this question to Davis, who puffed his chest, straightened his uniform shirt, and removed papers from a manila folder resting in front of him on the conference table.

"Yes, ma'am. The first fatality, Robert Violetto, age twenty-five, fell from an eighth-floor balcony at Bayside Towers, a local apartment complex here in San Rafael, last Thursday, May 9. Dispatch received a 911 call at approximately 9:50 p.m. from a resident who was parking his car in the complex's parking lot and heard the body hit the ground. Pronounced dead at the scene. Our deputies found no evidence of foul play, but no suicide note either." He glanced upward at Pearson, who was motionless, listening.

"Fatality number two, Indigo Murray, age twenty-six, lived alone in a small rented house on Marine Drive. Reported missing from work by his employer on Wednesday. We sent a patrol car and he was found deceased on our arrival, that was Wednesday afternoon. Lots of marijuana around the house. Toxicology found a high amount of fentanyl, many times the lethal amount. We suspected accidental overdose. We're seeing an influx of bad weed, lately. No ability to trace where he got it from." Mike rocked in his chair, pursed his lips and raised his eyebrows in agreement, eyes fixed on the table before him.

Shuffling his papers, the Sheriff continued. "And the third fatality. Peter Greene, age twenty-five, also here in San Rafael. He resided in a rented villa on North San Pedro. We received a 911 call this morning from his fiancé, a Cindy Caldwell, also of San Rafael, who found him unresponsive at his home. Paramedics arrived and pronounced him dead on scene. Coroner says it's definitely poisoning. Still waiting to find out what type, but a heavy dose, for sure."

"And you believe these are related." Pearson said this as a statement, not a question.

Schmidt took over. "Well, I think Morita can add some context here. All three deceased had been classmates, at First Principles. And she received anonymous emails, after each of the first two deaths, that make some reference to the school, or a particular course, or some book. I'll let her explain." Schmidt gestured to me. My throat suddenly turned dry.

"Well," I stammered, "first of all, it's an honor to meet you, Agent Pearson. I...I'm a huge fan of your work. Your books, I mean." *Those eyes.*

"Tell me about the emails," the mouth below the piercing eyes directed.

"Right. So, Rocky—that's Violetto—Indigo, Peter and myself, and also Peter's fiancé Cindy, by the way, the one who found him," I glanced at the Sheriff, "we were all in the first graduating class of First Principles College, here in San Rafael. Are you familiar with First Principles?"

Pearson blinked. "Andy Freel's pet project. Very exclusive. Heavy emphasis on technology and business."

"Exactly," I said. *She's good,* I thought.

"Andy and I have a number of mutual acquaintances," Pearson explained, canvassing the others seated. "Go on."

"Andy recruited Doug Mallory away from New York, to run the school," I started.

"I have heard of Mallory, as well," Pearson said.

"Right, and so Mallory, in addition to running the school, teaches one seminar a year, just for a group of seniors, who he hand-picks based on grades and interview. The seminar is called Business Strategy. It's the most sought-after class in the school. Anyone who gets in is pretty much guaranteed a great job after graduation, plus Mallory goes the extra mile with personal recommendations and introductions for the students who do well. Top companies recruit right out of his class."

"And all three of the alleged victims were in that seminar, with you."

"Correct."

"But *you* are not in high-tech."

I had not expected Pearson to show interest in me. Caught flat-footed, I stuttered, "I, um, thought I would go into tech, for sure, when I started at First Principles, like everyone else."

I regained my composure. "Mallory wanted to place me—I had done well in the course—but this opportunity came up in the Computer Crimes Task Force right here in Marin County, and I guess, at the time, I felt like...let the others chase the money, I'm going to do something meaningful, you know?" I realized too late that *at the time* might imply that I regretted my decision, and I grimaced without making eye contact with Schmidt.

"OK, proceed," Pearson said. "The emails."

"Here they are," offered Schmidt, and slid my printout of the two emails across the table to Pearson. She studied the text quickly.

"What is 'TBT'?" asked Pearson, still eyeballing the page.

"Throwback Thursday," I said. "Basically, it was Mallory's idea, for the members of the seminar to stay connected after graduation. We're supposed to pair up, and get together on Thursdays, one on one, round-robin style, to keep our networks healthy."

"So Violetto—Rocky?—fell from his balcony on Thursday night, and did he have a TBT that day?"

"Exactly, that evening."

"With whom?"

"With Peter Greene."

"And Greene himself is now dead as well," said Pearson. The Sheriff nodded.

Pearson was already peering back at the page with the two email texts.

"And, 'Helmer's Powers'?"

"OK, so that's the reference to the book, I believe," I said.

"A *book*."

"Yes. A book about startup growth strategies, called *7 Powers*, by Hamilton Helmer. Mallory uses it in his seminar. It's the primary focus of the course, essentially, that one book."

"Ms. Morita—may I call you Addison?"

"Addie."

"Addie, I am allergic to speculation. But given that we have very few facts so far here, what do you think is the possible connection between the book and these casualties?"

"Well, I guess someone could have a vendetta, against the school, or Mallory, or—"

"I did not ask about motive, Addie." It was more of a chiding than a scolding, but it stung nevertheless. "I never start with motive. I am just asking, how does the book specifically relate to the three deaths, in your opinion?"

Schmidt glowered at his watch, probably imagining his disappointed daughter winding up on some faraway pitcher's mound. Mike readied himself for the "Econ" lecture he had dodged a day earlier.

I explained. "Helmer's book defines the ways startups can achieve prolonged dominance in their markets and establish barriers to complement their benefits. He says there are only seven strategies that are effective, long-term. And he calls these strategies the 'Seven Powers,'" I said, and added, "That's also the name of the book."

The three men stared down at the table. Pearson's gaze remained fixed on me.

I continued. "I still remember the seven strategies clearly. Would you like me to explain them?"

"Not right now," said Pearson politely. "So the connection would be?"

"I'm guessing...and yes, it's just speculation...that the connection is to the victims' employers. So, for example, Rocky worked at Netflix. In Helmer's book, Netflix is Helmer's example of Scale Economies. Indigo worked for Intuit. That's probably Switching Cost. And Peter was at Twitter, that's Network Economies. I can explain all of this, but you're right, now may not be the time."

Pearson nodded. "And if we follow your theory to its logical conclusion, there are four more murders planned, and the seven victims will be employees of companies corresponding to the seven, what do you call them, powers?"

"Again, just speculation based on the emails, but yes, that's what it seems to me," I responded.

Hope Pearson's fingers drummed on her cheek, as she leaned back in her chair.

"And no third email?"

"Not yet—I mean, no," I stammered.

"OK." Pearson leaned forward, and tapped her fingers on the table. She turned to Schmidt. "Mr. Schmidt, I know you are pressed for time. Addie, Detective Bromley, please excuse us, I need to speak with the District Attorney and the Sheriff, privately."

CHAPTER 6

*DOUG MALLORY, BUSINESS STRATEGY SEMINAR, Lecture 4 –
Cornered Resource*

"You might assume that when Helmer refers to Cornered
Resource, he would mean a company that has a legal monopoly on
some right to use or produce something, like a patent, a copyright, or
mining rights. So that if any competitor wants to use that resource,
they can't, and that exclusive right gives the holder of the resource a
fully legal power to corner the market, and derive ongoing value from
that resource.

"But Helmer extends our understanding of the term, and that's
what I find fascinating. He says a Cornered Resource can be a person,
or people. In fact his primary example of Cornered Resource isn't

Pfizer with Viagra, or Google's PageRank algorithm, but instead Pixar and its management team. He says Pixar assembled a once-in-a-lifetime team of talented individuals that no other company could rival, and those uniquely talented individuals enabled Pixar to deliver hit after hit and dominate the animated film industry. It's a debatable point, and I want to discuss it today. But Helmer claims that sometimes people have such unique talent or skill at what they do, that those people become the cornered asset that generates the company's ongoing, competitive power..."

Ω

The conference room did not have a window, so from my desk Mike and I could not observe the continuation of the meeting between Pearson, Schmidt and Davis.

"Well, at least this time we don't need to find a quiet place to talk," I said, gesturing toward the empty cubicles surrounding us.

Mike chuckled. "Hey, I guess whether I like it or not, I'm going to have to brush up on my Econ. Sorry I blew you off yesterday."

"It's OK. What a difference another dead body makes," I said. "Two days ago Schmidt chucks me from his office. Now he's calling me in on a Saturday for an emergency meeting with Hope Pearson."

"You know her? You said something to her about admiring her work."

I leaned back in my chair with my hands behind my head. "You've never heard of Hope Pearson? I haven't even worked on a single homicide and I know all about her. She's famous, Mike. They say she's never lost a case. Always gets her man, that kind of thing."

"Who says?"

"I read a profile of her. You don't understand, she's my idol. I want to be Hope Pearson when I grow up. First of all, she breaks every stereotype—a black, openly gay, brilliant woman. She's investigated and solved some of the most complicated homicide cases in the State of California, including a bunch of serial killer cases."

"Wait...When you grow up, you want to be black and openly gay?" Mike asked with a grin.

"*Ha-ha.* Girl power, Zero Fox Given, know what I mean?" I said, flexing my biceps. "She's a driven, independent, accomplished woman. But what I really admire is she's also a best-selling author. You've never heard of Stella Westcott?"

"The crime writer?" asked Mike.

"Exactly. That's *her.* Stella Westcott *is* Hope Pearson."

"Whaa-at?"

"Yes. It leaked a year or two ago. And she admitted to it. For years, she's been writing crime novels, many of them loosely based on true stories. A bunch of her books have been New York Times bestsellers. The article I read said one of them is being made into a movie. I've read all of her books. She's a fantastic writer. *That's* what I would love to be when I grow up."

"Impressive. I wonder what she's—"

"Bromley!" Sheriff Davis' head protruded from the conference room doorway and we both jumped at the sound of the Sheriff's bellowing voice. Mike scampered back into the conference room.

The yellow legal pad, with my Mallory seminar class chart, still occupied the center of my desk. Pearson had not asked me any questions about the students in the class, their relationships, their personalities, their histories. I wanted to get to work on identifying suspects, potential targets, and motives. Matching the Helmer powers to the employer of each student, alive or deceased. There was much work to be done, and the clock was ticking.

About five minutes after Mike left me at my desk, I received another email from my mysterious pen pal, UnluckySevenFP:

> **From:** *unluckysevenfp@gmail.com*
> **To:** *Addison Morita*
> **Subject:** *Re: Investigate this*
> *Greene Petered out and went to heaven*
> *Color me done when I get to seven*

That's it. Proves my 7 Powers *theory*, I thought.

I copied the text of the email from my phone to my computer and printed it out, as I had done with the initial two messages.

Mike soon emerged from the conference room, followed by Schmidt, Davis and Pearson. The latter three proceeded down the corridor toward the second-floor exit, while Mike returned to my desk, one eyebrow raised.

I peered up at him questioningly.

Mike scratched his head and said, with noticeable discomfort, "Well, that was a bit odd. It seems like they were arguing while we were out here. I go in there, and Pearson is saying to Davis something like 'I told you I prefer to work alone' and he's answering back. And then Davis is like, 'OK, Bromley, you're going to be helping Agent Pearson with fact-gathering. Anything she needs, anything she asks you, you do,' that kind of thing. She did not look happy. I guess the Sheriff's office wants to keep a finger in this pie. And Schmidt said we'd be using the conference room as our office for the investigation."

"And me?"

"That's what I'm saying, it was weird, they didn't mention you at all. The meeting just kind of ended, and they all left. You saw them go. I don't know what to tell you."

"You would think I could be of some value to this case," I grumbled, tossing my pen onto my desk.

"I'm sorry, Addie."

"Whatever," I said. "Well, since you are an official part of the investigation, you will probably want to see this." I handed Mike the printout of the new email.

"A real poet," said Mike.

"He's not going to win any literary awards," I said.

"You assume it's a *he*."

"You're right. Or *she*," I said. "I guess we're not up to profiling a suspect yet. Or, *you're* not up to profiling, I should say, since I'm not on the team."

"Hey, chin up," Mike said. "I'm sure you'll get your chance to work on your first homicide case, Detective Morita. And prove yourself to your mighty idol, Hope Pearson."

Ω

No Hope. Literally. I strapped on my helmet and pushed off on my Mantis down Civic Center Drive, leaving the empty D.A.'s office behind me.

Along San Pablo Avenue, the Saturday afternoon traffic whizzed by on my left as my scooter hugged the shoulder on my way back to Bayside. A car's engine down-shifted behind me, and the vehicle slowed to keep pace with my scooter. I sped up, and the car accelerated, remaining what sounded like five or six feet behind me.

My heart picked up a beat and I quickly peeked to my left, while pointing the Mantis forward. At that moment, the car revved up, and its driver jammed the horn. I swerved frantically toward the shoulder.

As the vehicle shot past, a familiar voice called out from the open window.

"Buy a car, Morita!" Senior Investigator Marvin Hoag cackled like a gleeful hyena.

Ω

"Are you scared?"

My roommate, Carly Mendez, and I lounged on folding chairs Saturday on our balcony at apartment 6A in South Tower. On this clear evening, we could see a glowing sliver of bay on the horizon, the setting sun bathing the wide landscape in orange and violet splendor.

We were drinking Prosecco from disposable wine goblets. Carly kept a few bottles of La Marca chilled in the refrigerator right next to my stash of G Zero. I took a sip, as Carly waited for me to respond to her question.

"I don't like to live life looking over my shoulder," I said. "You?"

"I am scared, yes, not going to lie," Carly said. "I mean, Rocky, then Indigo, now Peter. Anybody saying anything in your office? Do they think something's going on?"

"Reminding you, Carly, I'm on the Computer Crimes Task Force."

"I know, but I just thought, you know, around the water-cooler or something."

"No Christie's tonight?" I asked, changing the subject.

"I had the afternoon shift today." We each sipped from our plastic cups. Carly put hers down. "Everyone at Christie's already knows about Peter. Cal was awful about it, before he left. He said it couldn't have happened to a better guy. I told him to shut up."

"I've warned you, Cal Forsythe is bad news."

"I know you don't approve of my dating him. You're always just jealous of my boyfriends. Maybe you should try to get one sometime." She laughed.

"First of all," I replied, "Cal is not your boyfriend, he's your *boss*. You are a server at Christie's and he owns the restaurant. And, you're not dating, you're..."

"Oh, pardon me, Mom, or are you the Sex Police?" Carly snapped. "Can I remind you I'm twenty-five? Would you feel better if we went out for ice cream every Wednesday after home room? And FYI, I'm not a server anymore. I've been promoted to *Greeter.*"

"Wow. Please explain to me how that promotion came about," I quipped.

"I'm living life, OK?" Carly said. "As soon as we get our startup funded, I'll ditch Christie's and settle down. Julie's almost done with our pitch deck, and we've got meetings scheduled with angel investors."

"Fantastic," I snorted. "Another First Principles grad, creating just what this world desperately needs, another online fashion startup. And then I'll have to find someone else to split the rent."

We were both gazing toward the sunset beyond the balcony. "Why was Cal so nasty about Peter?" I asked.

"It wasn't specifically about Peter. You know, Cal has always resented the First Principles guys, even though they basically support Christie's. He calls them stuck up, snooty, privileged, obnoxious. The only one he ever liked was Tyler Lukela. He's from your year right? Probably because of their shared obsession with guns. They still go shooting at the range over in Richmond, almost every Saturday. Otherwise, Cal can't stand the FP crowd. But on top of that, lately, Cal is really pissed at Andy."

"Andy? Freel? What does Cal have to do with him?"

"Well, you heard about the move, right?"

"What move?

"Oh, I thought people knew. Cal told me the rumor is that Andy wants to move First Principles out of San Rafael. Expand it to like a thousand students. There's crazy demand because the college has built a real rep over the last couple of years. And Andy's Endscape stock has doubled recently, plus the Chinese paid him four hundred million dollars cash for a piece of the company, so Andy has tons of money to pour into the school. Anyway, Cal heard that Andy wants to move First Principles to a corporate campus he found in Palo Alto, which will destroy Christie's business."

"Wow, that's big news. And you're right, Cal would be crushed," I said.

We sat in silence again, watching the sky above the bay turn deep purple. A few bright stars were already flickering overhead.

"You sure you're OK?" Carly asked, suddenly turning to face me.

"Why are you asking me that way?"

"Well," Carly said, "I mean, you've lost three friends in the past, like, ten days. You don't seem very, um...emotional, or upset."

"I don't know if I'd call them *friends*," I said. "It's not like I was so close with those three guys. I saw Peter around a bit, and Rocky too, though a lot less lately. Nobody was really in touch with Indigo anymore. So, I just...I guess, it hasn't really hit me yet. The finality of it."

"OK," said Carly. "Sorry, just asking."

"It's OK," I said. "Besides, you're right, I've probably been too focused on myself lately. There's this big case at work, and I really think I could contribute, and they don't seem to be interested in what I have to offer."

Carly downed the rest of her La Marca.

"Honey, they don't appreciate you. They'll see it. And I know you. You'll make them see it."

I swirled the wine at the bottom of my cup, staring into it.

Swirling, and staring. Staring, and swirling.

"You're right," I said, my focus submerged into the eddying bubbles. "I'll make them see it. First thing tomorrow morning. I'll show them."

"Tomorrow's Sunday," Carly noted.

"I'll have the office to myself, then," I replied, already envisioning my surprise for Hope Pearson.

CHAPTER 7

I SPENT SUNDAY ALONE IN the newly commandeered conference room at the D.A.'s office, leaving a memento for Pearson to find the next morning. She would ignore me no more. Returning home in the afternoon, I encountered Tiffany and Elyse standing at the edge of the Bayside Towers traffic circle.

"You guys heard about Peter, right?" Tiffany asked. "I'm headed over to Cindy's, to keep her company."

"She's the one who found him?" Elyse asked.

"Ya, she said they were supposed to get together Friday night, at her house. Peter didn't show up. He had messaged her on Friday that he wasn't feeling well, so she just figured he had a stomach bug or something, and had gone to bed without telling her. But he didn't answer her calls or messages Saturday morning either, so she went over to his house and let herself in. She found him on the floor and called an ambulance. Seems that he had been lying there for a while."

"He was a healthy guy. What happened? Do they know?" Elyse asked.

"Poison. That's what the police told Cindy today. They don't know where it came from, or if he possibly committed suicide. No note, like Rocky. No way to know," Tiffany said.

"Poor Cindy," Elyse said.

"Send our wishes," I called as Tiffany walked off.

"What's going on here?" Elyse asked me. "It's like a horror movie."

"Yeah..." I said, distracted. A familiar figure stood across the circle in the Bayside parking lot. "Is that Tyler Lukela? What's he doing here?" I asked, as I squinted in his direction.

"He called me," Elyse said. "Asked to come over and talk. He wants to know if I can help him get a job at Carrie's Cosmetics."

"At Carrie's?" I repeated. Tyler had opened the trunk of his Hyundai sedan. Inside was a large duffel bag, and he bent down to remove something that he put into the pocket of his black windbreaker. The object was the size and shape of a handgun.

"Yes," Elyse said. "Even though his startup failed, Tyler has quite a bit of know-how about branding, and branding is what we do."

Tyler shot a glance over his shoulder and slammed his trunk shut.

"Branding!" I blurted. "Oh god. Oh god. You're Branding! Come with me now!"

I grabbed Elyse's arm and dragged her, startled, into North Tower. "Hurry, before he sees us!"

"What's going on?" Elyse stammered as I pulled her.

"I'll explain! Oh god." I threw open the lobby door and yanked Elyse toward the elevator. I punched seven, Elyse's floor, and then the Close Door button repeatedly.

"What's going on? Addie..." Elyse snarled breathlessly, as the elevator rose. I still held her wrist tight.

"Do you remember the *7 Powers* book we studied with Mallory?" I asked.

The doors opened on Elyse's floor, and I pulled her past her apartment door toward the far emergency exit stairwell.

"*7 Powers?* We had to know that by heart. What does that have to do with anything?"

"Get in here." I kicked open the metal exit door, and it banged against the cement brick stairwell wall. I shut the door and kept watch through its small glass window into the hallway as I quickly tried to bring Elyse up to speed.

"Rocky worked at Netflix. If you remember, Netflix is Helmer's example of Scale Economies, right?" I said.

"Something about being able to amortize large investments in original programs, over many more customers," Elyse said.

"And Indigo was at Intuit. Massive accounting software company. Once you install their software, it's expensive and difficult to switch, right? Switching Cost."

"Yes, but what does that have to do with me, and why are we hiding from Tyler?"

The elevator bell dinged and Tyler stepped out. He marched down the hallway and knocked on Elyse's door. I gestured to her, with a finger to my lips, to stay quiet.

"Elyse!" Tyler called, and knocked again. Elyse crouched, watching me. I pantomimed a slow, shooting motion with my thumb and forefinger, and mimicked holstering a gun at my waist, then pointed toward the door. I mouthed the word *gun*. Elyse's face transformed with fear.

I peeked again through the window. Tyler removed a phone from his pocket. Suddenly, beside me in the stairwell, a jingle sounded in Elyse's pocket.

DO do do do

DO do do do

DO do do do, do

The vintage Nokia ringtone.

"Elyse? You there?" Tyler called from the hallway, and his footsteps approached us.

I ducked below the window, and shoved Elyse toward the stairs. As Tyler pushed the door open, I threw my shoulder against it and the door hit Tyler's head with a loud *clanggg*. He fell back into the hallway, moaning.

"Run!" I shrieked, and we dashed down the stairs. Above us, steel banged against concrete as Tyler, back on his feet, staggered into the stairwell.

"Elyse?" Tyler yelled. We were already a flight-and-a-half down.

"In here!" I hissed to Elyse. I snatched her arm and we bolted into the hallway on the fifth floor. Tyler wouldn't know which door we had opened.

I led Elyse quickly across the hallway and down the opposite stairwell adjacent to the elevators. We raced out of the North Tower lobby, around the Mini Mart wedged between the two buildings, and into South Tower. The elevator doors were open at the lobby and I swept Elyse inside and jabbed the Close Door button, then pressed six.

"We'll hide you in my apartment until he leaves," I said.

Carly was out at Christie's. I slammed our door and bolted it shut. Elyse stood with her hands at her sides.

"You either just saved my life, or you're stark raving mad," she said, panting.

I stepped into the kitchen. "Where was I," I said, pouring a glass of water for Elyse. "Right. So Rocky's Scale Economies, Indigo is Switching Cost."

"Peter? I am still so confused," said Elyse.

"Peter's an easy one," I said. "The more users Twitter gets, the more valuable the platform is for each user. That's classic Network Economies."

Elyse flopped onto my couch, and I handed her the glass. "Addie, wonderful business strategy lesson. Now, before I call the mental health hotline, please explain to me what, in God's name, is going on."

I stood at the entrance to our kitchen. "I can't tell you how I know. But I think Rocky, Indigo and Peter were murdered. By someone targeting our class. There's been communication from someone, about the deaths. And he refers to the number seven, and something like 'guess which of Helmer's powers Indigo was,' something like that. So we—they—think it has to do with the book, *7 Powers.*"

Elyse listened, wide-eyed. "So there will be seven murders."

"That's what we're guessing."

"I'm also starting to gather what this has to do with me." Elyse rubbed the wrist I had grabbed, which was bright red.

I elaborated. "I made a list of our class, and the companies where everyone works, and which, if any, powers those companies would represent, according to Helmer."

"To try to anticipate."

"Right," I said. "Who the killer might go after next. There are four left. And I have you down as Branding."

"Are you sure? Let me see if I remember this," Elyse said. "Helmer says Branding power isn't just brand awareness or advertising, I remember that."

I cut in. "He says it's where the customer pays a higher price, for an equivalent product, simply because of the brand name. Its prestige, its reliability, or," I pointed to Elyse, "its having a famous celebrity's name on it. So Carrie's Cosmetics would be Branding."

"And you think Tyler—"

Bang, bang. My door reverberated with a loud pounding.

"Elyse? You in there? Addie? It's Tyler! I want to talk to you!"

Elyse covered her mouth and I motioned her away from the couch. I tiptoed into the kitchen and quietly opened our knife drawer, removing the largest kitchen knife we owned.

Bang-bang-bang. "Addie! Elyse!" Tyler bellowed.

I gripped the knife handle, keeping Elyse and the door in view.

"Addie! Come on." The door shuddered as Tyler kicked it.

After a few more moments, Tyler cursed loudly and his footsteps receded down the hallway. I padded across the room to the balcony, still holding the knife, and swept back the blinds.

"There he is," I said to Elyse after a minute. "He's leaving." I returned the knife to the kitchen drawer.

Elyse slumped back onto the couch and swallowed a deep gulp of water. "And you think," she said slowly, "that it might be...Tyler?"

"I don't know," I said. "Honestly. But he was so angry at Peter's, at the memorial. Vicious. Worse than usual. He's pretty imbalanced to start with. Could be that his startup fails, and he gets jealous. Could want to take something out against the school, against Mallory, against his successful classmates. And I'm telling you, he had a pistol in his pocket just now. I saw him take it out of the trunk of his car."

Elyse held her empty glass out to me. "I'm going to need something stiffer."

CHAPTER 8

DOUG MALLORY, BUSINESS STRATEGY SEMINAR, Lecture 10 – Process Power

"...In Process Power, Helmer's talking about a process that is so unique, or so complicated or complex, that even if other companies know about it and try to copy it, they won't have the same result. And if we use the same logic Helmer uses in Cornered Resource—that the process or resource could be a person or people—then I would argue that a person within the company could have a special process, usually developed over much time and experience, which even if other people tried to study and understand, would be impossible to replicate..."

Ω

I had parked my scooter outside the District Attorney's office on Monday morning at 8:30. It was already 10:15 and my legal pad was covered with hand-scrawled Japanese *kanji* letters.

Hope Pearson had emerged from the second-floor elevator at exactly 9:00 and swept straight into the conference room without a glance in my direction. Mike had entered the conference room three *kanji* characters before Pearson.

"Is that the memo you owe me, in Japanese? Because I don't read Japanese." The left side of Marvin's butt was planted on my desk.

"Forgot to tell you, Marvin, I do all my rough drafts in Japanese," I said, rubbing my eyes hard with my fingertips.

"Well, you better get on it, Morita, because—"

"Addie?" Mike called to me from the conference room doorway. I jerked my head up and blinked. Mike beckoned to me twice, urgently. His expression was grave.

I sprang from my seat, leaving Marvin teetering on my desk as my empty chair twirled in place.

Mike's face was sullen. He rocked his flex-back chair back and forth, with his arms folded, like a child who had just been scolded by an angry parent.

Pearson's elbows were on the conference table, her fingers holding her temples. Both of their chairs faced the whiteboard.

On Sunday, I had covered the whiteboard with a chart of the twenty-four Mallory seminar students, their residential locations and employers, and my analysis of which of the seven powers, if any, matched each employer. The chart appeared as follows:

Name	Residence	Employer	Potential Power
Andreyev, Maria	Seattle	Amazon - Seattle	Scale Economies, Process Power
Bluth, Elyse	San Rafael - BT	Carrie's Cosmetics	Branding
Briller, Heidi	Salinas	DripLogix	Cornered Resource
Butler, Chris	San Rafael - BT	Novato Organics	Process Power
Caldwell, Cindy	San Rafael	Netflix	Scale Economies
Chen, Tiffany	San Rafael - BT	Elektryk	none
Friedman, Jason	NYC	(biz school)	none
Greenberg, Perry	San Rafael - BT	GenPharmix	Cornered Resource
Greene, Peter	San Rafael	Twitter	Network Economies
Hudson, Janet	Union City	Facebook	Network Economies
Joshi, Vineet	Palo Alto	Cybergetic	Cornered Resource?
LeBleu, Vanessa	Seattle	Amazon - Seattle	Scale Economies, Process Power
Lukela, Tyler	San Rafael	SoleSurvivors	Branding?
Monroe, Brian	San Rafael - BT	Apple	Branding
Murray, Indigo	San Rafael	Intuit	Switching Cost
Naranja, Oscar	San Rafael	Apple	Branding
Newton, Marcus	San Rafael	CA Housing Partners	none
Redstone, Shanice	San Diego	SpaceX	Cornered Resource?
Rojas, Victor	San Rafael - BT	Liferr	Counter-positioning
Tresko, Jimmy	Tiburon	TradePeek	none
Violetto, Rocky	San Rafael - BT	Netflix	Scale Economies
Wei, Caroline	Union City	Facebook	Network Economies
Yelovich, Bill	San Rafael	Google	Scale Economies
Zhang, Warren	San Rafael - BT	Goldman Sachs	none

Pearson spoke in a low voice, without looking up. "Ms. Morita," she began. *Uh-oh.*

"Not forty-eight hours into this investigation, and I am already losing control," she said, massaging her temples. "I told the Sheriff, and I told the District Attorney, that I have my process. I work alone."

She paused. Mike rocked like a metronome, setting a dour beat to Pearson's blues.

"I have a junior detective whose expertise is busting suburban teenagers for smoking marijuana, foisted on me by the Sheriff. And now, I have a computer crimes researcher playing dress-up as a homicide detective, mapping out my suspect list."

"It's a target list," I began. But Pearson lifted one palm from her forehead, indicating she was not done.

Pearson inhaled and exhaled, deeply, slowly. She placed both of her hands flat on the table, and swiveled toward Mike, which caused him to lose his beat.

"What did you say to me before, about that corner?" She pointed to an empty corner of the small room.

"I said, uh, that we should, we could keep our files in that corner," stammered Mike. He eyed Pearson with trepidation, readying himself for the outburst which followed immediately.

"My files are up *here!*" Pearson growled, tapping the side of her head with her index finger. "Maybe you need lots of cardboard boxes for your vandalism or glue-sniffing investigations. But that is not how I work. I have my own method, and it works just fine for me."

Then the High Priestess of Homicide faced me. Her forehead furrowed. And the eyes—*those eyes*—opened, and they bore holes straight through me.

"This is my investigation, Addie. Yes, it is a complex scenario. Yes, you will say 'I just wanted to help.'" She said that in a singsong voice. "But I could get you fired for a stunt like this. I have that power. Nobody tells me how to do my job. Nobody."

I'm melting, I thought. *Like the witch in The Wizard of Oz.*

Mike sported a deep frown, and his chair squeaked with an annoying, *EE-ee, EE-ee* as he marked double-time. "Stop that," Pearson snapped at Mike and the squeaking ceased.

Silence ensued, as Pearson cooled to a low boil.

Pearson's eyes shifted to the whiteboard. "I repeat, this is my investigation. It will be done my way. If I trip over someone, there will be trouble. If someone gets in my way, I will run them over. 'Move fast and break things' may work in the startup world, or the First Principles world, but not in my world. Not in a Hope Pearson murder investigation." *Mike probably doesn't even recognize the Facebook motto,* I thought.

"Is this clear?" snapped Pearson.

"Yes," we responded in unison. *No,* I thought. *Does this mean I'm part of the investigation?*

"Mike, there will be many facts to gather here, and you will help me with those. I always start with the facts. You will present me with your updates daily, and I will file them away in our file area." She tapped her head again, and Mike smiled sheepishly.

"So, start with the facts," she continued. "What evidence do we have on Greene and Murray? Very little, I believe."

Mike spoke. "We got the toxicology back on Peter Greene. Ethylene glycol."

"Antifreeze," said Pearson. "Colorless and sweet-tasting. Very deadly in moderate amounts, and difficult to detect."

"Exactly," Mike said. "Timing-wise, Peter Greene and Indigo Murray are both similar. Time of death is not exact, time of poisoning is not known, and could have happened over a wide range of hours, if not days."

"Right," Pearson said. "Also, there was a large gathering of most of the Mallory class, including Mallory himself, at Greene's house

Thursday night. So in both cases, there were many opportunities for someone, particularly someone known to either of them, to make contact, plant the poisonous element, and leave without any specific record or evidence. We could investigate further, of course, and we will have to at some point, but right now those two would be huge drains on our resources."

Mike took over. "Violetto, on the other hand, fell from his balcony at a very specific time. At or close to 9:50 p.m. on Thursday, May 9."

"If Violetto was thrown from his balcony," Pearson interjected, "anyone we suspect will have to have an alibi for that exact place and time. So let's start there, and rule people out in order to narrow our suspect pool."

Pearson handed Mike a folder. "Mike, you are going to start with the Mallory class list. Here you go, though it's a far less attractive version of the original work of art on our wall." Mike unsuccessfully tried to stifle a snicker.

"This list has everyone's phone numbers," she noted. "I received them from Katherine Meadows, First Principles' alumni director. She will cooperate in any way you need. And I am sure Addie can be helpful with finding updated contact information as well. Get started on that immediately. I hope we can cover all whereabouts and alibis by the time we meet here tomorrow."

"I'm on it," said Mike.

"And now, to our lovely *object d'art.*" Pearson faced the whiteboard. "First of all, Addie, since you are in the computer crimes group, get one of your people to see if they can trace the sender of the emails you have received."

"I'll do that today," I said. *Can't wait to turn the tables on Marvin.*

"We see this sometimes. A serial killer taunts the authorities with hints or clues to a pattern. So, Addie, your theory is that the killer is signaling to us that the victims represent the seven business strategies described in that book."

"Hamilton Helmer's *7 Powers*, that's correct," I said.

"So there would be four more targeted victims," she continued. "And what you have done here is suggest that the victims are targeted based on their employer matching one of the seven powers."

"Right," I confirmed.

Pearson stroked her chin, then said, "Too many assumptions here. For example, in terms of suspects, you are just focusing on the class itself. The killer could be someone outside the class. We have to remember that. And in terms of targets, you are assuming as well that the only targets are former students. And why assume that the seven powers map to current employer? Maybe there is some other matching characteristic. A personality trait perhaps? We cannot be sure." She paused again.

"I agree, but—"

Pearson cut me off. "And it seems that you have identified the first three powers, matching the first three victims, but there are still many possibilities for the other four, even if you are correct. More than half the class are still potential targets."

"You're right," I said cautiously. "At least it's a start."

"But not something we can work with right now," Pearson said. "We cannot just go around following a dozen or more people, in different states, just because they might be murder targets based on your chart."

"That's why I included *Residence*," I said.

"Explain," said Pearson.

"Well, just noting that all three deaths so far have been local. Some of the people on the chart live far away. So I figure they're less likely targets."

"Careful about the assumptions. I keep repeating myself," cautioned Pearson.

"How about a column for *Motive*?" asked Mike. "Who might have an ax to grind, or the like?"

Pearson's brow furrowed deeply. "Mike, I am going to say this loud and clear, for the last time. I have a method, a tried-and-true process. Facts first. Then motive."

She exhaled deeply. "Let me tell you a story, OK? A short story. A homicide, down in Napa. A wealthy doctor. Not much evidence but definitely a homicide. And lots of motive. Motive everywhere. The young third wife, gold-digging. The children and stepchildren already fighting over inheritance before he died. Dozens of dubious business relationships. On and on. And guess who did it?" She paused for effect. "I figured out it was the gardener. The damn gardener. Doctor owed him $1,640 and was withholding payment. *Boom*. The end."

Mike shook his head in disbelief.

"What I am saying, Mike, is that this is not the Juvenile Crime department. At this level, you have to let facts guide you to motive. You do not chase motives trying to match them to facts. In complex cases like this, under every rock you lift up, you will find plenty of maggots. Plenty of potential motives, distractions and dead ends. And we will be lifting up plenty of rocks. Stay focused on the facts. Start with the alibis for Violetto. I have arranged with the District Attorney for you to work at the empty desk next to Addie's out on the floor."

"Got it," said Mike.

I remained standing next to the whiteboard. Pearson was checking her phone.

"Agent Pearson," I ventured, "I just want to understand. Am I now officially part of the investigation team?"

She glanced up from her phone. "Is that very important to you, Addie, to officially be part of the investigation team?"

"Well, yes, I guess it is."

"Then I am sorry to disappoint you. You have not been officially transferred to me by the computer crime task force."

"But you have the power to—"

"And, I cannot allow myself to do that. You have no formal training and no experience in homicide investigation. At least Mike has some homicide exposure, however minimal."

I bit my upper lip.

"Addie, we cannot let ourselves get hung up on titles, or ego. I am sure you will be able to contribute when called upon. For now, just go about your regular day-to-day. I know where to find you. You are just a shout away."

Hope Pearson picked up her phone and car keys from the table, and walked out of the conference room toward the elevator.

Mike shrugged, and I hit him with an angry glare.

CHAPTER 9

"WHAT ARE YOU STARING AT?" Mike asked, as he scribbled in a notebook at his new desk next to mine. A few hours had passed since our meeting with Pearson.

"Sorry, sorry," I apologized. "It's just so stupid, so arbitrary."

"What's so stupid?"

"'You can't be on the team, you don't have homicide experience, Mike does,'" I said in a falsetto tone. "And then, she plunks you right next to me. I can hear every single one of your calls, to every one of my friends. It's like she's rubbing my face in it."

"Wanna switch?" Mike asked, holding Pearson's folder out to me. "I told you, I don't even like this work."

"*Arrrgghh,*" I moaned, dropping my head into my hands. "It's not fair."

"No, I get it," Mike said. "I'd be jealous too. These phone calls, I'm tellin' you. Cloak and dagger stuff." He scanned the room furtively, and whispered, "I'm risking my life out here. Cover me."

"*Ha-ha.* You know what I mean. All I want is to contribute. To be part of it, to help catch this guy. To have her take me seriously."

"I thought all you wanted was to be a black lesbian," Mike said. I threw a pen at him and resumed typing my report for Marvin.

Toward the end of the day, I marched over to Marvin's desk and leaned on its edge, testing whether Marvin would get the joke. He did not.

"I finished that intrusion study, Marvin. It's in your inbox." He did not react. "Oh, and also, I'm going to need you to try to trace some emails I received. They're related to another case."

"Huh?" Marvin had separated his nose from his monitor.

"I. Said," I repeated in a slow cadence, as if I were talking to a two-year-old, "I. SENT. You. Three. EMAILS. That. I. Received. I. NEED. You. To. See. If. You. Can. Trace. The. SENDER. Or. Find. Out. Anything. About. His. Identity. Or. LOCATION."

"Is this approved?" Marvin's eyes flashed toward Gonzalez's office.

"Schmidt needs it. Urgent," I said. I uprooted my rear from Marvin's desk.

When I returned to my desk, my phone buzzed with a message from Tiffany:

You & Elyse, my place, 8pm, for a surprise. See you there.

Ω

I had just arrived at Tiffany's apartment when Elyse let herself in.

"Sorry I'm late," Elyse said.

"You're good, Addie just got here," called Tiffany from her kitchen.

"I'm so curious. What's the big surprise?" asked Elyse.

"Please be seated," said Tiffany, entering her sitting area and motioning toward the two loveseats. She perched on the edge of her couch, hands clasped on her lap over her short skirt.

"So I've been wanting to try this for a while, and I thought now would be a good time to start," Tiffany continued. "A couple of years ago, my family took a tour to Japan, and when we were in Kyoto, we went to this ancient place that does an incense ceremony, called a Kodo. It means 'The Way of Incense.'"

"Ever hear of that?" Elyse asked me. I shook my head.

"If you're familiar with the Japanese Tea Ceremony, it's kind of like that," said Tiffany. "It was magical. Spiritual, almost. You're supposed to 'listen' to the smells."

"That's so Japanese," I cracked.

"But it works," insisted Tiffany. "And it's like a game. You're supposed to smell the different flavors, and then write down what you think the aromas are."

"I love it," said Elyse.

Tiffany rose elegantly from the couch. "Now, of course, The Kodo we did was conducted by an expert, and I'm not an expert. But you guys don't know the difference anyway, so we'll do the best we can, and we'll have fun. I thought we could use a little diversion, with everything going on."

"That's for damn sure," I said.

"Great! I'm so excited," Tiffany said. "I stopped by an incense shop downtown on the way back from work. They sold me everything: flavors, cups, the works. I'll get it set up. It'll just take a few minutes. Meanwhile, talk amongst yourselves." Elyse and I laughed, and Tiffany stepped back into the kitchen.

"Good for you," called Elyse after her. "This is a great idea. I feel like my head is exploding. Since, you know, Rocky, and Peter."

"And Indigo," I added. "And yesterday." I mimed a gun with my thumb and index finger, and Elyse frowned.

"Tiff, how was Cindy when you went over there yesterday?" I called toward the kitchen.

Tiffany placed an incense cup down on her kitchen counter, and straightened her shoulders.

"Well, it was pretty intense. I thought she'd be hysterical, but she was, you know, almost stoic. Maybe it still hadn't sunk in. Or maybe she'd gotten it out of her system since she found Peter on Saturday morning. I don't know. Anyway, she told me some strange things."

"Like what?" I asked, rising from the love seat and stepping toward the kitchen.

"Well, first of all, it turns out that the delayed engagement had been mutual. I had always thought it was Cindy who had been pushing it off, but she said Peter was also having doubts. Cindy told me—she got emotional about this part—that Peter suspected she had been cheating on him. He even thought Rocky might be back in the picture, and part of the reason he had a TBT with Rocky was to ask him, man to man."

"So it's possible they fought," Elyse said.

"Why would Peter schedule a TBT to go fight with Rocky?" I asked.

"No, see, that's the thing," said Tiffany. "Cindy said Peter was convinced about the cheating part, but he didn't really believe it was Rocky, so he just wanted to be casual about it, in the context of a

TBT. Peter told Cindy that Rocky had totally laughed it off, and Peter put it to bed. Plus, Cindy had sworn to Peter nothing was going on with Rocky. But the key is that she said Peter was already long gone from Rocky's apartment when Rocky fell. Peter was at Christie's."

"How do you know that?" Elyse asked.

"Well, Cindy told me. But also, remember, Addie, when we were standing outside with the police cars? I'm pretty sure I saw Peter with the group that ran up from Christie's."

"Who else was there?" I asked.

"I remember seeing Malcolm, Perry, Victor and Warren, for sure. There was some baseball game on, and a bunch of the guys went to the bar to watch it, and Peter joined them."

"OK, interesting," I said, making a mental note of the names.

"The other strange thing, is that Cindy mentioned that Tyler Lukela has been, basically, harassing her. He called while we were sitting there, and she was like, 'he's terrible, he's making me insane.' She wouldn't say what it was about."

Elyse and I exchanged glances and I put my finger to my lips, as Tiffany continued to work in the kitchen.

"Anyway, enough about all that," said Tiffany. "The point of this Kodo is to take our minds off any negative energy." She was carefully arranging five ceramic incense cups and some other paraphernalia on a wooden tray resting on the kitchen counter.

"This should be fun for you, Addie," Tiffany remarked, as she delicately spaced the five cups on the tray. "You're legit Japanese."

"My dad's Japanese," I corrected her. "I'm *Nisei*, second generation, and barely that. True though, my dad always pushed the Japanese heritage stuff. All the years my parents were together, and even after the divorce, it was like a battle for my soul. My dad wanted his daughter to be proud Japanese, and my mom pushed the German side. So by ninth grade I was an orange belt in judo and I could bake a mean *butterkuchen.*" Elyse chuckled.

I stepped toward Tiffany's buffet. "What are these things?" I asked Tiffany, holding up some plastic cartridges with yellow stickers stacked on the narrow buffet.

"EpiPens," answered Elyse from her loveseat. "Tiffany has those crazy allergies. Remember, at Mallory's end-of-semester party, when Heidi brought her peanut brittle? Tiffany started to go into shock, and gave herself the shot right there in front of everyone?"

"How could anyone forget that?" I murmured.

"The last thing we need is another person dropping dead around here," Elyse said.

"I need those EpiPens for work. I'm super careful at home, but I never know who's brought what into the office," said Tiffany, entering the sitting area with the wooden tray.

"OK, we are ready to begin," Tiffany announced, shifting to a soft, soothing tone. She slowly lowered herself to a kneeling position and gently placed the tray on the floor before her. "Elyse, grab those papers and pens next to you, and each of you kneel down, just like me. We'll make a triangle."

Elyse and I complied.

"Now, it's not a seance or anything. You're allowed to talk. But try to really focus on the scent. I'll light one cup at a time, and pass it around. Take your time with it, like I said, *listen* to the smells. You'll see what I mean."

Tiffany gracefully leaned forward and lit the first incense holder. "Then, when you think you've identified the smells, take a pen and write down what you think they are."

Elyse distributed the papers and pens.

"OK, here we go," Tiffany said, and slowly lifted the first incense receptacle with two cupped hands, to just underneath her nose. She closed her eyes and inhaled, meditatively and deeply, then exhaled slowly. She opened her eyes.

"Nice," she said. "I'll start them around, so I don't hog them. I'll come back to this one." She passed the cup to me, on her left, with both hands.

I mimicked Tiffany's movements and lifted the cup to just under my nostrils. *A rushing mountain stream. The sound of wildflowers, and lavender.* Tiffany was right, I could *hear* the scent of the wildflowers and the lavender.

The next cup sounded like snow-covered pine trees. And another one sounded like my mother's voice, whispering to me to be calm, not to worry, that everything would be all right. A tear welled up in my eye.

We passed the incense cups to each other in almost total silence. After what seemed like two hours, but had actually been about forty minutes, Tiffany softly said, "OK, I think we can stop." She gathered the cups and placed them back on the tray. I had covered my paper with poetic phrases, and Elyse and Tiffany's pages were full as well.

"How was that?" Tiffany asked expectantly.

"Wow. Amazing," said Elyse, smiling broadly.

"Transcendental," I said.

Ω

I descended from Tiffany's floor in the North Tower elevator to the lobby, exiting toward the traffic circle for the few strides to South Tower. Those strides led me past the Moskva Mini Mart, a small convenience store operated by two cousins, Sergei and Vlad.

As I passed the unlit store, an unfamiliar figure leaned against the corner of the Mini Mart dragging on a cigarette. He was older than the typical Baysider, balding with a steep forehead and angular nose. The collar of his jacket was upturned and he watched me as I walked past him into the South Tower lobby.

I lingered at the row of mailboxes in the lobby and slowly unlocked and opened mine, pretending to take great interest in the five envelopes I found inside. I unhurriedly opened each letter, one after the other. I made a show of finding each utility bill and credit card offer more intriguing than the last, and as I perused them, I intermittently peeked over the pages at the stranger. The spy, or hit man, or whatever he was, just glowered at me each time our eyes met.

After a few minutes of our visual cat-and-mouse charade, loud running footsteps drew near. Sergei crossed from the far side of the traffic circle and greeted the stranger apologetically in murmured Russian. The interloper stomped his cigarette on the ground with the heel of his shoe and eyed me one last time as Sergei produced a ring of keys and unlocked the door to the darkened shop. The two men disappeared inside.

CHAPTER 10

HOPE PEARSON APPEARED ON THE second floor of the District Attorney's office mid-morning on Tuesday, and made straight for the southwest corner. She deposited herself into the firm gray chair alongside my desk, the old chair that in two years, Marvin had never used.

Pearson crossed one charcoal-colored pant leg over the other, and turned her back to me. "What do you have for me, Mike?" she asked.

"OK, so I've reached just about everyone on the list," Mike said, stretching to pick up a folder. "Most people check out, but there are some holes, and some question marks."

"Start from the top," instructed Pearson.

"OK. Maria Andreyev. Works for Amazon, lives in Seattle. So she's ruled out—"

"Incorrect," Pearson cut him off. "Someone can orchestrate a crime without being proximate. This exercise is just to help us decide where to concentrate our investigation in the near term. There is a difference between low chances, and completely ruled out."

"Understood," Mike said, shifting in his seat. "Elyse Bluth, she lives at Bayside Towers, and she was with Addie in Elyse's apartment from after work until they heard the sirens." Pearson did not acknowledge me when Mike mentioned my name.

Mike continued. "Heidi Briller, she lives in Salinas. She says Jimmy Tresko had gone down that night to see her. But I have to say she was a bit vague. As to why they met, what they did that evening in Salinas, etcetera. Her voice was...shaky. She didn't sound confident."

"And Tresko?" asked Pearson.

"Lives in Tiburon. He said he went down to Salinas to talk to Heidi about her company. He does some kind of stock trading thing, and he was researching the company Heidi works for," said Mike.

"Jimmy doesn't have a job, per se," I cut in, over Pearson's shoulder. "He invests in shares of publicly traded companies, on a social stock trading platform called TradePeek. I guess Heidi's company is publicly traded."

"Right," said Mike. "But I'm just saying, Heidi sounded hesitant about Jimmy's visit."

"Noted," said Pearson. "Keep going."

"Butler, Greenberg, Naranja, Rojas, and Zhang were all at Christie's, which is a sports bar just down the street from Bayside Towers. Sorry I'm going out of order—"

"Proceed," said Pearson, waving him on.

"So they were all at Christie's, watching the Oakland A's game. First pitch was 7:08 p.m. and it was a fast game. The A's hit a walk-off home run to win it. I checked the box score, and the game ended right around 9:50 p.m."

"Which is significant, because that's the precise time of the 911 call about Violetto," said Pearson.

"Exactly," said Mike.

"And they claim that they were all at Christie's, the whole time, until the game ended?" asked Pearson.

"Not only that," said Mike. "But a number of them said that Peter Greene was with them at the end of the game. Meaning, he had left Rocky's and joined them at the bar."

"Are they certain?" asked Pearson.

"Yes. Well, at least one was. Zhang says he remembers high-fiving Greene when the game-ending homer was hit."

I don't care if her back is turned on me or not, I thought. I spoke up again. "Tiffany Chen told me the same thing. She recalls seeing the group of guys walk up from Christie's just after the police cars pulled in to Bayside, and she's sure Peter was with the group."

"All right," said Pearson to Mike. "Continue."

"Cindy Caldwell says she was home, uncorroborated, so question mark. The same goes for a bunch of others: Tiffany Chen and Brian Monroe, who both also reside at Bayside Towers, and Vineet Joshi who lives in Palo Alto, so they're all question marks. Marcus Newton and Bill Yelovich share a house in San Rafael, they say they were home together, playing video games. Janet Hudson and Caroline Wei share a condo in Union City, they say they were home together. I think that's it for the locals. Noting what you said about Maria, the remaining ones are Jason Friedman, who lives in New York, Vanessa LeBleu in Seattle, and Shanice Redstone in San Diego—she works for

SpaceX, which is super cool by the way. I spoke with all those out-of-towners just for good measure, and they were all home then."

"You skipped one," said Pearson, her eyes closed.

Mike stared at his notebook. "Well, Indigo Murray, but he's—"

"No, another one."

Mike's eyes were still fixed on his notes. "Oh, yeah, of course. Tyler Lukela. Wow, you're good."

Pearson smiled at Mike and tapped her temple.

"Yeah, Lukela...Lukela..." Mike said, rapping his pen on the pad. "Weird dude. He shares a house in San Rafael with Oscar Naranja, but he apparently wasn't with Oscar and the other guys at Christie's that night. Basically, Lukela refused to talk the minute I introduced myself. Practically hung up on me."

"If I may," I interjected again. "Tyler is a very problematic guy. He was acting really strange at the memorial for Rocky at Peter's house. I wasn't the only one who noticed it. Plus his startup just failed. And Tiffany tells me that Cindy told her that Tyler has been harassing her. Her, meaning Cindy." I paused. "I know that sounds like teenage gossip, but it could be relevant. And Tyler likes guns. I saw him on Sunday at Bayside Towers, and I'm pretty sure he had a handgun in his jacket pocket."

"*Hmm...*" murmured Pearson, digesting the nuggets of hearsay. "Well done, Mike."

Marvin suddenly interrupted us, standing at my left elbow because Pearson encroached upon his usual parking space.

"Excuse me. Um, Addie, I ran the check on those emails," he said haltingly, making brief eye contact with my two guests. "We can't tell you much. IP address is masked, probably a burner phone using a VPN. Sorry."

"Thanks, Marvin. Appreciate the fast turnaround," I said with false sincerity as Marvin turned and left.

Pearson's fingers were at her temples again. "Mike, what was the name of that stock platform Jimmy trades on? TradePeek?"

Mike consulted his pad. "Yes. I think I'm going to drive down to Tiburon to see Jimmy on Thursday. Try and get him to open up a bit more, see why Heidi was acting strange about his alibi."

"Excellent," said Pearson. "And Lukela, we need to find out more about him. What was the name of his startup?"

"SoleSurvivors," I said. "It was a marketplace for collectible sneakers."

"I will look into that a bit more," Pearson murmured as if to herself. Then she addressed me directly for the first time. "Do you recall if Tyler started that company right after graduation? Do you know who funded it?"

"I believe it was right after school," I said. "But I don't know who his investors were."

"Worth checking," she said. "And Mike, I need you to get me the toxicology and coroner reports on Murray and Greene."

"Got it." He jotted a note on his pad.

Pearson blinked and shifted back toward me. "Why do so many of you still live at Bayside Towers, and in San Rafael in general? Two years since you finished school and...one-third of the Mallory class still essentially lives in the school dorm."

"That's an interesting question," I said. "I never really thought about it."

After a moment of contemplation I added, "I guess we each had our different reasons for staying. I mean, I work five minutes away. For Elyse and Tiffany, they like the safety and security of Bayside. Which seems ironic now...Also, it's cheaper than other places, certainly than downtown. Andy Freel owns Bayside Towers, and he wants the buildings to be full, and it's good for the students to have some alumni around, so he keeps the rent low."

"Fair enough," Pearson said. When you watched her you could almost hear file cabinets opening and closing in her brain.

Pearson rubbed her hands together. "All right, good work, Mike. I have some meetings to get to. Tomorrow morning I will be meeting with Doug Mallory to hear what he has to say."

She swiveled again in my direction. "Addie, you will join me. I will pick you up, here, at 9:30." She vacated the chair and walked off, toward the elevator.

I searched Mike's expression for an explanation of Pearson's behavior. "'You're not on the team. But come with me tomorrow to Mallory.' It's crazy. I wonder what her game is," I said.

"Beats me," Mike said. "Maybe, you have to be a little crazy to want to be a homicide detective."

CHAPTER 11

DOUG MALLORY, BUSINESS STRATEGY SEMINAR, Lecture 14 – Branding

"You want a good example of Branding? How about this one standing right up here. That's right, me, Doug Mallory. Why do startups want me as an investor, or on their boards? Is my advice that much better, my cash any greener? Probably not. They want me for my name, my reputation. If you get Doug Mallory on your team, you get immediate credibility, my name alone is instant value-add. It's that simple..."

Ω

"Wow, I just realized, I haven't been back here since graduation," I remarked to Pearson as we entered the Descartes Building at First Principles College. The small school housed all of its administrative offices and most of its classrooms in the post-modern octagonal structure encased in glass windows.

Our footsteps echoed as we traversed the cavernous open atrium, which rose to the skylight at the top of the sixth floor. "Nice," said Pearson, beholding the ornamental California Palm trees that ringed the entrance and stretched upward past the balconied hallways that overlooked the lobby.

The elevator carried us to the sixth floor. "That's Euclid Hall on the left, where Mallory taught our seminar," I pointed out to Pearson, and we proceeded in the opposite direction down the hallway toward the administrative offices.

A receptionist's desk guarded the two offices that comprised the Executive Suite. The door to the larger office, Mallory's, was closed. The smaller room to its right, with its door open, belonged to Danny Armstrong.

"Good morning?" The young woman at the receptionist's desk greeted us earnestly.

"Hope Pearson, here to see Professor Mallory. And Addison Morita. She will be joining me."

"Yes, of course. You're right on time. Unfortunately, Professor Mallory is on a call. Something to drink?"

"No thank you," said Pearson, checking her watch.

"OK. Please make yourselves comfortable on the couch. You can go right in when he's done."

At that moment, Danny Armstrong stepped out of his office and toward the receptionist's desk holding a huge, inflated beach ball.

The girls in my First Principles class had nicknamed Danny "Mini Mallory." Danny dressed like his mentor, generally in jeans and a Brooks Brothers oxford with sleeves rolled to the elbows. Danny was about an inch shorter than Mallory, with dirty blond hair rather than brown. And blue eyes. Deep blue eyes, that you could dive into and swim in...

"Addie? Is that you?"

I rose from the couch as Danny bounded over. "It's great to see you! I'd give you a hug, but...I'm holding a beach ball."

"I can hold it for you," offered Pearson from the couch.

"*Ha*, that's OK," said Danny. "How've you been, Addie? What brings you?" His questioning gaze shifted from me to Pearson.

"Hope Pearson. We are here to see Professor Mallory," she said cordially but without elaboration.

"Oh. Cool," he said. "Danny Armstrong." There was an awkward momentary silence and Danny quickly realized neither of us was going to explain further.

He bowed his head obsequiously. "Nice to meet you. Addie, great to see you. Come by, we should catch up."

Danny turned to the receptionist's desk. "Caitlin, I think we'll order these white and purple ones for Orientation." He handed the beach ball to the startled receptionist and hurried out into the hallway.

"Danny is Mallory's Chief of Staff, his right-hand man," I whispered to Pearson as I settled next to her again on the couch. "Mallory can't make a move here without him. Danny is also the Teacher's Assistant for Mallory's senior seminar."

Pearson's eyes had followed Danny as he scurried off. "He's cute." *Thanks, Mom? Or are you jealous?* I thought.

We remained stranded on the couch for another fifteen minutes. Pearson leafed through an issue of the *Harvard Business Review* that basked on the coffee table in front of us while Caitlin clattered on her keyboard.

The phone on the desk buzzed, and Caitlin uttered a low "Yes?" into her headset. Facing our direction, she announced, "You may go in."

Pearson opened Mallory's door, and my mouth suddenly became pasty in Pavlovian apprehension. The King of First Principles College remained seated at his spacious yet uncluttered desk as we entered.

"Ms. Pearson, welcome, sorry for the delay. I was live on CNBC, they always have me on to comment when Facebook does something stupid." He laughed.

"And...is that Addison Morita?" he asked, noticing me, suddenly confused.

"Ms. Morita is with the District Attorney's office," Pearson said quickly. "She is lending us a hand."

Mallory shifted his attention back to Pearson. "And you're with the D.O.J. This is about the recent, um, misfortunes with our former students?"

"Precisely. I would just like to get some additional background information from you."

"Certainly," said Mallory. "I have about," he checked his watch, "twenty minutes or so."

Pearson blinked. "I will keep it brief. I am respectful of your time, Professor." Mallory bowed his head in gratitude.

"The three young men who are deceased—Violetto, Murray and Greene—I understand they were not merely students here, but they were also part of a special seminar you taught?"

"Yes, my Business Strategy seminar. I think they were my first year...Your year too, Addie, right?"

I confirmed.

"What makes the seminar so special? I understand the students compete fiercely to get in," asked Pearson.

Mallory, looking perplexed, answered. "Well, I mean, it's exclusive because I teach it myself, right? You'd want to be in the course if the head of the school teaches it, I should think."

Mallory chuckled haughtily, and continued. "I select the participants personally, based on their grades and other factors—"

"Such as?"

"I call it 'leadership aptitude.' Some tangible, some intangible characteristics."

"I understand that you are helpful in advancing the students' careers," Pearson said, and Mallory nodded. "So any student completing your seminar should be expected to have a good strategic mind and strong leadership skills."

"Yes, exactly right," said Mallory.

"Like Ms. Morita here," Pearson said.

I shot a startled look at Pearson, who continued to face Mallory.

"Uh...I guess so," Mallory said, flustered. "Addie was one of my better students."

"And do you follow up with students after they graduate? Any ongoing relationships?"

"Relationships?" Mallory asked uneasily. "I mean, I see some of them from time to time. They're always welcome here, you know. And if you mean business relationships, I sometimes help them out, give them some seed funding for example, if they're starting a company. I think Tyler was your year, right Addie?" I nodded again, and he turned back to Pearson. "Lukela, I put some money into his sneaker startup. And Jimmy Tresko, I placed some funds with him, too."

Mallory chuckled, and continued. "I don't expect to see much from those investments. They usually bomb. I just try to be nice, and help them out. Sometimes they think I really believe in what they're doing, like it's some kind of Doug Mallory endorsement, but I can't help that. So be it." He leaned back, putting his hands behind his head.

"And Violetto, Murray or Greene? Any recent contact with them?"

"No, not really. The first time in a long time that I saw the rest of the guys was when I stopped by Peter's house for Rocky's memorial. God, that must've been right before—"

"And the women?" interrupted Pearson.

"Excuse me?" Mallory coughed.

"You said you had not seen 'the *guys*' in a long time, what about any of the women from the class?"

Flustered again, Mallory said, "Well I...I don't distinguish, I mean...I meant I hadn't seen most of the *students* in a while. Sorry for not being politically correct. You're right, I should be more careful."

"No worries," said Pearson, waving her hand casually. She gazed out the window for a moment. Pearson's aimless questions, and my presence at the meeting, remained odd mysteries.

"One more question," she said. "I understand that Andy Freel brought you in to run the college. I do not know him personally, though we have some mutual acquaintances."

"Andy put me in the driver's seat and handed me the keys, for better or for worse," Mallory bragged with a smile.

"Do you still speak with Andy often? Do you have other business dealings with him?"

"Not so much, actually. We've started to see the world very differently. Andy's quite an opinionated guy—*person*, sorry—as you may know, and some might say I am too." He winked at me.

"So can you think of anyone that might want to harm Andy, by harming his school?"

"Wow, I...I don't know," stammered Mallory. "That would be very hard to believe. Gosh. I'd have to think about it."

"Think about it," said Pearson.

"Well," said Mallory, consulting his watch again, "we need to wrap up. I have to do a podcast at the top of the hour. Take my card, and please contact me if you have any other questions." He handed Pearson a business card from a small golden tray on the desk.

"I certainly will," said Pearson politely.

"Listen," Mallory said, standing up. "I want you to figure out who did this. It's very troubling. I want you to find out the truth."

"The truth is always painful for somebody," Pearson retorted.

"Absolutely, of course," replied Mallory firmly. "Say, Ms. Pearson, do you have a card? I apologize, I did most of the talking today."

"Quite all right, Professor Mallory," Pearson said as she produced a card from her sweater pocket and handed it to him. "You are in the business of talking, and I am in the business of listening."

As we left Mallory's room, Caitlin, who had been standing outside, inserted her head into the doorway behind us. "Professor Mallory, the IT consultant you hired just left. He installed that new software program on my computer, he said not to bother you."

Pearson froze.

From his office, Mallory called out. "IT consultant? What IT consultant? I didn't hire any IT consultant."

Pearson rushed out of the Executive Suite to the hallway guardrail, and I hurried after her. Six floors below, a male figure with a leather motorcycle jacket and spiked black hair dashed across the lobby and out the main exit door.

"Addie, call your boss Marvin, and tell him to get over here," said Pearson, watching the man as he sprinted toward the parking lot.

CHAPTER 12

MIKE'S HARLEY RUMBLED INTO THE circle at Bayside Towers the next morning, Thursday, at nine o'clock. Mike cut the engine and hopped off where I stood, about ten paces away from where Rocky's body had rested two weeks earlier.

"You sure she's not going to be pissed that I'm coming with you?" I asked.

"She took you with her yesterday to Mallory, didn't she? Why can't you come with me to talk to Jimmy Tresko?"

"Anybody asks, it was your idea," I said.

"Heard you had an interesting time at Mallory's," Mike said.

"It was nuts. A guy walks straight in, as we're meeting with Mallory, and says he's an IT consultant, and Mallory's assistant lets him install some software on her computer, and he runs out. Mallory's about to strangle her, and Pearson tells me to get Marvin. I was there all afternoon. Pearson left, of course. Marvin's pretty sure it's malware. He's analyzing it right now."

"You think it's related? To the murders?"

"No idea. But Pearson was on it right away. She told me to get her Marvin's take as soon as he has something."

"See? You are contributing."

"Shut up. How about you? Anything interesting yesterday?"

"Not much. Pearson's really focused on the Violetto alibis. Turns out Zhang isn't certain anymore that Peter was at Christie's at the *end* of the game. He remembers high-fiving Peter, but it might have been earlier. And all of the other guys are fuzzy on the exact timing."

My gaze shifted to the top of North Tower. "So Peter could've left Rocky, gone down to Christie's, and then run back up to Rocky's and surprised him?"

"In theory," said Mike. "But your friend, what's-her-name, says she saw Peter with the group from the bar."

"Tiffany. She said she saw Peter *standing* with them. She assumed he walked up with the group from Christie's. But I guess maybe—"

Mike cut me off. "Peter could've just snuck around the gathering crowd and mixed back in with the Christie's guys, once he came back down."

"File that away in your file cabinet," I said, and tapped my temple.

Mike chuckled. He circled to the rear of his bike and unhooked a helmet secured to the seat by a cargo net. "Are you ready to ride bitch?"

My jaw dropped. "Excuse me? What did you call me?"

"Punctuation saves lives, Addie. Would you like to ride bitch, not would you like to ride, comma, bitch. 'Riding bitch' means riding on the back seat." He belly-laughed, then switched into a faux British accent. "Or perchance you would prefer the proper term, 'ride pillion'? *Ha-ha-ha.*"

"You probably rehearsed that line the whole way over here, sicko."

"I did, I did," he said, still giggling. Handing me the spare helmet, he recited in a gravelly voice, "Just wrap your legs 'round these velvet rims, and strap your hands 'cross my engines." He straddled the Harley and gripped the handlebars.

"*Ha-ha*, Springsteen. You're hysterical. You sure you don't want to go into stand-up comedy instead of social work?" I buckled my helmet and mounted the pillion seat.

"Thanks. You're too kind. Hang on." He twisted the throttle and I grasped his sides.

"Where does Jimmy live? I've never been to his place," I yelled to Mike, as he piloted the bike toward the Highway 101 South on-ramp.

"Tiburon. It's only about 20 minutes, and we're early. You have a strong grip. Do you work out?"

"If I didn't know you better, I'd say you were flirting with me."

"No way! I have a girlfriend already," Mike called out.

"Really?"

"Yeah. Hope Pearson. What do you think we do in that conference room all day without you?"

"You really are sick," I yelled, and he cackled and accelerated down 101.

Ω

When you round Blackie's Pasture on Tiburon Boulevard, the road narrows from four lanes to two. From there it's a scenic drive for a few minutes along Richardson Bay toward the tip of the Tiburon Peninsula.

We exited onto a winding lane that led to Jimmy's villa near the water. Mike parked his Harley next to another motorcycle.

"Honda," declared Mike with contempt.

"I'm around back," called Jimmy, who apparently had heard Mike's bike come to rest. We skirted the side of the small cottage and found Jimmy on his deck in shorts, a T-shirt and sandals. He was chewing gum and balancing a laptop on his knees in a brown wicker patio chair.

"Welcome. Hey, Addie." Typing, Jimmy glanced up at me briefly, then gestured toward two identical wicker chairs to his right. We crossed in front of him and Mike settled into the chair closer to Jimmy.

"So, what can I do you for today?" asked Jimmy as his fingers tapped on the keyboard.

"Nice place you got here, Jimmy," said Mike with an artificial smile, appraising the deck and the view of the bay.

"Listen, let's cut the small talk. I know you're a detective, so why don't you just detect?" Jimmy snapped.

"OK man, you the boss," said Mike calmly, palms up in a peace gesture. "It's your home court. We're just trying to figure out who might want to cause harm to people who went to First Principles. Wanted to get your input."

"Wow, you're some crackerjack detective," said Jimmy, squinting at his laptop screen and shaking his head.

"You have any thoughts on that?" Mike pressed.

"Nope. Try Tyler. He hates everyone. He's really pissed at Mallory about something. He despised Peter. Does that mean he would kill someone? Don't know. Who else? Victor's got a mean streak. Dunno."

"Victor was at Christie's when Rocky fell from his porch, so he's accounted for," said Mike. "Speaking of, I want to ask you a bit more about that night."

Jimmy closed his laptop slowly, and met Mike's gaze. "I told you I was down in Salinas."

"Right, with Heidi Briller. Tell me again what you were doing there?"

"Research. Man, what kind of Dick Tracy are you? We went through this shit already."

"We did, but Heidi, she was a little vague when I spoke with her," said Mike.

"Look, man," Jimmy said angrily. "Heidi's a good girl. I don't think she's ever talked to a cop, or detective, or whatever the hell you are, in her life. Probably would freak out if she got pulled over for speeding. Probably would never even break the speed limit in the first place." He chortled at the thought. "She told me she was real nervous when you called, it surprised her. She was out of sorts, in the moment."

"So you were down there to talk about her company?"

"Yeah. Heidi works for this agriculture technology startup, DripLogix. They went public last year, and the stock has been bouncing around. Small stock, nice volatility, good for trading. I trade in the shares. I wanted to ask her some questions."

"Inside scoops?" I asked.

"Look Addie, don't get all high and mighty on me. Is this the S.E.C., or a homicide investigation? I'm telling you both, you're barking up the wrong tree. I sure as hell didn't kill anybody. You're wasting your time. And frankly, I don't like you snooping around my business. I think we're done here."

Jimmy abruptly rose, clasping his folded laptop in one arm, and extended the other toward Mike. "Thanks for stopping by." Jimmy slammed his screen door behind him, leaving us standing on the deck.

"Swell guy," said Mike, cracking his knuckles. "Let's go."

Mike's Harley rolled down the short, tree-lined slope from Jimmy's house. Soon after we turned back onto Tiburon Boulevard, another motorcycle revved its engine behind us. Glancing over my shoulder, I saw it approaching quickly as we proceeded west on the two-lane road, hugging the waterline to our left.

Our helmeted pursuer gunned his engine again, and his bike pulled alongside us, on our right. The motorcycle was a Honda, and the rider's shorts matched Jimmy's. Without looking at us he gradually angled his bike to the left, forcing Mike to pull the Harley further to the left to avoid contact. We were soon on, then over the double yellow line. As Mike accelerated and then decelerated, trying to slide back over the divider, the other rider copied Mike's actions, pinning us in the oncoming lane. I gripped Mike tightly.

Mike and I simultaneously noticed the oncoming RV. Approaching slowly, it blocked the entire width of our lane. Mike throttled, matched immediately by the other bike, then braked, mirrored again by the other rider. The RV's horn was blaring, getting louder. My adrenaline spiked. The RV was about three seconds away. *Two, one...*I buried my helmet hard into Mike's back, eyes squeezed shut.

At the last instant, the other biker sped up. Mike slammed his brakes and swerved sharply back into the right-hand lane. The RV roared past, its horn still sounding. Mike slowed to a crawl as the Honda disappeared ahead.

After a few moments a patch of wider shoulder presented itself and Mike swerved the Harley off the road, and planted his feet on the ground. I whipped off my helmet.

"That was Jimmy! He could've killed us!" I shouted.

Mike removed his helmet slowly, and ran his hand through his hair, "He *could* have killed us," he said. "But he didn't."

"Meaning?"

"That was just to scare us." Mike removed his phone from his chest pocket and dialed. "Hi, it's Mike. Yeah, just finished with Jimmy Tresko. He stuck with his Salinas story. Says Heidi was just nervous when I called. Said he had nothing to do with any murders. Then he chased us on his motorcycle and ran us off the highway." He paused. "Yes, off the highway...Us, meaning me and Addie, she's with me...Yeah. OK, see you there." He hung up.

"Pearson," he said. "She's at a cafe on B Street in San Rafael. She wants us to meet her there."

Ω

Mike and I entered the Courtyard Cafe on B Street in San Rafael. We scanned the tables inside for Pearson.

"There she is," Mike said, pointing to an outdoor patio with a few tables sheltered from the overhead sun by blue umbrellas. Pearson occupied a small round table in the corner, alongside a trellis of quilted white lattice covered in pink and purple climbing roses. As we approached, a man seated across from Pearson with his back to us, rose and collected a pack of cigarettes and a phone from the table. Bidding farewell to Pearson, he brushed past us on his way out of the garden toward the street.

I recognized him immediately. He was the Russian spy I had seen with Sergei at the Moskva Mini Mart on Monday night.

Mike pulled a chair from an adjoining table and I claimed the seat the Russian had vacated.

"So, we have all had an interesting morning," Pearson said, and sipped her iced tea.

"Who was that man?" I asked. "I recognize him."

"That, Ms. Morita, is your landlord."

I stared at her. "I've met Andy Freel. That wasn't Andy," I insisted.

Pearson placed her iced tea on the table and leaned back slightly, folding her arms. "Andy Freel does not own Bayside Towers. That man does. His name is Alex Andreyev. Russian billionaire. Friend of Andy's. Andreyev's money funded the purchase of the apartment buildings, but Andy wanted the students to think he owned them himself. Alex was happy to keep a low profile. Probably some money laundering involved."

"How did you find that out?" asked Mike.

"Real estate records, some other connections," Pearson said. "Not rocket science. Andreyev admitted it. But he did not want to talk about Andy. He is hiding something."

"I bet he's angry about Andy moving the school to Palo Alto," I said. Pearson peered at me inquisitively.

"I heard a rumor, just this week, that Andy is considering moving First Principles to a new campus, near Palo Alto," I continued eagerly, as Pearson's eyebrow rose.

"That would really hurt rental income at Bayside Towers," Mike said.

"Wait a minute. Is Andreyev related to Maria? At Amazon, from my class?" I asked.

"Her father," said Pearson. "I told you, Mike, you cannot rule someone out just because they are not local."

"Jeez," Mike muttered. "So Andreyev could be using his daughter, her knowledge about the other students, to get back at Andy."

"Did you learn anything else from Jimmy Tresko?" Pearson asked Mike.

"Before he drove us off the road? No, not much. He fingered Tyler, but not based on anything concrete. Jimmy swears he wasn't involved in any deaths, but I don't know why he chased us down like that."

"Probably has something to do with his trading account. You have seen his portfolio, haven't you?" asked Pearson, looking at Mike, then me.

Mike and I exchanged looks, then shook our heads.

"Well, that surprises me. It's right there, on the internet. That website, TradePeek, posts all of Jimmy's positions and trades. Here, look." She produced her iPhone and after a few taps of her manicured fingertips, rotated it so that we could view the screen.

"A First Principles reunion," Pearson said. "His largest holding is a long position in Cybergetic—"

"That's where Vineet works," I added.

"Right." Pearson turned to Mike. "'Long' means Jimmy makes money if the stock goes up. And look at the second-largest position."

"He's short Endscape Labs," I read.

"So he makes money if Andy's stock goes down..." Mike said, processing.

"And on and on," said Pearson. "Third is Heidi's irrigation company, long. Fourth is Apple, where two other classmates work. Also long. You get the picture."

"Insider trading," I said.

"His portfolio is probably a hornet's nest of inside information," Pearson said. "But also, look at the total amount he has invested. I cannot believe neither of you looked this up."

I frowned sheepishly.

"Portfolio value, eight hundred and eighty-six thousand dollars," read Mike.

"A lot of money for such a young person. Is he from a wealthy family?" Pearson asked.

"Not that I know of," I said.

"So in addition to insider trading, he is probably managing other people's money. Without being a registered financial adviser. Those could be adequate reasons for him to try to scare you away," she said.

"Damn," Mike said.

"And what about this," Pearson said. "The eight-eighty-six, the current value. His trading history shows that he started off with over one and a half million dollars under management. So he likely has a number of unhappy investors. He has already lost almost half their money."

"And therefore, resorting to insider trading to guarantee a rebound," I added. Pearson placed her phone on the table.

"So he collects intel from Vineet and Heidi and the Apple guys, about secret good news, before the stock pops," said Mike. "And Andy's Endscape shares—"

"Go down if there's a serial murder scandal at Andy's school, and Jimmy makes money on the short," I said.

"Wow," said Mike. "Jimmy's not off the hook at all."

"Exactly," said Pearson. "What else do we have?"

Mike crossed his legs. "I have some new stuff from Warren Zhang, a bit of a setback. Now he's not sure Peter Greene high-fived him at the game-ending homer, it may have been earlier. And the other guys from the Christie's group aren't a hundred percent sure either that Peter was with them at the end of the game, though they're certain he was with them earlier."

"I see," Pearson said. Then she asked me, "Addie, where do we stand on *7 Powers?*"

"I, um..." I stammered, caught off guard. *Had she asked me to continue that work? Was I on or off the investigation team?*

"I'm working on it..." I stalled. "I probably need to...to re-read the book. I'll do that this weekend."

"Get on that. We need to identify the next potential targets in order to anticipate the next attempts. Time is of the essence." *Maybe Mike's right. Maybe she's schizophrenic*, I thought

"On it," I said, confused about my role, but happy to be called upon.

Pearson's phone rang, and she answered. "Pearson. Yes, OK, thank you."

Pearson stirred her iced tea, as her brow creased momentarily. "That was Marvin. They completed the trace on the malware that was installed on Mallory's computer yesterday."

She reached for her glass, and took a long sip. "The code traces back to Endscape Labs."

CHAPTER 13

"BOOK OF THE MONTH CLUB?"

I knew the speaker's name was Tim. Assistant District Attorney, perhaps? I had once heard Marvin talking to him on our floor.

I placed *7 Powers* on the picnic table, holding my place with my finger. "Excuse me?" I responded.

"What you're reading there. Good book? Murder mystery or something?"

Tim had brought his bagged lunch out to the patio, apparently to enjoy the Friday afternoon calm. I had been so engrossed in my book that I had not noticed him eating at the next table.

"Yes, kind of a murder mystery...No, just kidding. It's a business strategy book, actually."

"Ugh," Tim playfully shooed me away. "Can't stand that stuff. Read some of it. There was a time I thought I might go for an M.B.A. instead of law school. Bought a couple books like that. Jim Collins, and who's that other guy, Gladwell. You know what? It's all B.S. They just come up with a bunch of provocative theories, then back-end 'em into historical examples. Total crap, that's what I say. A lot of innocent trees have died for that crap."

Tim vigorously shoved the rest of his sandwich into his mouth. "You're in Marvin's group, right?" he asked with his mouth full.

"Yes, computer crimes."

"That's good stuff. The future, I tell you. You're in a good place. Good career choice."

"Thanks for the tip."

"No prob." He crumpled his brown bag and stood up. "Don't mind my rant about business books. I'm sure some are good. You like that one?"

"It's to die for," I said.

Ω

Saturday morning I stretched on the living room floor, lacing up my Brooks for my long run. Out of Carly's bedroom stepped a curvaceous, bohemian beauty in a floppy straw hat, scoop-necked blouse ringed with lace and ripped blue jeans.

"I'm off to Richmond, to the flea market," Carly proclaimed, as I pulled my calf tight under my thigh.

"*Quaint,*" I said. "Your boyfriend—um, boss—should be right nearby, with his buddy Tyler, at the firing range. You can browse for knick-knacks to the sweet sounds of their automatic gunfire. Maybe you could meet them for lattes in between."

"I hope you get hit by a truck on your run," said Carly.

"Unlikely. They don't let trucks on the running path."

I had so much tangled brainwork to unscramble on today's run. Why was Hope Pearson dangling my formal involvement in the case like yarn before a cat? How could I complete the *7 Powers* column of my chart and figure out the critical question of who might be next? And, could I do anything to show my value to Pearson, on the suspect side of the equation?

The breeze, the steady *pop-pop-pop* of my Brooks on the pavement, the regular soft *thwacking* of my nylon backpack, gradually did their work. By the time I jogged back into the traffic circle at Bayside an hour and a half later, I had sorted out a few new ideas.

What I really needed was someone to confirm, or critique, my *7 Powers* evaluation of each of the employers on my chart. During my run, I had realized who that someone was.

Stepping out of the shower in my apartment, with the towel still wrapped around my hair, I texted Danny Armstrong:

Hey, great to see you this week. I could use your help with a case I'm working on. Can we meet? - Addie

You do not want to leave a new message to an old acquaintance unsigned, in case he has not saved your number.

Next, I dialed Mike. Carly had given me my second idea.

"Hey, Addie, what's up?"

"What are you doing today?" I asked.

"Oh, you know, a little bit of this, a little bit of that."

"So, staying at home watching TV."

"Wait—what? Are you outside my window?" he said. We both laughed.

"Listen," I said. "I've got an idea. Tyler Lukela is at the top of your list, right? He's got good motive, possible resentment of the class because his startup just failed, and everyone else is successful. Or maybe something went south between him and Mallory over his investment in Tyler's company. And he's got major aggression and anger issues."

"OK, so?"

"So, he's not going to talk to you, he's made that clear. But I know where he hangs out. Maybe we can eavesdrop."

"Eavesdrop?"

"Tyler is very tight with Cal Forsythe, the owner of Christie's. Every Saturday they get together and go shooting at a firing range in Richmond, then they come back to Cal's house here in San Rafael."

"How do you know all that?"

"My roommate, Carly. She's dating Cal, at the moment."

"So you think we can—"

"We go over to Cal's today, before they get back, and hide out where we can hear them. Carly says they barbecue, drink beers in the backyard and stuff, until late. She doesn't enjoy being there, so they hang out by themselves."

"And you think we'll be able to hear them talking?"

"They're both really loud guys, Mike. Cal's house is secluded, quiet. If we sneak around and find a good place to hide, before they get back, I bet we'll be within earshot."

Mike snickered. "A stakeout. Well, aren't you the homicide investigator now?"

Mike took on a tone of gravity, and through the phone I could hear him scratching his goatee. "I'm not sure about it...We can't trespass on Cal's property."

"I want more on Tyler, and I just don't know how we're going to get it otherwise," I said. *And I want to prove myself to Pearson,* I thought.

Silence, for a moment. Then Mike prompted me.

"So what I'm hearing you tell me, Addie, is that we're not going to be on their property, but we still might be able to overhear them?"

"Exactly," I replied, following his lead.

"OK, what time?"

"Pick me up here at Bayside at, say, four o'clock? That should give us time. I have Cal's address."

"See you then. Wear dark clothes."

I brought my phone down from my ear. Danny had replied to my message:

Happy to chat. Come by the Happy Hour at FP on Monday @ 4pm, we can talk then.

Ω

"Can we get any closer?" I asked Mike, as we crouched behind a large, rotting woodpile behind Cal's house.

"Totally up to you, babe," Mike said, and snickered. I punched his shoulder.

"This is as close as we can get, with a path back to the bike if they see us," he said. "I figure it's about twenty-five yards to the patio, and it's quiet out here. Should be good enough. Best we can do."

After some circling on the Harley, we had located Cal's bungalow in the wooded outskirts of San Rafael. A gravel road led to the house, which sat on a ridge thick with maple and oak trees. Behind the rear edge of the ridge, where our woodpile stood, a rocky slope the height of a small maple tree ran down to a lower service road. After briefly surveying the vacant property, Mike had decided we should park the Harley on the lower road, and scale the incline to position ourselves behind the woodpile, which obscured us from the house and its rear patio.

We did not have to wait long. After less than an hour, a silver Hyundai snaked up Cal's driveway and parked. A short, burly, olive-skinned man stepped out on the driver's side. "That's Tyler," I whispered to Mike. Cal Forsythe, a foot taller and fifty pounds heavier than Tyler, wearing a black Metallica T-shirt and a khaki hunting vest, exited the passenger side and retrieved a duffel bag from the back seat. The men were animated and energized after their afternoon of gunplay.

"Steak and burgers?" Cal called out to Tyler, as he stacked charcoal briquettes into the barbecue.

"Yeah, let's do it," Tyler replied, and he opened the back door to Cal's house. "I'll get the beers."

Mike made a thumb's up sign. We could hear their conversation clearly.

The two men drank and talked, while we remained motionless behind the stacked lumber. Most of their chatter was unremarkable other than for its vulgarity, misogyny and homophobia.

The sun sank behind the trees and the temperature dropped perceptibly. My black, hooded sweatshirt kept me adequately warm, but Mike's visible discomfort intensified. He would reflexively start to shift his body to generate heat, then immediately restrain himself from further movement.

Tyler and Cal's inane banter had carried on for what seemed like hours. Suddenly, I lifted my finger to my lips and locked eyes with Mike.

"...Those candy-ass rich kids, they got what was coming to them," Cal said, jabbing a barbecue fork into a large piece of meat sizzling on the grill.

"Yeah," Tyler replied, leaning against the back wall of the house, holding a beer bottle. "I can just see poor little Peter, squirming on the floor, holding his throat. 'Cindy, Cindy, save me!'" The men guffawed as Tyler staggered around the patio clutching his throat.

"Fuck 'em. Fuck First Principles. Fuck Andy, too, that's what I say," Cal said.

"You know what would make me happy?" said Tyler. "Someone putting a bullet right through Mallory's chest, that's what. Today, at the range, that's what I'm thinking. 'Hey, Doug.' *Bam.* 'How you doin' today, Doug?' *Bam.* 'What, you don't want to put any more money into my company, Doug?' *Bam. 'It was a lifestyle investment? What the fuck is a lifestyle investment, Doug?' Bam.* 'What about *my* lifestyle, Doug?' *Bam.* All day, man."

Cal cackled as he flipped a hamburger. "Yeah, I saw Andy Freel in those targets today, man."

Mike stiffened and sneezed, loudly, then covered his mouth, wide-eyed. Too late.

"What was that?" yelled Cal, wheeling toward our woodpile.

"Someone's there! Get the guns!" barked Tyler. He dashed toward his car and Cal ran inside the house.

I froze with fear.

"Run!" Mike shouted, and shoved me backward.

We scrambled down the rock-strewn hill toward the Harley. I heard commotion overhead and behind us on the ridge.

"Get on the bike!" yelled Mike, slipping and scraping his legs as we tumbled down. We sprang onto the motorcycle and I grabbed Mike around his waist. He frantically threw the bike into gear. Its rear wheel spun in the dirt, and as we peeled away, loud gunshots rang out behind us. A bullet whistled past my ear. Another ricocheted off the pavement next to the front wheel.

We hurtled down the road, the echoes of the terrifying salvo soon fading into the distance.

CHAPTER 14

THE WHEELS OF MY MANTIS slowed, and rolled to a stop outside the Descartes Building.

Monday afternoon Happy Hour at Descartes transformed the towering atrium into a seething pit of amateur hubris. Students mingled in clusters of overconfidence. They practiced their *tee-hee-hee*s and *ha-hah-ha*s, like lion cubs play-acting for their future roles in the great startup savannah. The conversational buzzing reminded me of Rocky's memorial. Perhaps this was a kind of memorial, for me, of my simpler days at First Principles.

I found Danny next to a folding table that supported two enormous bowls of unnaturally red and yellow punch.

"Heeeeyyyy, Addie, you made it!" he greeted me warmly.

"We didn't have this stuff when I went here. Hope it's non-alcoholic," I said.

Danny introduced me to two female students as he ladled fluorescent fluid into their oversized plastic cups. "Guys, this is Addison Morita, one of our alumni. From our first graduating class."

"Cool," one of them said, tearing her adoring gaze from Danny. "Where do you work now?"

"At the D.A.'s office, here in Marin County," I told her. "Computer Crimes force."

The girl shared a confused glance with her partner. "I didn't know people go there," she said, and they wandered off.

"Not the success story a First Principles student wants to hear," I remarked to Danny.

"They don't know anything," Danny said. "So what's new? It's really great to see you."

The background music from the speakers next to the punch table blared with an annoying *oots-oots-oots* beat. "Is it just me getting old, or is that music freaking loud?" I complained over the din.

"*Hah.* Two years out, and already a cranky old-timer." Danny placed his cup on the table. "So you wanted to talk about something? And hey—what were you meeting with Doug about last week?"

"That's what I need to talk to you about. I'm sure you heard about Rocky and Indigo and Peter."

"Yeah, terrible. You want some punch by the way?"

"No, no thanks. Anyway, it seems pretty clear that they were killed. Murdered."

"Whoa. Really?" Danny ran his hand through his hair.

"Heeeeyyyy, Danny, bro!" Two other 'bros' had ambled up to us and one offered Danny a fist-bump.

"Hey, Bryce, Ian. Meet Addie."

"Heeeeyyyy," the bro brayed. My nostalgia for First Principles was plummeting by the second.

"Hey, guys," Danny said, "I'll catch up with you soon?" The discouraged pair drifted off.

"Go on," Danny said to me.

"Long story short, it seems that someone has targeted people from my Mallory seminar."

"Your Mallory seminar?"

"We don't know why. Maybe a vendetta or something, Maybe it has to do with Mallory. But the thing is, the killer seems to be picking his targets, based on Helmer's book."

"*7 Powers*? I don't get it."

"Employers, probably. People at companies that represent each of the seven powers, most likely."

"That's sick."

"Killing them randomly would make more sense?"

"No—no, I'm sorry, I'm just saying...Wow. That's insane. So that's what you and that woman were meeting with Doug about."

"That woman is Special Agent Hope Pearson. She's a homicide investigator with the D.O.J."

"I thought you did computer crime," Danny said, picking up his cup.

"It's complicated," I began.

Another young female student interrupted us. "Hiii, Danny," she flirted.

Danny plastered on a smile. "Hey, Lori, this is Addie. Addie, Lori. Addie's a former student here, she's back to visit."

"Cool. Catch up with you later?" Lori winked at Danny.

"Uh, sure. I have office hours tomorrow." He emphasized the words *office hours*.

"Sorry," Danny said to me.

"No. it's OK. They practically throw themselves at you, don't they? Special friend?" I asked, keeping my eye on Lori as she departed.

"No, absolutely not," Danny protested indignantly. "I don't, I wouldn't, date students. And, just by the way old-timer, do you think you guys were any different?" Danny smirked, as I blushed.

"Listen, Addie, I want to hear more, and I am happy to help. Maybe this wasn't the best forum for us to talk. I didn't realize you wanted to discuss something so, you know, heavy. Let me do my job, mingle with these kids until it's over at five. Then let's get out of here, to someplace quiet. Circle back to me at five? Or maybe let's just meet outside?"

"Meet you outside at five," I said. I wouldn't be able to stand waiting my turn as any more sheepish sophomores cooed and clucked at him. I poured a tall cup of red punch and sauntered to the edge of the crowd of *huh-huh*-ers and *oh-my-god*-esses. I leaned against a tall palm tree, and my eyes flickered toward the sixth floor, toward Euclid Hall. *I was one of the best of the best. Now I'm a stranger in a strange land*, I thought.

Ω

Emerging from the glass doors of Descartes, with his backpack slung over one shoulder, Danny easily could have been mistaken for a First Principles upperclassman. I waited for him next to my folded scooter.

"Sorry again, Addie."

"Everyone wants a piece of you."

"It's called being accessible to students, actually. You've forgotten already," he said. "Anyway, we're free now. I'm over this way," he said, motioning for me to follow him to his green Prius. The sign over his front-row parking spot read *Reserved - Chief of Staff.*

Danny opened the trunk and I slid my scooter inside. "OK, so, murder, and *7 Powers.* I'm all ears," said Danny, as he gentlemanly opened the passenger door for me. I pulled on my seat belt, wondering where we were going. Danny dropped into the driver's seat.

"Let me double-click on what you told me. You want to go through the class list, and map every student's employer to one of Helmer's seven powers," he said.

"Some companies might have more than one power," I said.

"Right, and some might not have any. Because the person, the..."

"The killer."

"Yeah, I just, I just can't wrap my arms around it. The killer is, you believe, picking his victims to match all seven powers, for some twisted reason." Danny had not yet started the car. He snapped his fingers. "Like that movie, that twisted one, with Morgan Freeman, and Matt Damon, and the seven deadly sins..."

"Brad Pitt, I think it was," I said.

"Right," Danny said, wagging his finger at me. "But why...why would he...someone...wanna do that?"

"Sending some sort of message, perhaps," I said. "Or maybe a vendetta? Dunno. Pearson doesn't want to talk about motive."

"Mm-hmm." Danny gazed at distant emptiness through the windshield. He put one hand to his chin, his other resting on the steering wheel. "OK, so it's, how many, twenty-five students, so about twenty-odd companies...And you figured, you'll ask me for help."

"You've taught that book for the past couple years, Danny. You know it back to front. I need to make sure I'm not missing anything. Pearson is counting on me."

"Because if you can figure out who's next..."

"We can save lives, and possibly catch him. You realize I'm telling you all of this in confidence, right?"

"Of course, absolutely," said Danny solemnly. "So. Quiet place, nobody bothering us...How about Lagoon Park?"

Ω

"Love this place. Great views. Those Civic Center buildings over there? Frank Lloyd Wright," said Danny.

We had found a picnic table near the water. Aside from a gaggle of geese waddling aimlessly on the grass about a stone's throw away, we had the area to ourselves.

"Let's see what you've got," said Danny.

I placed my yellow legal pad, with the Mallory class list I had copied from the conference room whiteboard, on the table. Danny settled in on one end of the bench and pulled the chart closer as I parked beside him.

While Danny scanned the page, I explained. "My thinking is, that we've already got Scale Economies, that's Rocky at Netflix, and Peter is Network Economies."

"Where's Peter?" asked Danny, running his finger down the list. "Oh, here. Twitter. Uh-huh."

"Indigo is Switching Cost, I think." I said.

"Intuit," said Danny, locating *Murray, Indigo* beneath *Greene, Peter.*

"Because it's costly and painful to switch accounting software," I said. "Intuit has a built-in barrier, so—"

"Wait, slow down," said Danny. "Let's go power by power, and see what matches."

He leaned back and stretched. "This is actually kind of morbidly interesting. How much time do you have?"

"I've got all night," I said, smiling. "It's life and death, and frankly, I'm stuck."

"OK." Danny placed his hands behind his head. "Let's take the ones that are rarest, first. Process Power."

"Amazon?" I asked.

"Good thought. Process Power is not just Michael Porter's Operational Effectiveness. It's a deep understanding of your business, a process, that even if other people try to copy, they can't imitate. You could say that about Amazon, for sure."

"You're so pedantic," I said.

"Drives the girls crazy," Danny said.

Geese mingled near the water's edge. "Ever see the famous Jeff Bezos interview, with Charlie Rose?" Danny asked.

"Must have missed it," I said.

"So there's this great Charlie Rose interview of Bezos, really early, I think 1998. Bezos still has hair then, you know? And Rose asks him, 'What's stopping other booksellers from just doing what you do, selling books online?' or something like that, and Bezos just laughs. This evil, *mu-ha-ha* laugh. And he answers, 'Nothing. They can do what we do, tomorrow. But we know things about our business today, that will take our competitors two years to figure out. And by then we'll be two more years ahead.' So yeah, that's classic Process Power."

I jotted that down on the pad. "How about Malcolm Butler? Novato Organics. I don't know much about them but their website says they have a proprietary process for diffusion of cannabis."

"Proprietary process. Sounds a lot like Process Power to me. Yup, could be," said Danny.

I pulled my ponytail band out and shook my long hair loose. As I raised my arms and rearranged my hair into a tighter tie, I caught Danny watching me, and he hastily averted his eyes.

"Branding is also rare," he said. "Who do you have there?"

"Easy," I said, pushing the pad back to him. "Just Brian and Oscar at Apple, and Elyse at Carrie Carmezian's cosmetics company."

"You might say Tyler is Branding, too. His startup sold branded sneakers, I remember. Doug invested in it. And Goldman Sachs might be a brand, at least on Wall Street, so that's Warren."

"Damn," I said. "Some help you are. Hey—are you looking down my shirt?"

Danny jerked his head up and stammered "No!" with Puritan shock, then grinned. "Why? Anything in there?"

I shrieked, and punched his arm as he threw his head back and cackled.

"My brain is up here, wise guy," I said.

Danny caught his breath. "Is there anybody we can rule out completely? Not any one of the seven powers? That would help," he suggested.

"Sure. Tiffany's at a software marketing firm, nothing special. Jason Friedman's at Columbia Business School, in New York. Marcus Newton's at a housing nonprofit. And Jimmy Tresko's trading stocks."

"Great. They're off."

"You agree that Twitter is Network Economies, right?"

"Definitely."

"So that one's off the board, with Peter, and we can rule out any other Network Economies companies."

"That would be Facebook," said Danny.

"So Janet, and Caroline are off," I said.

"And Bill is Network Economies, too," said Danny.

"Yelovich? At Google? I had Google as Scale Economies," I said.

"Disagree," said Danny, arms crossed.

"The bigger Google gets, the more searches, the more money they make, the bigger they get, etcetera. Scale Economies," I asserted.

"Ah, but that's not what Helmer means by Scale Economies, is it? What makes Google a better search engine is that more people use it, so more people put in all their wacky searches, and the algorithm *learns* from those searches. It's called a long tail. And therefore Google's search results are more robust. They get power, not because their scale gives them greater economies. But rather, because their scale means more searches, which makes the algorithm smarter, which allows all subsequent users to derive more incremental value. That's Network Economies, not Scale Economies." Danny bowed, and a goose honked nearby.

I clapped for his effort. "Well done, even the goose liked it," I said.

"Besides," Danny said offhandedly, settling back onto the bench, "I heard Helmer on a podcast, and he said Google is Network Economies, not Scale Economies. Did you think I was actually that smart?" he said, grinning.

"Yes," I said. "That's why I want to have your baby."

Danny gagged and coughed, and laughed, and laughed more, and I laughed, and geese *honk-honked* overhead, dispersing the lingering fog of mayhem, and murder.

We watched the geese. A large, aggressive one chased another, its wings spread wide.

"Mating season," I said.

"No, it's passed. That's in the spring," Danny said. "I wonder how they pick. They all look the same."

"Biggest honker?" I giggled.

Danny winked. "Size doesn't matter, Addie."

The sinking sun brushed the edge of the lagoon and Danny squinted toward the horizon. "Hey, you hungry? How about we continue this at my place and order in? Chinese?"

"OK, sure," I said. Danny opened an app on his phone and we made our selections.

"Twenty minutes," he said.

Ω

"It's not much, but it's home," Danny apologized, as he unlocked the door to his condo on Marin Center Drive.

"It's great," I said, studying the renovated apartment. The decor was minimalist, with off-white walls in the living and dining room and a spotless, steel-blue kitchenette with white cabinets. His narrow, white dining room table had two Scandinavian-style, upholstered vinyl and steel chairs on each side.

Danny's doorbell rang, and we spread out at the dining room table. I quickly ate my two eggrolls while Danny worked on his Moo Goo Gai Pan.

Danny waved at me with a chopstick. "Keep going, don't let me stop you. Where were we?"

"You said Google is Network Economies. So Bill's off, because Peter already is Network Economies," I said, noting that on the pad.

"Great, so we knocked out a bunch, see?" said Danny. "How about Cornered Resource?"

"OK. So I have...Heidi, at DripLogix. Patent-pending ag-tech. Something about artificial intelligence for irrigation analysis. And Greenberg, at GenPharmix. Also patent-pending, gene therapy for macular degeneration. Those could be Cornered Resource. I'm not sure about some others."

"Which ones?"

"Vineet, for example. Cybergetic. Edge network intrusion detection."

"Nah. Them and five hundred other startups founded by bald-headed, former Mossad hackers. Next?"

"Shanice Redstone, SpaceX–"

"Shanice is at SpaceX? Cool," said Danny.

"Why does everyone say that? Yes, it's cool. But is it Cornered Resource?"

"I'd say no. SpaceX is awesome, but there are a couple of other companies that shoot rockets into space. If anything, maybe they're Switching Cost, because once NASA signs a contract with SpaceX, it's hard to switch to another rocket ship vendor."

"But we have Switching Cost already, with Indigo," I said.

"Right. So Shanice is probably off."

I gathered the empty take-out containers and carried them into the kitchen. "Danny, by the way, I really appreciate you doing this with me," I called back. "It's really nice of you."

"My pleasure. I usually eat alone. And this is super interesting. Trash is under the sink, thanks."

"What's left?" asked Danny as I returned to the dining room.

"Just one left. Counter-positioning," I announced.

"Ah, the tough one. I'll get the wine list while you tell me what you have on Counter-positioning." He reached into a cabinet and brought two glasses and an open bottle to the table.

"Well, not many, which is why I'm sure I have it wrong. All I have is Victor, at Liferr."

Danny poured a glass of white wine and handed it to me. "What's Liferr?"

"Commission-free life insurance. Like Robinhood for insurance. So my thought is, it's Counter-positioning, because the life insurance companies—the incumbents—can't permit themselves to copy Liferr's business model. It would cannibalize their current commission business."

"Good," Danny said as he poured the second glass. He swiveled the pad around.

"By the way, if we're wrong about Indigo, Apple could be your Switching Cost. Helmer mentions Apple in that chapter. Ever try to switch from Apple to Android? You'll lose your whole library of iTunes music. That's a good enough reason to upgrade to the next phone Apple wants to sell you, instead."

I scrawled on the pad as I touched the glass to my lips.

"And, I'm going to make you upset again," Danny said. "You have Rocky as Scale Economies, of course, because Helmer uses Netflix as his primary example of Scale Economies. Helmer goes total fanboy on Reed Hastings."

"So?"

Danny circled around the end of the table to my side. "So you're forgetting, toward the very end of the book, Helmer's like, oh yeah, by the way, Netflix could also be Process Power, and Counter-positioning too, because of their origin story. The way they disrupted Blockbuster's business model by mailing movies to people, and Blockbuster was too paralyzed to adapt and copy them."

"Helmer says that?"

"Yup, it's in the book. Trust me."

My chart was now more jumbled than when I started. Outside, the moon illuminated Marin Center Drive. I dropped my forehead into my hands and groaned.

"Hey, sorry." Danny rested his hand on my shoulder. After a few seconds he lifted it up suddenly. "Sorry, I didn't mean to do that."

I reached up, replaced Danny's hand onto my shoulder, and caressed it.

Ω

In my dream, my father was perched on the edge of my bed.

Addie, have I ever told you the story of 'Saiou ga uma'?

No Father.

Listen closely. There was an old man, Saiou. One day, his only horse ran away. The neighbors consoled Saiou on his bad luck. "How do you know it is not good luck?" he said.

The next day the horse returned, and it had brought another horse with it. The neighbors congratulated Saiou on his good luck. "How do you know it is good luck?" he said.

Saiou's son took the new horse out for a ride. He fell off the horse and broke his leg. The neighbors comforted Saiou. "How do you know it is not good luck?" he said.

That week, the Emperor demanded that all the young men in the village join the army to fight in the war. Saiou's son did not join them, on account of his broken leg.

Everything is Saiou's horse, Addie.

I opened my eyes. Sunlight streamed through Danny's bedroom window. I untangled myself from the sheets in the empty bed. The sound of a coffee bean grinder emanated from the kitchen.

My clothing was somewhere on the floor. I found Danny's oxford first and slipped it on, loosely buttoned, and rinsed out my mouth with toothpaste in the bathroom sink.

Danny, wearing only boxers, noticed me and smiled as I entered the kitchen.

"Good morning, sleepyhead. You wear it well. I put up coffee."

I reached around his trim waist from behind. "I'm glad I asked you for help."

"Not every day I get to solve a murder," he said, as the espresso machine whirred.

Danny handed me a steaming black and orange mug with *Eat. Sleep. Data.* printed on its side. "Here, try some. My favorite coffee. Doug brings it back for me from Paris."

"Doug." I snickered. "Are you going to stay with him forever? You know you could get an amazing job tomorrow, at any venture capital fund on Sand Hill Road. You'd be great at it, and you'd probably triple your salary." I sipped from my mug. "This is great, by the way. I see why you like it."

Danny poured a second cup and turned to face me. "First of all, not sure I agree, about salary I mean. Doug is very generous." Danny raised his coffee mug, as evidence. "Second, he's been a mentor to me, and I've been loyal to him. It's that simple."

"You'd never leave him?"

"It's funny you mention it, because I suddenly thought, over the past few days, that Doug was going to leave *me*. Or First Principles, I mean. Now I realize, no wonder he's been acting strange. Must be because of the murders. I figured it was Andy. Andy's been giving him a hard time lately."

"Really?" I peered down into my mug. "About what?"

Danny took a luxuriant sip of coffee and licked his lips, savoring the taste. "Not sure. Sometimes I overhear Doug's conversations, or pick up snippets. I think someone's made him a big job offer, but Andy won't let him out of his contract. You know, Doug's pretty calm, usually very much in control, right? The other day, he's on the phone, and I suddenly hear him get all agitated. He's yelling, 'Andy!'—I think he said 'Andy'—'You can't do that to me! It's blackmail!' Over and over, he's yelling. 'It's blackmail, you're so goddamn manipulative, who do you think you are,' that kind of thing. Anyway, he comes out of his office, and I say, 'Everything OK, Doug?' And he's shocked. He says, 'You heard that? Oh, it was nothing.' And that was it."

Danny placed his mug on the counter. "So after that, when he was still acting strange, I thought he'd lied to me, that it was about that call with whoever it was. But maybe he was telling me the truth, and that phone call was really not a big deal, and something else has been troubling him. You know. If word gets out about a serial killer targeting people from First Principles, it could be really bad for the school."

"*Could be...*" I said. A drawer opened and closed in my brain.

I embraced Danny again. "Yesterday, I thought everything was turned against me," I said.

He reached out and stroked my hair.

Everything is Saiou's horse.

CHAPTER 15

"CAL WANTS TO SEE ME?" I gulped, facing Carly in our kitchen on Tuesday evening as she prepared to leave for Christie's.

"He wouldn't tell me why," she said. "He just said you should come by later tonight, around 9:30."

Carly eyed me suspiciously, then asked, "By the way, where were you last night?"

"You won't believe me if I tell you," I said, as I leaned against the kitchen wall. "Danny Armstrong."

"Danny Armstrong, what?" Then her eyes widened. "You *slept* there?"

"Excuse me, are you the Sex Police or something? I'm twenty-five now, last I checked," I said smugly.

"Well, well. That's big news. Check you out." Carly zipped her sweatshirt. "See you at work."

You only like Christie's if you're a male sports fan in your twenties, or if you're sleeping with the owner. Otherwise, it's an over-lit, clamorous, house of worship, serving the gods of athletics and alcohol. Vintage A's and Raiders memorabilia mix with garish neon lights and beer signs in a decor designed to smother any empty wall space at the expense of style.

Carly greeted me at the entrance to Christie's, seated atop a round stool. She was wearing tight capri trousers and a top that left so little to the imagination that it would have gotten her removed from a commercial flight.

"You working tonight, or on the menu?" I asked Carly as I studied her outfit.

"*Ha-ha.* He's in the back, waiting for you."

I located the closed door marked *Business Office* by following the pungent odor of the restrooms and continuing past them, and knocked.

"Come in!" Cal bellowed. The tight office was littered with unkempt stacks of papers, piles of parking tickets, and filthy ashtrays.

"Welcome to the Inner Sanctum. No smoking, please," Cal said, as he lit a cigarette.

"How can I help you today, Cal?"

Cal puffed and placed the cigarette on his cluttered desk, next to an empty ashtray. "I have a couple of problems, maybe you can help me out. As a member of the law enforcement community, since I try to generally avoid that type."

"Tell me your troubles, Cal."

Cal pulled deeply on the cigarette. "Well, I think someone has stolen a hundred and fifty thousand dollars from me. Also, I think someone might be trying to kill me."

"Whoa, Cal. That's not a joke."

"Did Carly say it was a joke?"

"No, I just...Why don't you start from the beginning?"

"OK. My buddy, Tyler Lukela. I think you know him."

"Tyler? We were classmates."

"Right. He's my buddy, we shoot and hang out and shit. So I'm talking with him one day, and he says we should do something together. He's in between things, like."

"I heard, his startup shut down. I saw him recently."

"Anyway, I'm like, listen Tyler, I have two big issues with the restaurant. One, the mortgage. Two, I'm anticipating a, what do you call it, shift in democratics."

"Demographics?"

"Yeah, yeah. That." He puffed again. "So I'm thinking of changing the restaurant, from you know, a sports theme to like a family theme, more upscale."

"Sounds like a great fit for you, Cal." My sarcasm glanced off him like a mosquito off an oblivious windshield.

"Exactly. So Tyler's like, hey man, I got a plan. I'll spare you all the technicals, Addie, because Tyler's really the business brain."

Cal tapped his fingers against his temple as he mansplained, and I threw up a little bit in my mouth.

Cal went on. "Basically, Tyler says, we open a new company, new bank account. Tyler has this big investor in Tahoe, he'll put in a hundred fifty, I put in a hundred fifty, we pay off the mortgage. Then Tyler gets a business development loan from the city at a low rate and we redo the place. We split everything fifty-fifty."

"So what happened?"

"Well, I deposited my one-fifty. Tyler said the other half is coming any day. And then..." Cal snuffed out the cigarette on his boot.

"And then," he continued, "my money disappeared."

"Disappeared."

"Yeah. Tyler calls one day and says someone hacked the bank. Took our money. I don't know shit about that kinda stuff. Carly says that's what you do, right? Hacking crimes?"

"I can open up an RFA—I mean, a Request for Assistance— with our team."

"I'll have to get you the account details," Cal said. "Tyler was working on it, but now he's gone."

"Gone?" I stiffened.

"Yeah, that's the second part of my problem. So you know about the suicide here two weeks ago, and the other guy that died."

"Two others," I said.

"Yeah. So Tyler was sure they weren't accidents. He got all paranoid and shit. And I'm telling him, dude, relax. Shit happens. Then last Saturday..."

My hair stood on end.

"Last Saturday, we're out at my place. Nobody around, so we think. We're grillin' and chillin' and all the sudden Tyler hears someone and there's two people hiding behind my woodpile. A guy and a girl. We chased them." *And shot at them,* I thought.

"Did you get a good look at them?" I asked coolly.

"Nope. It was getting dark. Tyler got the bike's license plate number, I have it right here. It was definitely a Harley, I know my bikes." Cal produced a small piece of paper. "So Tyler freaks out. Says someone's been following him, attacked him at Bayside or something. He thinks it's all related to the other guys that died. Conspiracy theory, like. So, he takes off."

I breathed a soft sigh of relief. "He took off from your house, on Saturday."

"No, I mean he split. Left town. Nobody's seen him. Left without a trace. Car still in the driveway. Phone's dead. *Poof.* Into the wild blue yonder. So I need help."

I shifted in my chair. "I can definitely help you, Cal. Get the bank account information to me, and I'll look into it. And, tell you what, give me that license plate number too. Little things like tracing a bike can get lost in the shuffle. I'll make sure it gets top priority."

"Appreciate it," Cal said, handing me a torn scrap with a number written on it.

I took the paper from Cal and secured it in my jeans pocket. I stood to leave, and said, "Cal, has it occurred to you, that possibly, there was no hack? That Tyler swiped the money and ran off with it?"

Cal thought for a moment, and frowned. He placed both of his hands firmly on the table and grumbled, "If Tyler did that...if he did that, I'll kill him."

$$\Omega$$

"How was work?" Carly asked as I opened our apartment door Wednesday afternoon.

"Annoying," I said. "Remember that big case I told you I was working on? I had this big breakthrough on Monday, and the two people I'm working with have been AWOL for two days. I haven't even been able to present it to them."

"What did Cal want last night?"

"Oh, I have a message for him, if you see him tonight," I said, as I crumpled a piece of paper I pulled from my pocket. "Tell him I'm sorry, but we checked the license number, and the bike had been reported stolen. Untraceable. He'll know what I'm talking about."

"Untraceable. Stolen. Got it," Carly repeated. "Seeing Danny tonight?"

"Hoping to," I said.

My phone chimed. It was Pearson.

"I've made real headway on the seven powers," I reported. "I updated the whiteboard—"

"No time to hear about that now, Addie," Pearson interrupted. "I will be stopping by to see Cindy this evening. She told Mike that she will be visiting her parents in Lake Tahoe this weekend and I want to ask her a few questions before she leaves. I would like you to join me."

"What time did you tell her you'd be there?"

"I did not tell her we are coming. Just want to drop in. I will see you at Bayside at eight."

Sorry, Danny.

Ω

A Tesla Model S? My shock must have been evident as I slid into the white, sculpted, synthetic leather passenger's seat. Pearson smiled. "Book royalty money, honey. The D.O.J. does not get you a Model S." I buckled, and the Tesla rounded the traffic circle.

"I asked for leather, but they said no leather anymore. Environmentally friendly," she continued, patting her seat. "I always wanted a nice car. This was my present to myself after I signed the movie deal and broke up with Janice."

Pearson confounded me. *Ignore me for days, and now you're Chatty McChatterson?* In protest of her sudden display of friendliness, I remained silent for the short drive.

As we pulled into the cul-de-sac leading to Cindy's house, Pearson explained, "I assume she will be home. Packing for a long weekend, no fiancé to go visit."

Two cars were parked in Cindy's driveway. One of them was a red Porsche Boxster. *Didn't Mallory drive a Porsche?*

"You introduce me," said Pearson as we approached the home's entrance and I sounded the doorbell.

Footsteps approached with a *slap-slap, slap-slap* and Cindy opened the front door. Her usually straight blond hair was stringy and wet, a loose tunic covered her slender figure, and she wore flip-flops. We had startled her, which I gathered was Pearson's intention.

Cindy greeted me with surprise. "Hi...Addie?" Cindy said, eyeing me quizzically, then Pearson.

"Cindy, this is Special Agent Pearson of the Department of Justice. She's investigating Peter's death. And the others."

"Just a few minutes of your time, Cindy," said Pearson. "May we come in?"

"Um, sure." Cindy wavered, looking over her shoulder. We followed her into the wood-paneled hallway.

I had been to Cindy's house many times. It was a remarkable Alpine-style home with an open, two-story living area topped by a huge skylight. Three plush built-in sofas faced a giant fireplace, cradled in a hexagonal, sunken living area. A number of bedrooms were off to the left, and a large, open kitchen stood to the right. You had the feeling that the Caldwells had air-dropped a ski chalet directly from Switzerland into San Rafael. In the backyard, off the kitchen, was the in-ground pool where I had spent many evenings and weekends with other First Principles classmates.

And standing in the kitchen holding a towel, in shorts and a T-shirt, his hair damp, was Doug Mallory.

Cindy awkwardly began to make introductions as Mallory stared at Pearson. "Uh, Doug, this is—"

"We've met," Mallory said, regaining composure. "Nice to see you again, Agent Pearson, Addie."

I studied Pearson's face for a reaction. None came.

"Doug was just over for a swim," Cindy explained to Pearson, trying too hard to make that sound normal. "Father encourages me to let anyone come over to swim. Addie can tell you, people come over all the time. Doug comes a lot. Right, Doug? You come a lot." She plucked a piece of lint from his shirt.

Mallory coughed, like he had been punched in the solar plexus. "Uh, yes, I come...often."

"Doug's been helping me lately with a big decision. I'm happy at Netflix, but I have a fantastic job offer in New York. Peter and I were really torn about what to do. Poor Peter," Cindy bowed her head. "So Doug came over for a swim, and to help me sort things out."

"Well, I'll be going," Mallory said. "Good to see you all again." Cindy accepted his towel, and Mallory let himself out the front door.

"He's really been terrific," Cindy said facing me. "He's not nearly as scary as he seemed, up on that podium. Once you get to know him. Let's sit in the kitchen,"

Pearson and I settled onto high stools alongside the kitchen's island, while Cindy produced glasses and a cold bottle of sparkling water. Cindy perched on a stool at the head of the island, facing us.

"Cindy, I would like to ask you a few questions about Rocky and Peter," began Pearson. "But first, tell me a bit about what you do."

"Well, I'm at Netflix, they recruited me straight out of school. Rocky too, by the way. Doug introduced us to the company. I'm sure you've heard that he's very helpful, with his network, for the students he likes."

"I am aware."

"So I'm on the Netflix Originals side, working with management to screen ideas for new programming. Rocky was a Project Manager in the subscriber division."

"And the new job offer?"

"Well, it's a media startup, I can't say much more about it. Mobile-first, their own content. A bunch of former HBO and Disney people. And they want me to basically run original content. It's a huge, huge opportunity."

"And Peter wanted you to stay here in California."

"Yes, we argued about it, a lot. That's mainly why we kept pushing off the wedding. Trying to figure out where we were going to live. Which coast."

Mallory's still-wet footsteps remained on the kitchen floor, leading out the back door to the pool.

"Tell me about Peter's relationship with Rocky. I understand it was, well, rocky, no pun intended," Pearson said with a prodding smile.

"Not really, actually. Peter and Rocky were really fine, by the end." Cindy took a sip of water. "Basically, I dated Rocky in college, and we work at the same company. At some point, Peter gets this crazy bug in his head—I guess, as we kept pushing off the wedding—that somehow Rocky and I are, you know..." Cindy trailed off and lowered her head, circling the lip of her glass with her finger.

"Of course, nothing like that was going on between me and Rocky. So Peter went to ask him about it. Rocky told him he was nuts, which is what I'd been saying all along, so Peter dropped it. That was the night Rocky died."

"What can you tell me about Tyler Lukela?" asked Pearson.

Cindy had raised her glass to her lips again, and she coughed and set it down. "Tyler. Oh, god. He's unhinged.

"So you know Tyler had this sneaker startup, right?" Cindy continued. Pearson nodded. "He started it straight out of school. He got to some big celebrities right away to endorse the company and promote it. Some of them were Peter's dad's contacts. Doug invested. Father invested. I think they were his two largest investors. Something like two hundred and fifty each."

"Two hundred and fifty thousand dollars," repeated Pearson.

"Right. So Tyler launches, and revenue spikes at first, then sputters. He needs more cash. Doug says no. Father says no, he's put in what he wanted to put in. Tyler gets really mad."

"How long ago was this?"

"About two months ago. Father won't take Tyler's calls anymore."

Pearson sipped her water slowly. "Tell me about the night Rocky died."

"That was a Thursday night. I think it was, yes, it was Peter who called to tell me. From Bayside. He'd gone over to Christie's."

"Yes, we know he was there. And you were...?"

"I was here, at home."

"Alone?"

"Why, yes," stammered Cindy.

Pearson drank from her glass again, then set it down gently on the table. "Very well. I think we have what we need for right now."

Pearson stood up, which startled both Cindy and me. "Thank you very much for your time, Cindy."

I followed Pearson as she strode to the door. Cindy *flap-flapped* after us. "Pleasure meeting you," Cindy called toward Pearson. "See you, Addie." She closed the door behind us.

Pearson, back in her chilly silence, started the car.

"What was that, with Mallory?" I asked with excited curiosity.

"Everybody is hiding something. Cindy is hiding something. But she *wanted* us to see *that*," Pearson said, peering over her shoulder, old-fashioned, ignoring her dashboard camera as she backed the Tesla out of Cindy's driveway. "That was not the interesting part. I already suspected there was another man between Cindy and Peter."

What I would give to understand how this woman's brain operates, I thought. "And why did you bring up Tyler?" I asked.

We were heading west on North San Pedro, back toward Bayside Towers. "You told us that Tiffany said that *Cindy* said that Tyler had been hounding her. I wondered if it had to do with SoleSurvivors. So I got the cap table."

"The cap table?" I asked.

"The list of the company's shareholders."

"How did you get that?"

Pearson smirked. "This is still the easy part, Addie. Found the company's filings with the Secretary of State. Saw its lawyers are Henderson, Gellmer. Called a friend there. Got the cap table."

"Nice," I said.

"Saw Doug Mallory and Dennis Caldwell listed as investors. Checked Cindy's Facebook page, and saw her father's name is Dennis. There you have it."

"Impressive."

"Really, Addie? That is not even basic homicide investigation. More like the kind of research you do, is it not?"

That stung. "So presumably, Tyler's been chasing her to try to get back to her father?" I asked.

"I doubt it. The company is dead."

"Then what?"

Pearson exhaled, as she continued to face the road ahead. She spoke more quickly. "Why did Cindy introduce Tyler to her father for investment? Why? Why would she do that?"

"Because...she thought it would make money?"

Now Pearson broke into a wide grin. "Addie, Addie. Did you study Darwin in high school, or in your exclusive college perhaps?"

"A bit." I said, confused again.

"Do you know what Darwin described as, 'the most human of all expressions'?"

"Smiling?" I guessed.

"*Blushing*," Pearson stated emphatically. "Humans are the only animals that blush."

"I'm lost," I said.

We had reached the Bayside Towers traffic circle, and Pearson stopped the Tesla in front of South Tower. "You have to always watch, watch, watch. The clues are often right in front of you, in plain sight. Cindy did not blush when we caught her red-handed with Mallory, no, not at all. She practically dangled him in your face, 'Look who I got.' No. But when did she blush? Only one time."

I shrugged. Pearson purposefully kept me in suspense.

"When I mentioned *Tyler*."

"Wow," I said. I opened the Tesla's passenger door.

"Have a good night," said Pearson.

I did not see Hope Pearson again until the next body was found.

CHAPTER 16

FRIDAY AFTERNOON. THE LAST DAY in May. Almost two weeks had elapsed since Cindy had discovered Peter's lifeless body, and Special Agent Hope Pearson had assumed leadership of the murder investigation.

"Where've you been, stranger?" I asked Mike as he plunked himself down in the square chair that separated our desks. "I haven't seen you since, what, Monday?"

"Pearson had me running around all week. Chasing my tail."

The word *tail* reminded me of Marvin. "Let's go outside, and catch up?" I said.

I grabbed my legal pad with the class list, and Mike followed me down the stairway. We exited to the patio, and to the same picnic table where we had first met. Tim, the Assistant D.A. and part-time book critic, was taking his Friday lunch outside again, wrestling with a twist-tied plastic bag at an adjoining table.

"So what's new?" I asked Mike. I stood alongside the table as Mike swung his legs over one of its benches and clasped his hands, shaking his head.

"It's all about Rocky, that first night. She just keeps saying, that's the only one we have an exact time on. She needs to know exactly where everyone was. You know what she made me do? Get this, she had me sit with each of the guys who was at Christie's that night, and I had to watch the replay of the freakin' A's game with each one of them, and ask, 'OK, when that guy hit that double, do you recall who was standing next to you,' 'when that play happened, who reacted, are you sure,' and so on."

"She's trying to see if anyone could've slipped out and gone up to Rocky's and come back," I said.

"I know what she wants. I'm not dumb. But it's so time consuming. And so far, nothing. I'd say there's consensus that Peter was down there with them for the last two or three innings."

"When Rocky fell," I said.

"I still don't know much about these murders, but if you want to know the pitch count to Carlyle in the bottom of the eighth, right before he tripled, I'm your guy." Mike laughed. "Truth is, it was nice hanging out with Malcolm, Perry, Oscar. They're good guys."

"First name basis now, huh?" I teased.

"Watch a ballgame with a guy, friend for life," Mike said, holding up his crossed fingers. "Oh, and I did find out some other things, potentially more relevant. Remember Jimmy Tresko's Endscape trade, the short on the stock?"

"Yes?"

"He placed the trade on Monday, May 20th."

"That's the Monday after Peter died," I said.

"Correct. So I call Jimmy. And you know what he says? He says, 'I know why you're asking me about the date. Yeah, as soon as I heard Peter died, I figure, this is going to go bad for the school, bad for Andy, so I short his stock. Why shouldn't at least someone benefit from all this?' What a guy."

"Did you ask him about our little motorcycle chase?"

"Yeah, he was a jerk about that too. He pretended he didn't know what I was talking about."

"Maybe you should drop by and watch a baseball game with him."

"*Ha-ha*. Oh, and another thing. Tyler's gone off the grid."

"I know, I heard that from Cal. The good news is Cal and Tyler didn't get a good look at us. Cal had no idea it was me."

"Pearson's not happy about it," Mike said.

"You told her about our stakeout?"

"Yeah, she asked if I'd been in contact with Tyler so I told her what happened. She was mad. I couldn't tell if she was upset we went over there, or just frustrated that I haven't been able to find Tyler since. You know, you can never tell what she's thinking."

"Tell me about it." I told Mike about my visit to Cindy's with Pearson, the awkward encounter with Mallory, and Pearson's unusual pattern of questions to Cindy.

I picked a pink flower off the branch of a plum tree that hung alongside the picnic table. "I just don't get her. She talks about her process, her method, but she just seems so erratic. Then she disappears for days." I flicked the flower to the side. "This case is a lot more complex than a typical homicide investigation. I just don't understand how she's going to solve it this way."

"Who knows," said Mike, rotating my pad to face him. "But she's never lost one yet."

Tim spoke up from the next table. "Don't mind me butting in, but I couldn't help overhearing. You know that's B.S."

Mike swiveled to face Tim. "What's B.S.?"

"Never losing a case." Tim stood up from his bench. "Tell you a story. When I started out in the prosecutor's office, about fifteen years ago, there's the public defender's office, right? And there's this young lawyer there, in the public defender pool, named McClanahan. Trying to make a name for himself, you know. And the rumor is McClanahan's never lost a case, just like you said about your lady." Tim pointed to Mike.

"How's it possible that one guy never loses a case?" Tim went on. "So we check it out. Turns out, whenever McClanahan draws a defendant where he sees the trial isn't going to go his way, he's gonna lose, suddenly, his kid breaks an ankle. His grandma dies. The guy buried five grandmas. Dog ate his brief. You get the picture. He begs off the case, gets replaced. Keeps his perfect record. You know what they call that, in legalese?"

"What?" I said.

"Quitting." Tim laughed. "*Nolo continue-ay.* We used to call it 'pulling a McClanahan.' All he cared about was his record. So I wouldn't buy the whole 'never lost a case' crap, if I were you."

Tim crumpled his empty plastic bag and tossed it into a trash can. "Good luck with your McClanahan."

Tim left the patio. I watched two chickadees flittering between branches of the plum tree.

Mike was staring at my handwritten chart. "Addie, did you notice this weird thing about the names? The students' names?"

"What weird thing?"

Mike jumped up from the table and snapped his fingers. "What's that acronym, the colors of the rainbow?"

"ROY-G-BIV?"

"Right," said Mike. "Red, orange, yellow, green..."

"...blue, indigo, violet," I finished. "So what?"

Mike swiveled the pad toward me. "Look." He pointed to my chart, and I bent closer.

"*Violetto, Indigo,* Peter *Greene*," he read. "There's your green, indigo, violet. And remaining, you have a whole bunch. You have *Red*stone, *Gree*nberg—no, we have Greene already—Yelovich could be yellow..."

"Oh, come on," I protested.

"No, wait, you've got LeBleu, and you could say Bluth too. What's left?"

"You're missing orange," I said with a smirk.

Mike peered closer at the pad. "Naranja," he said, firmly. "Naranja means orange, in Spanish. And Rojas means red. So you've got two options for red." He straightened up triumphantly, hands on his hips.

"I don't understand. You're saying he's targeting people by the seven powers *and* for some reason also filling in the colors of the freaking rainbow?" I asked.

Mike flailed his hand. "Killing people because their employers match the strategies in some book is totally normal? But killing people based on the colors of the rainbow is completely out of the question?"

"What would a rainbow have to do with anything?" I stopped short. "Wait a second," I said, covering my eyes with my hand.

"What?" Mike asked.

I opened my eyes. "The motto. Andy's stupid motto, for First Principles College. We always made fun of it. 'Truth is as diverse as the colors of the rainbow.'"

"See?" Mike slapped the pad. "And one of the emails you got from the killer, talked about colors."

"*Color me done when I get to seven,*" I quoted. "I still don't buy it. But you're saying, we should focus on...who's missing? Bluth and LeBleu. Naranja. Yelovich, and...Redstone."

"Or Rojas," added Mike.

"I need to see how they match the seven powers," I said. "Naranja's the only orange, he's at Apple, which is probably Branding. Yelovich is Google, Danny says Google is Network Economies—"

"Who's Danny?" asked Mike, but I ignored him and continued.

"But if Yelovich is Network Economies, what is Peter? We needed Network Economies for Peter. Unless I was right, and Google is really Scale Economies. And then Rocky at Netflix isn't Scale Economies, but instead one of the others that Helmer says at the end of the book..."

"You've lost me. I think you've lost yourself too. You need the whiteboard," said Mike, smiling.

"In theory...in theory, the rainbow idea could fit with the seven powers," I admitted. "I need to look closer at the chart. But you'll have to convince Pearson about your cockamamie color theory, and that these are the only people to focus on. I don't buy it and I doubt Pearson will."

Mike was not listening to me. He was pacing in a tight circle. "First Principles' motto is about rainbows. I hadn't even thought of that."

"You've already sold yourself on it, Mike. I'm telling you, it's a ridiculous theory."

I reached up and picked another flower from the plum tree, twirling it in my fingers.

"The reality is," I said, "Pearson doesn't care about any of our ideas. She's just off on a frolic of her own. I can't figure her out."

"Can't help you with that," Mike said. "I'm not a social worker yet."

Ω

"You seem down," Danny said, in an uncertain tone. After my morning run we had spent Saturday together, and then driven west late in the day to find the perfect seaside overlook to watch the sunset.

"Oh, I'm sorry," I said. "You're so perceptive. It's not you. It's...it's just work. It's this damn case. It shouldn't be on my mind, now, when I'm with you."

"It's fine." Danny put his arm around my shoulder. "Talk to me."

"You know," I said, leaning my head back, against Danny's arm, "it's all your fault." I rolled my head to face him.

"How so?" he asked, one eyebrow raised.

I turned my head and eyed the darkening sky. "You probably don't remember it. Senior year, Mallory wants to recommend me to one of these big tech companies, like everyone else, for a nice job after graduation. And I see this opportunity at the Computer Crimes Task Force."

"Right?"

"So you're our T.A. I book an office hour with you. And I tell you I'm not sure about the whole rat race thing, ask you what I should do."

"And let me guess, I probably encouraged you to follow your heart, do something fulfilling." Danny laughed. "And now you're unfulfilled."

"I'm just teasing you. It's not really your fault. But now, I've got my big break, and she's holding me back."

"Pearson," he said.

"Yes, all I want is to help solve the case, right? And she's so capricious. She'll disappear, or ignore me, and suddenly she'll be like, I have this meeting with so-and-so tomorrow, you're joining me. And then we go, and she asks a bunch of random questions, and I do absolutely nothing, and then she disappears again, and I'm back on the shelf 'til next time."

Danny thought for a moment. "Maybe you're a decoy."

"A decoy?"

"I read this book, a crime novel. The detective, she has this ruse, this *shtick*. Whenever she has a confrontation with a suspect, she takes someone else with her. Then while the suspect is distracted by the decoy, the detective observes. Body language, other subliminal signals she'd miss if the suspect was talking only to her."

A sudden wave of déjà vu swept over me.

"I can't remember the name of the author..." Danny continued.

I raised my head off Danny's arm and pressed my palm to my forehead.

"Stella Westcott," I uttered softly.

Ω

Sunday evening, I reclined on my balcony with half a plastic cup of Carly's La Marca while Carly was at work. I had joyfully immersed myself in Danny Armstrong over the weekend.

My phone, face down on the chair beside me, vibrated.

"Where are you right now?" It was Pearson.

"Home, why?"

"Get to Cindy's. As soon as possible." She hung up.

Ω

Flashing lights illuminated the cul-de-sac as I approached on my scooter. Next to two sheriff's cars and an ambulance was a van whose sideboard read "Master Electrician" in large letters. Pearson's Tesla was parked next to the van.

As I braked the Mantis next to Pearson's car, the electrician appeared at the rear of the van. He wore a yellow hard hat, gray overalls and heavy, insulated safety gloves. I hurried over to him as he tossed his tools, hat and gloves into the back of the van.

"Sir, what happened?"

"Pool electrocution," he called over his shoulder. "She didn't have a chance. Haven't seen one of those in a long time." He slammed the rear doors and marched past me to the driver's door.

I sprinted around the side of Cindy's house. Two paramedics were hoisting a blue plastic body bag onto a wheeled gurney. Pearson and Mike stood next to a uniformed Sheriff's deputy, listening intently as he pointed to the pool, a utility shed and past the backyard to a slope that led toward the bay.

Mike broke off and rushed over to me. "It's Cindy," he said. "Someone ran an ungrounded extension cord into the pool, from that shed next to the house."

"Who found her?" I asked. *Mallory?* I thought.

"Neighbor heard her screaming, but by the time the medics got here, it was too late. They saw the wire and called the electrician. They wouldn't touch her."

"A wire can electrify a whole swimming pool?" I asked.

"Water doesn't conduct, usually, I remember that from high school physics. But the electrician explained that there are enough chemicals in swimming pool water for it to energize when the live wire touches it."

Pearson approached. "I spoke with Cindy's parents. She left Lake Tahoe early this morning, so the house was empty for the entire weekend. We have no idea when the cord was planted. It could have been anytime over the past few days. No other physical evidence, once again." She shook her head.

"So strange," said Mike. "I had actually started to suspect Cindy when you told me about finding Mallory here, and the conflict with Peter."

"Cindy and Rocky both worked at the same company," Pearson said to me.

Mike regarded Pearson's comment. "Oh, you mean the *7 Powers* thing? Yeah...how could that fit?" he asked me.

"I have to go back to the chart," I said. "Netflix has more than one power, according to the book, so Rocky could represent one, and Cindy the other."

Pearson abruptly said, "All right. I will meet you both in the office tomorrow."

"You aren't sticking around?" Mike asked, as Pearson strode away.

"Nothing more to see here," she said over her shoulder, and she disappeared around the side of the house.

The remaining officer circled the property, snapping pictures and scribbling in a small notepad.

CHAPTER 17

THE FOLLOWING MORNING, MONDAY, JUNE 3, Pearson arrived at the District Attorney's office about halfway through my first cup of coffee and summoned us into the conference room.

I passed a printed page to Pearson. It read:

From: unluckysevenfp@gmail.com
To: Addison Morita
Subject: Re: Investigate this
Now that Cindy's truly smokin' hot
Two from the same company thickens the plot

"I received it this morning," I said, as Pearson wrinkled her nose at the bawdy rhyme.

"Someone told the others?" she asked, passing the paper to Mike.

"Tiffany did," I said. "When I got home last night, I told her about Cindy. Just that Cindy was found dead in her pool. I didn't give Tiffany any other details. She emailed the TBT group."

Pearson assessed her fingernails. This week, they were a light turquoise.

"I have something, also," said Mike. "Oscar Naranja called me this morning. He shares the house with Tyler. Or, I guess, he used to. He told me Tyler's disappeared. Left without a trace last week, and hasn't been back, which Oscar says is very unusual. Tyler didn't say anything to him, and Oscar doesn't know where he could've gone. Oscar called Tyler's parents and they haven't heard from him either. It seems he's totally vanished."

"Also, Tyler may have stolen a hundred and fifty thousand dollars from Cal Forsythe, just before he disappeared," I said. "They had money in a joint account, and Tyler told Cal the account was hacked."

Pearson continued to examine her nails, with a slight frown. Mike glanced at me.

Pearson suddenly addressed me. "How tall or strong is Tyler? Rocky was a large man. Could Tyler have thrown Rocky off the balcony?"

"Tyler's short, but powerfully built," I said. "I remember he used to brag that he was all-state in football, and turned down an athletic scholarship to Fresno State to come to First Principles. He said his friends at home still call him 'Fifty-Six' which was his uniform number in high school. I'm sure he could get quite a bit of leverage on Rocky, if he surprised him."

Pearson mused, "I keep coming back to Rocky. All the other ones, Cindy too, the contact could have been made anytime. The murderer must have thought that through. Clever, though a horrible poet." She tapped the printed page. "But Rocky, we know exactly when that happened. We must find Tyler."

"I'm not giving up," said Mike.

"Addie, how does this new development impact your analysis of possible targets? We are down to three," Pearson asked.

I stood up and approached the board. "Well, Cindy and Rocky both worked at Netflix. Helmer uses Netflix as his example of Scale Economies in the book. Ironically, the Originals business is the division Helmer says gives Netflix that power, and Cindy worked in that group." I paused to look at the chart.

"But the killer can't be using Scale Economies twice. So someone—I mean, I realized—that later on in the book, Helmer writes that Netflix might be Process Power, or Counter-positioning as well, based on how they disrupted Blockbuster's business. A company can have more than one power, according to Helmer."

I gestured to the names on the board. "So we already have Network Economies, Peter. Switching Cost, Indigo. Two of either Scale Economies, Counter-positioning or Process Power, with Cindy and Rocky. That leaves the remaining one of those three, then just Branding and Cornered Resource."

"Only a few people match those last two," said Pearson, studying the board.

"Even fewer, if you use the color theory," said Mike. I shook my head furiously, mouthing *no*, but Mike ignored me and rose to the other side of the whiteboard.

"ROY G BIV," he announced to Pearson. "The First Principles motto. Truth as diverse as the colors of the rainbow. Violetto, Indigo, Greene. And you've got LeBleu, Redstone—"

"But Cindy Caldwell? What color is she?" I countered.

He smiled and pointed to his hair. "She was the only blonde in the class, so she could be yellow. And Peter had orange hair. So maybe Greenberg is green, and Peter was orange, and we don't need Naranja—"

"Mike, cut it out, now you've completely lost it!" I shouted. "That's ridiculous!"

"Yeah? Well, your stupid little Econ course is getting us real close to the answer, *huh*?" Mike yelled, as he jabbed a finger at me.

"Children. Settle down," said Pearson, who had remained imperially still. "Mike, I understand your desire to help narrow down the list. Very noble. But put the color theory aside for a moment. Addie, according to your analysis, who would still be remaining targets?"

Mike retired to his chair, still red with rage.

I pointed to the top of the board. "For Branding, we have Elyse at the celebrity cosmetics startup, and also Brian and Oscar at Apple. Tyler sold branded sneakers, but his company closed, and perhaps Warren at Goldman Sachs, but I'm not sure either of those would really qualify as Branding."

"Ridiculous," muttered Mike. "Trying to figure out how a psychopath would interpret a book—"

"Stop it, Mike. Continue," Pearson directed me.

"Cornered Resource, I think it's just Perry up here in San Rafael, at his genetics startup, and maybe Heidi at her irrigation company in Salinas. So maybe we should keep a close eye on Perry since he's the only local one that fits Cornered Resource? The other victims have been local."

"We do not have the ability to keep Perry under surveillance," said Pearson, shaking her head. "Not justifiable. There are too many other possible targets. And the last two murders were weeks apart. We cannot protect or watch someone for weeks."

She continued. "Going back to the remainder of the two Netflix powers—let me see, that would be either Scale Economies, Counter-positioning or Process Power—that could still be another five or six people."

"Some of those are in Seattle," I offered.

"But we have to consider them. I recognize the first four were local, but we may not make any assumptions based on geography. In fact, I am intrigued by the Maria Andreyev piece, and her father's connection to Andy Freel. And Maria is not local."

Turning in Mike's direction, Pearson said, "Give Maria Andreyev a call, and see if you can find out anything more about her relationship with her father, and his relationship with Andy."

"Fine," said Mike, straightening from his sunken position.

"And, speaking of Andy Freel, Addie, we will be going to see him on Wednesday."

Ω

"Sorry about losing it in there, Addie."

Mike and I were back at our desks on the second floor on Monday afternoon, a few hours after our showdown before Pearson in the conference room.

"Better learn how to control your temper before you become a social worker," I teased him. "It's fine. If I can handle Pearson, I can handle you."

"*If* you can handle Pearson," Mike retorted, smirking.

Mike picked up his phone. "Yes. OK, we'll be right over." He snatched his keys and helmet. "First Principles, let's go."

Ω

Pearson, Danny and Mallory stood side by side on the small stage at the base of Euclid Hall. They were facing the wall behind the podium. Mike and I descended the few steps to join them.

Seven eight-by-eleven-inch papers were taped to the wall. The first four were enlarged portraits of Rocky, Indigo, Peter and Cindy.

Danny noticed us as we approached, and greeted me with raised eyebrows.

"Those photos are from our First Principles yearbook," I said, and Pearson and Mallory pivoted toward me.

Alongside the four pictures were three white pages, each covered with a large question mark printed in red. And underneath the seven pages hung the *7 Powers* hardcover book jacket, secured to the wall by four pieces of masking tape.

Mallory's arms were folded and he frowned. "Our AV guy was in to do a sound check this afternoon. He saw this and came to get me. I called you right away," he said to Pearson.

"When was the last time the room was used?" Mike asked.

"I can check," said Mallory.

Danny said, "We only use it for special occasions, and for Doug's seminar. So probably not for the past few weeks. But it's always open."

"This had to be done in the past twenty-four hours," I said, pointing to the wall. "Cindy's picture is there." Mallory's face paled when I mentioned Cindy's name.

"Any cameras?" Pearson asked.

"We don't have much in the way of security here at First Principles," explained Danny. "It came up at our last executive meeting a few months ago. We discussed purchasing some cameras, maybe hiring a security guard. But Doug and Andy both felt we didn't need to spend the money. Security has never been an issue here." Mallory studied his shoes as Danny spoke.

"So anyone could have come in here, at just about any time," said Pearson.

"We keep our facility open as a matter of principle," said Mallory. "Like Danny said, we've never had an issue. I guess we need to rethink it. Our students are not aware of what's happened here in San Rafael the past few weeks. I can't let them see something like this."

CHAPTER 18

A KEYCHAIN JANGLED OUTSIDE THE door to our apartment as I prepared to leave for work Tuesday morning. Carly opened the door.

"Morning, sunshine," I said. "Cal's?"

"He actually took me to Gary Danko for dinner, to celebrate our three-month anniversary. He can be nice, sometimes, you should just know."

"Every three months, apparently."

"*Ha-ha.* Let me know where Danny takes you for your three-month anniversary."

"I'll make a note. Well, I'm glad you had a good time."

"We did. But it almost went off the rails. When Cal started shooting at a woodpile behind his house after we got home."

My head whipped back. "What did you say?"

"We had this romantic dinner at the Wharf. Everything's great. We're driving back up to San Rafael, after dinner, on 101. And you know how Tyler Lukela has disappeared on Cal? Cal told me he told you about it. So we're on 101, and a motorcycle flies past us in the left lane. Two guys on it, I barely noticed. And Cal jerks up in the driver's seat and says, 'That was Tyler. I swear it was him.' He tried to catch up but they were long gone."

I peered at Carly. "Are you sure?"

"I'm not sure it was Tyler, I didn't see them. But Cal was definite. He said Tyler was on the back seat, and the guy in front was Jimmy."

"Tresko?"

"Yup, Cal said he recognized him. Jimmy used to come to Christie's all the time. Cal said, 'It was a Honda. Jimmy has a Honda.'"

"I assume they were both wearing helmets," I said.

"Yes. But Cal said it looked like them. And he swears it was Jimmy's bike. So we get home, and Cal is steaming. I mean, he just couldn't calm down. He kept saying 'I'm gonna kill him, I'm gonna kill him.' Next thing I know, he takes out a pistol, goes out back, and shoots at a woodpile he has back there. *Bam-bam-bam.*"

"Whoa, that's intense," I said.

"Helped get it out of his system, I guess," Carly said. "That and the two shots of Jack Daniels I poured him. After that, he calmed down."

Ω

When I arrived at the office, Mike's legs were crossed, his feet resting on his desk. "I don't think she's coming in today," he informed me.

I relayed Carly's report about the mysterious motorcycle. Mike retracted his legs and stiffened in his chair.

"I gotta find that guy," he said, pursing his lips.

"Unless Cal finds him first," I replied.

"Meanwhile," Mike said, "get this. I called Maria Andreyev in Seattle, got her into a nice conversation. Everything's going smooth. Then, I bring up her father. *Click.* End of conversation."

"What's that about?" I asked.

"Not sure, but then I decide to poke around about Alex. Very little on the internet. But when you Google his name, look what *does* come up." He slid a printed article from The Guardian across his desk to me.

RUSSIAN ACTIVIST DIES AFTER SUSPECTED POISONING

(London) Russian journalist Sofia Andreyev, 54, died after being rushed to St. Mary's Hospital earlier today. Authorities believe the dissident journalist may have been poisoned with a substance placed in her tea when she met with an unidentified Kremlin official earlier this week.

An outspoken critic of the Russian president, Vladimir Putin, Andreyev fled Moscow for London in 2017 after a number of "credible threats" were telephoned to the office of her employer, the opposition newspaper Novaya Gazeta. Andreyev continued to pen critical essays that she published independently under the banner "Free Moscow."

Sofia Andreyev is the former wife of Russian businessman Alex Andreyev. The couple separated in 2016 and Alex Andreyev and their daughter, Maria, currently reside in the United States. Sofia Andreyev had recently filed suit in United States Federal Court, claiming rights to one-half of her former husband's assets.

"Surprises me that Pearson didn't see this," Mike snickered. "It's right there on the internet."

"At least she was right about one thing," I said. "You can't rule out someone just because they're not local."

Ω

Facebook reminded me that Tuesday, June 4th, was Elyse's birthday. I stopped at the Garden and Gift shop on my way home and bought an indoor plant I thought she would like.

When Elyse greeted me at her door and I presented her with the birthday gift, her face lit up. "You're so sweet!"

I relaxed on the sofa as Elyse unwrapped the plant and displayed it on her kitchen table.

"I'm so happy to see you. I've been so down about Cindy," she said.

"I figured we could both use a pick-me-up," I said.

"What are they saying at work?" Elyse asked from the kitchen as she poured two glasses of water. I did not respond.

"Addie, I know you're working on the case," said Elyse, hands on her hips. With her brown hair in a loose bun and narrow rectangular glasses, she loomed over me like a schoolteacher.

"You know, I always said, you were the smartest one in our class," I said smiling. "I'm helping with the case, not officially working on it. They don't have any strong leads. Not enough clues."

Elyse parked on the sofa beside me. "Tyler didn't do it. I know you think I'm crazy for agreeing to meet with him, but I'm sure he didn't do it."

"You're his biggest defender. Only defender, maybe."

Elyse placed her hands on her lap. "He's troubled. He's often angry. I'm not stupid, or naive, I just think his bark is worse than his bite. He didn't come here that night to kill me, I'm positive about it. He really wanted a job. That's all."

"How can you know that?"

"I don't know anything," she said. "I just...believe it." Elyse fingered her necklace.

"You believe it."

"A matter of faith, I guess. I used to talk to Tyler, at school," Elyse said. "I know that sounds odd. But I found out we belonged to the same church. His family, at least. We used to talk about life, about beliefs. He had plenty of questions. A difficult childhood. But I don't think he's capable of killing someone."

"He shot at me, Elyse. He's probably stolen money from Cal Forsythe. And I'm telling you, he had a gun in his jacket when he came to see you. I saw it."

"Look, you're the expert," she said. "But I was thinking about it. Everyone—except Rocky—died non-violently. As in, the killer didn't run up and stab them, or shoot them. Like you thought Tyler was going to do to me."

"What difference does it make, how they were killed?" I protested. "Could you kill someone? Could I? What difference does it make, how it's done? You have to be very disturbed, whether you shoot someone, or stab someone, or poison someone. I don't begin to understand what you're saying."

"I'm just saying," said Elyse, "I think it's someone who's afraid to actually be there when the victim dies. If you're suspecting Tyler because he's violent by nature, he wouldn't fit that profile. But it's not my field, so just forget it." She waved her hand. We each took a drink.

"So, how's work?" I asked, and Elyse chuckled.

"Yes, please, change the subject. Work is great, actually. Carrie's Cosmetics is growing like crazy. Carrie's Instagram is exploding and that drives tons of e-commerce revenue. Mostly teens, obviously. I heard a rumor that we're about to raise a huge round, at over a billion-dollar valuation."

"The next unicorn," I said.

"Which is why we need more branding people on board, which is why I wanted to meet with your violent murderer before you dragged me off down the stairwell."

"Hey, I didn't say he did it!" I exclaimed, and Elyse laughed.

"Enough about work," Elyse said. "How's your love life?"

"Working on it." I blushed. "Yours?"

"Nothing to declare. I need to lose twelve pounds," she said, straightening her skirt. "Then I'll think about it."

"Come on, you look great. What do you want, to be a pouty anorexic like Cindy? Lots of good that did her."

Elyse frowned. "There you go. I thought you came here to help me forget about that. *Ugh.*"

"Actually, I have the perfect guy for you, Elyse. His name is Mike. I know him from work. You'd love him. He's working on the murder case."

"A detective? No way."

"No, he's getting out. Going into social work. I'll have to introduce you sometime."

"Fine. Let's make a deal. You solve the murder. I'll lose twelve pounds. You'll introduce me to Mike the detective-turned-social-worker. We'll all live happily ever after."

"Sounds like a plan," I said. "But solving this case is going to be tough. I'm not even officially part of the investigation."

Elyse put her hand on my knee. "Addie, your heart is in the right place. You are here for a purpose. Whatever that purpose is, you'll find it."

I wiped my eye. "Elyse, you're the best."

"I'm praying for you, Addie. You're going to do it. You're going to solve this."

"You *believe* it," I quipped.

"I know it," she replied.

I leaned over and hugged her. "I'm not sure there's anyone up there listening to your prayers. But if he is, I'm so glad he put you on this planet."

CHAPTER 19

DOUG MALLORY, BUSINESS STRATEGY SEMINAR, Lecture 2 — Scale Economies

"*...Scale Economies is not just a form of 'the rich get richer.' When Helmer talks about Scale Economies power, he does not simply mean economies of scale. Recall that Helmer's looking through his lens at innovation-driven businesses. A Scale Economies company, as it grows, uses its growing profits to invest in new business areas, in continuing innovation, in moonshots, that its competitors can't dream of investing in. This creates step function growth, rather than linear growth, and further distances the Scale Economies company from its competitors. Nobody does this type of moonshot investment better than my friend Andy Freel. His company,*

Endscape, is using its video game profits to build the world's largest quantum-computing-as-a-service data center..."

Ω

When you enter the Endscape Labs corporate headquarters in Palo Alto, you step into the future. As the sliding doors seal off the outside world, you find yourself in a low-ceilinged, midnight blue circular hall with a ring of soft white luminescence overhead. Suddenly a rectangular counter brightens at the edge of the rotunda, and behind it stands a fully lifelike, holographic figure.

"Good afternoon, welcome to Endscape," said the soft, synthesized female voice of our welcomer. She was a glowing, green humanoid with wide blue eyes and exaggeratedly long, thin limbs.

"My facial recognition software indicates that you are Hope Pearson and Addison Morita. Here to see Andy Freel. Please confirm," the computer voice asked.

"Yes," I replied to the image.

"Proceed." A waist-high plexiglass gate to the right of the desk lit up and opened, allowing us to enter. As we passed the partition, another visitor to our left activated a dormant reception desk and was greeted by a metallic, skeletal cyborg, "Good afternoon, welcome to Endscape..."

An elevator doorway swished open. The interior of the elevator cabin reflected on all four sides, creating an infinite effect. After a few seconds, with no sensation of movement up or down, the doors reopened.

Andy Freel's office occupied the entire top floor of the Endscape building. We were higher than any other structure within sight, with a panoramic view. The wide-open floor rounded with the contour of the building, and was almost completely vacant. To our right, a cluster of low, angular couches and chairs hugged the floor-to-ceiling window. And directly to our left was Andy Freel's desk.

Andy sat behind a white, crescent-shaped workstation that curved around him. The desk was bare except for two oversized screens to his left. He was typing directly on the tabletop, with no visible keyboard, as we drew near.

"Welcome, Ms. Pearson," he called out. "As you can see, like you I prefer to work alone. Please have a seat."

Pearson and I approached Andy's desk. I sank into the most luxurious chair I had ever experienced. Its elastic-strap back and seat seemed to adjust instantly to my weight and contours.

I recognized Andy's unique appearance from his occasional visits to First Principles College. His head was bald and disproportionately large relative to his undersized frame. Thick, post-modern purple glasses were the dominant feature of his pale face. Underneath the desk I could see the exoskeleton braces that supported his crippled legs.

"Thank you for your time, Mr. Freel," said Pearson.

"Andy, please."

"I believe you know my colleague, Ms. Morita—"

My colleague? I thought.

"Yes. Or, your decoy, perhaps, Ms. Pearson? Or shall I call you Ms. Westcott? I've read all of your books. Big fan." Andy smiled.

Pearson covered her mouth to stifle a dry cough.

"It's terrible, what's happening at the school," continued Andy. "You have my full support. How can I help?"

"How would you describe your relationship with Doug Mallory?" Pearson asked.

"*Ha.* Our little hacking escapade? That was just a joke. A message." Andy stared at his screen and tapped with his fingers on his desk as he continued to talk to Pearson. "A college prank, if you will pardon the pun. We didn't take anything. Doug needs to remember who's in charge. Not him."

"What message? Is Doug upset that you are moving the school to Palo Alto?"

If Pearson was hoping to surprise Andy with her knowledge of his plan, his reaction was even more surprising. "No, not at all. Doug's upset because he's forgotten that I own him." He continued to type away.

Pearson blinked. "You *own* him."

"Correct." Andy swung to face us. "Silly, Third-Universe contract matters. When I recruited Doug to First Principles, he was just finalizing his most recent divorce. Cash-hungry, you understand. I made him an offer he couldn't refuse. Three million dollars per year, to run First Principles College. Ten-year contract. Now he's got an offer from a large podcast company, PushPin Audio. They want to hire Doug away. Fifty-million-dollar deal."

"So he wants to break his contract with First Principles," said Pearson.

"Not exactly. When Doug signed with the college, I also personally paid him twelve million dollars for fifty-one percent of his production company. That company owns all of his personal intellectual property. The Doug Mallory personal brand. I own his brand, so I own him, so to speak. And I'm not selling." He folded his arms.

I spoke up. "Has Doug accused you of blackmailing him?"

Andy glanced at me and shook his head. "No. This is a very recent development. He emailed me the offer from PushPin just the other day, and I emailed right back saying 'no sale.' We haven't discussed it."

"Not by phone?" I pressed, as Pearson observed.

"Not by phone," Andy replied.

Andy placed his palms on his desk and continued. "Let me explain something to you both about Doug Mallory. Doug sometimes loses himself in his own reality distortion field. He is one of the most brilliant, but arrogant and self-destructive people I know. He cavorts around, gets into trouble with wives, ex-wives, students. I asked him, why? This is why I've built virtual worlds. I have no problem with fantasies, with suspending actuality. I've spent my life building imaginary worlds, to enable people to activate their illusions and fantasies. We're so similar, Doug and I, which is why I love him, I really do. But he feels the need to bring his fantasies into *this* universe, which gets him into trouble. I, conversely, want to explore *other* universes."

"Through your video games? Through Endscape?" asked Pearson.

"No, no," said Andy. "Endscape is, despite its name, just the beginning. It has provided me with incredible power. A massive, growing user base. Endless streams of what you, in this universe, consider currency."

"Not following you, Andy, when you say 'you in this universe,'" said Pearson.

Andy leaned back in his chair and placed his hands behind his head. "Ms. Pearson, you subscribe to a series of societal rules. You make a living enforcing those rules. Catching people who violate your rules."

"*Society's* rules," she said.

"Call them what you will. Society, in your case your employer, compensates you with currency, for enforcing those rules. And, of course, you earn additional currency for writing books about people who break the rules."

"So you are some kind of libertarian. Or anarchist?" asked Pearson.

"Oh, no. I'm a Universarian."

"A Universalist?"

"*Universarian*, very different. It's not a religion. I'm not searching for moral or ethical truths. I don't believe in that at all, actually. I believe that we live in only one of many parallel universes. And in those other universes, there may be other rules, other laws. Not just different societal laws, different laws of physics too. So you don't like the laws in one universe? You just move to another universe. Just as people move from one country to another today."

"So if you break the law in one universe, you can just jump to another one?" I asked.

"Absolutely," replied Andy. "I've never taken laws too seriously here. And now we're very close to the first portal."

"'Close to the first portal'?" Pearson repeated incredulously.

Andy shook his head and smiled, as if to say, *You ignorant fools, how can you not understand?*

"Come, I'll show you," Andy said. "Special treat."

The exoskeleton motors at Andy's hips and knees whirred, and he elevated stiffly from his chair. He rounded the desk jerkily, and bounded toward the elevator like an astronaut on the moon. "Follow me."

"Endscape Two, Mezzanine," Andy commanded inside the elevator, and the doors closed. Once again there was no sensation of movement, but given our starting point we had to be descending. Our descent lasted much longer than the ride up to Andy's office from the lobby.

The elevator opened into a narrow mezzanine that overlooked a sprawling, cavernous subterranean chamber lined with over a hundred computer terminals. On the far wall, display panels as large as stadium scoreboards flashed and blinked around a giant central screen that read: *Percentage Complete 95%.*

"Excellent, last week it was ninety-two percent," said Andy, rubbing his hands together.

As Pearson and I assessed our surroundings, Andy explained. "OK ladies, exposition. When I was a young pup, thirteen years old, I was severely injured in a snowmobile accident which as you can see, rendered my legs useless. My parents, feeling terrible for me, bought me a computer. They hoped it would keep me occupied. The rest is well-documented history. I learned to code, built some games, and ultimately produced the world's largest multi-player online game, Endscape. But what drove little Andy? What was Andy trying to do? Make lots of money? No."

Andy rotated to face us, his back to the humming activity below. "I got into books like *Snow Crash, Ready Player One, Luminarium.* The Metaverse. Like many young people, I had this feeling that there was a 'more,' a 'beyond.' But I didn't believe the 'beyond' was spiritual, it had to be something else. That's what I was looking for when I built a digital 'beyond,' which was Endscape."

"So you're still looking for The Great Beyond," Pearson said, scanning the formation of workstations below.

"Not looking. Found. There *is* a 'more.' Much more. We now know this, scientifically. Here's the first clue: Scientists discover that neutrons break down in a particle beam in 14 minutes and 48 seconds, but in a lab it's 14 minutes and *38* seconds. Not much of a difference, right? But these are atomic particles, there should be no difference at all. Explanation? Some of the neutrons are *disappearing.*" He made a *poof* gesture with his hands.

"Some maverick physicists, my kind of people, suggest these decay times are off because, believe it or not, some neutrons are disappearing. Vanishing into—you guessed it—a parallel universe. And the more they dig, the more they find. Oak Ridge, the Russians, the Italians, they're all on this."

Andy wheeled back toward the looming scoreboard. "So little Andy thinks this disappearing neutron stuff is really compelling. He's been dreaming of this his whole life. The real 'beyond.' Many 'beyonds,' even. Andy has hundreds of bazillions of dollars, he'll buy the best science Earth money can buy. And find the portal."

"The portal to a parallel universe," said Pearson.

"Not just 'a parallel universe.' I believe there's more than one. So we get busy. Now remember, I'm a software guy, and that's the big difference. Everyone else is using hardware, accelerators, huge machines. Linear iteration. Andy says, let's use software. A step function. Remember how those huge Eniacs used to fill a whole room, and now they're just algorithms? We'll go straight to the algorithms."

Andy gestured toward the floor below.

"So those people you see down there, on the left, those are my quantum computing guys. Over there, in the middle rows, is my artificial intelligence team. Those on the end, the ones that look like physics professors, that's because they're physics professors. They're my theoretical physicists, gotta have a few of those. And we are damn close. As you can see."

My eyes were drawn to the giant screen. "So you're saying you're ninety-five percent of the way to opening the first portal to a parallel universe," I muttered.

"I'm not saying it, science is saying it. So, ladies, you better hurry and find your murderer. Because pretty soon, criminals aren't just going to jump bail to another country. They'll slip off to another universe that won't give them such a hard time."

I tilted my head. "I thought you were building a quantum data center. Not a portal to a parallel universe."

Andy blinked repeatedly, then glared at me over his purple glasses. "Don't believe everything Doug Mallory tells you."

Andy reached past us and placed his palm on the wall next to the elevator doors. A section of the wall illuminated. "I'm going to stick around down here for a bit. The elevator will take you back to the lobby. Thanks very much for the visit."

The doors glided open.

CHAPTER 20

THE TESLA'S DRIVER-SIDE DOOR CLICKED shut, and Special Agent Hope Pearson showed the first visible crack of vulnerability. The icon of equanimity nervously drummed her manicured fingernails against the steering wheel as we drove away from Endscape headquarters.

Pearson tapped on the Tesla's entertainment console and displayed her music playlists under "Hope's iPhone." She quickly scrolled past the entries at the top of the screen to a tab titled "Nineties Hits." Celine Dion's "My Heart Will Go On" engulfed me as Pearson returned her distant gaze to the road ahead. Lost in some parallel universe of agitated contemplation, she twitched occasionally as she drove. I had an instantaneous, fleeting nightmare that I would turn to my left and observe a werewolf driving the car. Whatever galaxy or otherworldly corporeality she now inhabited apparently did not emit verbal communication, so we proceeded, wordlessly, up 101 for about half an hour. She did not appear to be paying attention to the music, and I attempted to shut out the awful teen-pop, country-pop and grunge-pop cacophony, watching instead as a wispy fog coated the coastal hills, heading toward San Francisco International's terminal buildings.

"I need a beer. Let's grab a beer," Pearson suddenly said as we passed the airport.

"A beer?" I asked.

"I have never—never—had a suspect interview like that," she said. "I need to reboot."

"So Andy's a suspect."

"I have to consider more than just those names on your whiteboard, Addie. For example, Mallory. I imagine you would agree he is a possible suspect. And yes, Andy needs to be considered. Certainly after that performance."

She turned off 101 onto 280 South. "Why did you ask Andy about Mallory, and whether they spoke by phone?"

I rubbed my knuckles. "There's something I should probably tell you, actually."

"What is it?"

"I've been seeing Danny Armstrong."

Pearson's eyes narrowed for a moment. "Oh, right. The cute T.A. from Mallory's office. So?"

"So, I thought you might be upset, with the investigation going on, and all."

"No issue I can see. But what does that have to do with Andy?"

I exhaled. "Danny told me that he overheard Mallory really upset on the phone with someone last week. 'You can't do that to me, it's blackmail.' That kind of thing. Danny thought he heard Mallory say 'Andy.'"

"I see," Pearson said.

We were off 280 now, and the Model S was winding through a quaint San Francisco neighborhood. "Bernal Heights," Pearson said, pointing toward my window. "I live five minutes from here."

We continued in silence for a few minutes as Pearson navigated the local streets.

"Danny has probably been helpful to you with the seven powers," she said.

"I'm glad you're not upset about it. Danny's been super helpful. He knows that book better than anyone else."

Pearson turned onto a narrow alleyway. "You said Danny heard Mallory say 'Andy' on that phone call, about the blackmail. Is it possible...," She paused. "Is it possible, that perhaps Mallory said 'Cindy?'"

"Interesting idea," I said.

Pearson eased the Tesla into a parking spot between two scuffed-up jalopies. "This should do."

We got out of the car and I followed Pearson down the block. The late afternoon sun reflected off the windows of storefronts advertising dry cleaning and a nail salon. The first two-story house had a wooden stairway on its side and a fading, hand-painted sign that read *The Last Dance*. I followed Pearson up the stairs.

Pearson opened the stiff door with a practiced push, sounding a chime.

We entered a dingy watering hole. Mismatched wooden tables flanked the boxy room lengthwise, and a bar with stools stood to our left. Drab, green-gray paneled walls, having lost their original intended color, were adorned with tin ornaments shaped as hearts and flowers.

"There is Hope!" A beefy man with a handlebar mustache greeted Pearson from behind the bar. At the bar's far end, a pallid-faced drifter nursed a Pabst Blue Ribbon, while an older man with his plaid shirt unbuttoned over a grimy wife-beater occupied one of the tables facing us. All three men sized me up cautiously.

"Hey, Frank," said Pearson.

"Where's Janice?" chided Frank.

"Behave yourself, Frank. Addie works with me. Janice is gone."

I followed Pearson to a table at the back corner of the room, next to a large planter that served as the final resting place of a lifeless geranium.

"Good for you!" Frank called out after Pearson. "Day Lorraine left me? Best day of my life. Got my freedom, and this place rent-free. We never liked Janice anyway. Ain't that right, J.D.?"

The man with the plaid shirt grunted.

Frank followed us to our table with two opened bottles of Stella Artois that Pearson had not ordered. He turned to me as he placed our bottles on the table. "Welcome to The Last Dance. No food on the menu, but if you'd like I could probably whip somethin' up."

I politely declined.

Pearson and I simultaneously placed our iPhones on the table, which, I realized too late, was covered in spill stains and grime. Pearson's bright yellow phone case and mine, which matched her turquoise nail polish, clashed hilariously with the decor.

My eyes widened as Pearson took a swig from her bottle of Stella. "*Ahhh.* Just what I needed, after that strange trip with Andy Freel."

Pearson gestured toward the front of the bar with her bottle. "This place is authentic," she explained. "Nowhere else in town where you can get a beer for under five dollars. Frank charges two, when he remembers." She motioned toward my bottle in invitation.

I slid my bottle closer and said, "No offense, but you are a very intriguing person."

"None taken." Pearson smiled pleasantly. "I never apologize for who I am."

Pearson leaned over the table. "That young man, the one sitting at the bar? My connection to Andy Freel."

My eyebrows rose. "He looks like a homeless guy."

"His name is Mark Hoffberg. Very wealthy. One of the first investors in Endscape."

"And next you're going to tell me the other guy, at the table, is the C.E.O. of Hewlett-Packard."

"No, J.D. is a janitor." We both laughed.

My mouth was parched. I hadn't had anything to eat or drink all day. I took a deep, confident swill from my bottle.

"Wait a second. Stella?" I pointed to my half-empty bottle as I set it down.

"Exactly," Pearson said. "My best friend, my alter ego. I have had many girlfriends over twenty years, but Stella has always been my steady."

Pearson leaned to her side and crossed her legs, facing the table sideways and propping her elbow on the planter.

"So, tell me about yourself, Addie. Where did you grow up?"

"Near Fresno. Only child. My dad was a technician for Japan Airlines, my mom a student from Germany. The airline flew him over here to fix a plane, and she was here for the summer. They met somehow, and decided to stay in California. I showed up about a year later, he started drinking and they started fighting, as the story goes."

I mindlessly rotated my bottle on the table. "They split up when I was twelve," I continued. "Then my mom died in a car accident a few years later, when I was in high school. I lived with my aunt and uncle until I got into First Principles. Now I'm here. That's about it."

Pearson's face radiated deep compassion. "Sorry about your mother. Are you in contact with your father?"

"Not really." I drank again. "Last time I saw him was at the funeral. He has an aircraft parts company in Bakersfield. Married someone from his AA group soon after the divorce, I don't really know her. He would call every year on my birthday, but I think after a while he realized I wasn't interested. It's complicated."

Pearson gazed past me at the wall. "My father was a policeman, in Chicago, where I grew up. Tough man, very set in his ways. I studied criminal justice undergrad at San Jose State. When I came out, during my Masters, he was devastated. He just could not get past it. He never spoke to me again before he passed." She sipped from her bottle.

"That's tough," I said.

"It hurt. He taught me so much when I was younger. Taught me how to drink beer, certainly," she continued, tapping her bottle with her perfect fingernails and chuckling.

"So you went into law enforcement," I said.

"Yes," she completed my thought. "Definitely psychological. Spiritual, even. Every working day, every beer, I feel like I connect with him. I disagreed with him, but I still miss him."

My beer had run its course. "I'll just be a minute," I said, and pushed my chair back.

"Cross your fingers and hope you find toilet paper in there," Pearson said with a grin.

I stepped into the hallway at the rear of the bar, passed a condom dispenser, and opened the restroom door. The small room contained a toilet with its seat partially detached, a discolored sink with a dripping faucet, and a shower obscured by a filthy plastic curtain. There was just enough toilet paper on the roll to cover the seat and have some to spare.

When I returned to the table, there were two more bottles of Stella. Pearson's first bottle was empty as was most of her second.

"Better catch up," she said.

I obliged. If this was a test, I would not fail.

"So what about you, how did you end up with the task force?" Pearson asked me.

"Also complicated," I said, putting down my second bottle. "I guess...well, you've gotten a good sense of what First Principles is about, by now. I just felt I wasn't like the others. The tech vibe, the rat race. I thought I wanted that. When I got accepted at First Principles College, my god, I was thrilled. Maybe because at the time, I was running away from my childhood, my dad. My mom's accident. I wanted stability. I got into school, worked hard, got into Mallory's course. Reached the peak. And then I guess, I ran away from that. I thought I wanted something else. Maybe I'm always just running away from things."

"Do not be hard on yourself, Addie. Despite what Andy Freel says, there is value in people like you and me serving the public."

I sipped my Stella again. "Want to know what I really wanted to be? You'll laugh."

"What?"

"A writer."

"Nothing wrong with that," Pearson said. "Writing is my outlet."

"I wish I could write like that," I said, "I've read all of your stuff. I even wrote a whole novel, last year. A financial thriller, about a startup founder who gets mixed up with the mob. But everyone rejected it. Nobody wants to publish startup fiction."

Pearson chortled heartily. "My first novel? I submitted it to thirty editors. And I got thirty-six rejections. That means six of them forgot they rejected it, and rejected it again." We both laughed.

"You know what you do when they reject your novel?" Pearson asked.

"What?"

"You start working on your next novel."

I twisted the neck of my unfinished bottle between my fingers. "I don't know. Maybe it's not just the genre. My roommate says my writing is too dry, unsentimental. Anyway, I don't think I have the strength anymore. Or the story."

Pearson uncrossed her legs and straightened. "Find it." She tapped our matching iPhones on the table. "See, who knew how much we have in common. When you write your next manuscript, I would love to read it."

"No, I couldn't," I stammered.

"My offer is sincere. Happy to give you my input. How else could you get free feedback from a published author?"

The beer must have been playing with my brain. And hers. "OK, I'll think about it."

Pearson leaned back again. "Great. Now, explain to me again, how both Rocky and Cindy can be two of Helmer's seven powers, if both of them worked at the same company?"

Ω

Darkness had fallen by the time the Tesla's headlights illuminated the traffic circle at Bayside Towers.

"Thanks for the ride," I said, as I opened the passenger door.

"Well, you were not going to go down to Palo Alto on your scooter, were you?" Pearson laughed. "It was nice to share some beers with you."

"Yes, thanks for that too. Drive carefully, Agent Pearson."

The Tesla's horn tooted as I stepped onto the sidewalk. Pearson ducked her head toward the opened passenger window.

"Hey. Call me Hope," she said, and the window slid closed.

CHAPTER 21

WHO COULD BE KNOCKING ON my door at this time of night?

I had just returned to our empty apartment after my drinking date with Hope Pearson. Carly was out, working.

"Who's there?" I asked as I squinted through the peephole.

"Doug Mallory. Do you have a minute?"

I cracked open the door.

"Sorry to stop by without notice, Addie. I was in the neighborhood. Can we talk?"

I opened the door cautiously. "Um, sure, come in."

Mallory shifted his feet nervously as he sized up our small apartment from inside the doorway. Both hands were concealed in the pockets of his Patagonia vest, and he was fidgeting with an object in one of them.

I retreated as Mallory entered our small sitting area, keeping my distance and monitoring my proximity to the knife drawer in the kitchen.

"It's...a surprise to see you, Professor Mallory."

"Please, it's Doug. May I sit?" He advanced toward the couch.

"Make yourself at home." Having him seated would be better, if he had nefarious intentions. I hovered near the kitchen. "So, what brings you?"

"I have a situation, Addie, and you might be the right person to help."

"What is it?"

Mallory reached inside his vest pocket and withdrew his phone. "I've received some anonymous communication. I recall you're in the computer crime unit. I'd like to know if your people might be able to trace it."

"What type of communication?"

"An email."

"What does the email say?"

Mallory sighed. "It says, the person is going to go to the press about the murders of a number of my former students. Insinuate that I had some involvement. Unless I transfer three hundred thousand dollars in bitcoin, within forty-eight hours."

"What's the name on the email account?" I asked warily.

"It's something like hedge." Mallory checked his phone. "Hedge300k."

"When did you receive the email? Have you done anything about it?"

Mallory placed the phone back inside his vest. "When I received the email yesterday. I quickly opened a bitcoin account, and transferred the money. I had to."

"You transferred the money?" I asked, startled.

"Addie, let me explain. Obviously, I have quite a reputation. And I have a very, very large business opportunity pending. Career-changing. I cannot afford any personal brand damage at this moment. I cannot afford for the school to have a public scandal. That would be disastrous for me. Three hundred thousand dollars is a lot of money, but a small price to pay for preventing that kind of harm. But I want you to try to catch the sender. Maybe I'd even recover the money, if the person was caught."

"You are aware, Professor, um, Doug, there's no guarantee that this case stays quiet, that it doesn't get out to the press on its own. Once it's solved, certainly, the news will get out."

"I know," he said. "But then at least I'll be cleared. You'll find out who did it. By then, my deal will be done. I just can't afford for someone to try to link me to the, to the..."

"The murders," I said.

"Yes. So, as I said, a small price to pay relative to the downside for me and my reputation. But I still want you to try to catch him. The blackmailer."

"Send me the file. I can't promise anything. We haven't had much luck tracing anonymous emails lately. Very difficult," I said.

"Well, do your best. That's all I can ask." Mallory stood up, and I remained at the entrance to the kitchen with one hand on the counter.

"This is a great place. Quaint. You live here by yourself?"

"No, I have a roommate. She should be home any minute," I lied.

"*Huh.* Great, great. Listen, I have a terrific place on the water in Belvedere, near Tiburon. You should come by."

"Tiburon's great, I was just down there the other day," I said.

"Happy to have you over for a coffee, or a drink. I love catching up with former students. Hey, one more thing." Mallory was at the door, so I relaxed cautiously. "Your boss, Agent Pearson."

"She's not my boss. I'm just helping out here and there."

"Right. Well, impressive woman." He chortled. "Aggressive type, though."

"A tough line of work requires a tough personality," I said. "But she's fine when you get to know her."

"OK, well then, if you've gotten to know her, maybe put in a word for me, for your old Prof? I get the feeling she's...She doesn't know me like you guys know me, see? I feel like she's suspicious of me or something, which is crazy of course. *Ha-ha-ha.*" His laugh was forced.

"Of course. I'll have a word with her, next time I see her."

"Fantastic. And I'll forward the email to you. Great to see you, Addie."

I closed the door after him, leaned against it, and exhaled.

Ω

Thursday morning, Marvin intruded upon my desk's airspace again.

"Reminding you, Morita, that you aren't officially part of that murder investigation. You still work for me."

"I would never leave you, Marvin," I said. Mike snickered at his desk.

Marvin dropped a mass of papers on top of my keyboard. "We got more Request for Assistance forms this week while you were gallivanting around with your new friends. I need you to review them and write a short recommendation memo for each one. Short." He uprooted his posterior from its corner of my desk and plodded away.

"Hey, Marvin," I called. "Anything more on that malware you found at First Principles?"

Marvin swung around and snapped his fingers. "Yeah. Forgot to tell you. A simple bot. The code was programmed to identify any file with the word 'Pushpin' in it, and send a copy to a server at Endscape Labs. But it doesn't look like it actually sent anything back before we disabled it."

I exchanged a look with Mike. "Interesting. By the way, Marvin, I have another email for you to trace. I'm sending it to you."

Marvin shuffled back to his desk.

"Marvin's a real keeper," Mike said. "What's the new email?"

I told Mike about Mallory's spontaneous visit the night before. Mike leaned back and cupped his hands behind his head.

"Wow, super, super interesting," Mike said. "I'm sure you're thinking—"

"Jimmy Tresko," I said. "A perfect hedge, hence the account name." I shifted Marvin's papers over and typed *tradepeek* on my keyboard.

Mike thought aloud. "If the news of the murders gets out, and Endscape stock falls, Jimmy makes money on his short. And if it doesn't, he still pockets the three hundred thou from Mallory. How much is his short on Endscape?"

I pointed to my screen. "Three hundred thousand dollars."

"Bingo," said Mike as he clapped his hands.

Mike pulled out his phone, placed it on his desk and dialed a number.

"Who are you calling?" I asked. Mike touched his finger to his lips.

"Hello?" a voice said on speakerphone.

"Hey, Jimmy, this is Mike Bromley, I'm here with Addie Morita. Have a minute?"

"Well, well, Maxwell Smart and Agent 99."

"*Ha.* Listen, I actually could use your help. Besides you, who else in your Mallory class knows anything about bitcoin?"

"I don't know. Never really discussed it with anyone. Maybe Jason, in New York. Or Yelovich, too."

Mike winked at me. There was no further response from the phone for a few moments.

"Wait a second. What makes you think I know anything about bitcoin?" Jimmy asked.

Mike frowned. "Well, I figure, with your trading expertise and all."

Jimmy's voice blasted at Mike through the speaker. "OK Columbo, lemme guess. You got some clue, something happened, and you want to trap me into saying I know something about bitcoin. You think I'm stupid? I don't know anything about bitcoin. OK?"

"Jimmy, slow down. Mallory got an email from someone, shaking him down for bitcoin. We're trying to figure out who it might have been."

"*Uh-huh.* Yeah. Listen, Mallory is a pansy. If I wanted to get money out of Mallory, know what I'd do? I'd go over there, bang on his door, and say 'Gimme some money.' OK? I wouldn't email him asking for bitcoin. I don't know what's going on, but I'm telling you, I'm not your guy."

The call abruptly ended.

Mike tapped the desk with his pen. "Get Smart. *Ha.* I would have said you and me are more like Remington Steele. Ever watch Remington Steele?"

"Jimmy's so defensive, he's hiding something," I said. I folded my arms. "Or, maybe..." I paused.

"What?"

"Maybe Mallory staged it."

"Staged what? The email? Why would he do that?"

I stood up and paced behind my chair. "Follow me here. You're Mallory. You need to get out of your deal with Andy. If there's bad PR for the school, let's say the killer isn't found, people panic, the school suffers or even closes. Andy loses his leverage over you, and that helps you get out of the deal."

"OK, I'm still with you," said Mike.

"You wouldn't want anyone to suspect you'd be the one to cause harm to the school. But now you're getting nervous, because this hotshot homicide detective is on your tail, and just found you getting out of the pool with your former student and secret lover, and oh by the way, your lover turns up dead a couple days later and so is her fiancé. So you need a good distraction, or cover."

Now Mike stood up. "Let me see if I get it. You want to make it look like you want to *prevent* bad news at the college. Like you'd be devastated if there was bad news, for you or the college. And look, you're even willing to pay three hundred thou from your own pocket to spare the school from such a terrible scandal. You'd be the last person anyone would suspect, who would actually have caused harm to the school in the first place."

"Exactly." I pointed at Mike with my pen. "And, you placed money with Jimmy Tresko. His trades are public for anyone to see, right? But you certainly know about them because Jimmy's running money for you. And you see Jimmy's got a short on Endscape. So you concoct a fake threat, as if it's from Jimmy. You make the demand the same amount, and name the account 'hedge300k,' to make it appear like Jimmy is trying to hedge his Endscape short, by profiting even if the short loses."

Mike chimed in. "It's beautiful. Make it look like you're willing to spend your own money to protect the school, not, heaven forbid, cause it any harm. And point the finger at Jimmy."

"And even if he proves that he sent the bitcoin," I said, "bitcoin isn't traceable, so if he staged the threat, Mallory could have simply sent the bitcoin to his own account."

Mike dropped back into his seat. "You're a smart, smart dude, Mallory."

"Thank you," I said with a grin.

CHAPTER 22

DOUG MALLORY, BUSINESS STRATEGY SEMINAR, Lecture 9 –
Switching Cost

"...Note the title Helmer uses for his chapter on Switching Cost:
'Addiction.' He's talking about more than just an economic cost of
switching to a competitor's product. Companies with Switching Cost
power make sure their customers are 'hopelessly hooked' on their
product. For these customers, switching to a different way of doing
things would involve what Helmer calls 'Intimidating uncertainty.'
That addiction or uncertainty is what prevents your customer from
switching to any new alternative..."

Ω

The second crack in Hope Pearson's veneer surfaced the following day, Friday, June 7.

I typed busily on my keyboard, working on the RFA memos for Marvin, when Pearson suddenly deposited herself in the chair alongside my desk. She wore white slacks and a purple-and-black-striped top.

"Is Mike here yet?" She checked her watch. "We arranged to meet here at nine."

"Haven't seen him yet today," I replied.

Pearson picked at a cracked fingernail. This was Agent Pearson of the drive from Endscape. Hope from *The Last Dance* had vanished into a parallel universe, as quickly as she had briefly appeared.

"Hey, sorry I'm late," Mike said breathlessly as he dropped his helmet and keychain onto his desk. "Conference room?" he asked Pearson.

"We can sit here," Pearson said. "Any new developments?"

Mike showed Pearson the article he had found about Sofia Andreyev's poisoning death, and recounted Mallory's visit to my apartment, the threatening email, and our conversation with Jimmy. Pearson acknowledged my theory about Mallory's subterfuge with only fleeting interest.

"Tyler Lukela. Do we have anything?" she asked Mike.

Mike leaned back stiffly. "Unfortunately, nothing to report. I've been searching for Tyler all week. Nobody's heard from him. Phone is off, nothing on social. No credit card transactions."

Pearson crossed her arms and her white-slacked leg, and leaned back. Her brow furrowed deeply.

"ATMs?" asked Pearson, staring at the tips of her shoes.

"Yup, checked. Withdrew a thousand dollars the Saturday they shot at us, then another thousand that Sunday. Then he disappeared."

We watched Pearson watch the unmoving floor. "We need to find him," she muttered.

A man cleared his throat behind me and Pearson raised her head. District Attorney Schmidt stood facing us, with sleeves rolled and reading glasses perched on his forehead.

"Good morning, Agent Pearson. I saw you walk in. I...I hope I'm not intruding," he said. He rubbed his hands together nervously.

Pearson said, "No intrusion, Mr. Schmidt. How can we help?"

"I, I...wanted to check in, and see how the investigation is progressing." He clasped his hands behind his back.

Pearson shook her head. "No breakthroughs yet. Plenty of leads. We are still sorting things out. Cooperation is hard to come by. Everybody is hiding something. I am accustomed to obfuscation, but this is worse than I have ever seen. Makes it very difficult. And one of our primary persons of interest has disappeared."

Pearson was gazing back at the floor and there was a moment of silence as Mike and I looked on.

"Well, I hope our office is being cooperative. Has Ms. Morita been helpful?"

"Yes, certainly." Pearson glanced at me. *Best decoy I've ever used*, I thought.

"If there's anything else we can do to be helpful..." Schmidt's voice tailed off, and Pearson nodded.

"I will be sure to let you know, Mr. Schmidt," Pearson said in a somber tone, and Schmidt retraced his steps to his office.

"I have not had a case like this in a long time," Pearson said, seemingly to herself, her glazed eyes fixed on the tops of her shoes. "I do not have a handle on it. Nothing is coming together for me."

More silence. Then Pearson slowly uncrossed her legs, and stood up. "I will be on my cell, if anyone needs me." And she walked off down the corridor toward the elevator.

Mike raised his eyebrows in disbelief and shook his head. "Strange bird."

"She's unsettled," I said, swiveling my chair to face him. "Wednesday, after we met with Andy Freel, we stop at this bar and she downs two beers, and tells me about her issues with her father...totally out of character. Then today, she says she doesn't have a handle on the case. I'm telling you, she's cracking."

"She is so darn obsessed with just a few details. The Violetto piece, and Tyler," Mike said.

I tapped my legal pad, with the chart of names and employers. "And what about the targets, the seven powers? Trying to think like the killer. She's doing none of that. Just facts, facts, facts, when we have none. And no talk of motive. There's so much to explore here, so many strings to pull on."

"You're right," Mike said earnestly. "She's always off by herself. We have no idea what she's doing, or where she is."

"Like she said in that first meeting. She works alone," I said.

Mike leaned toward me. "That's it. Reminds me of this nature show I watched. Know what the difference is between a leopard and a lion?"

"Spots?" I asked.

"Lions, they hunt in packs, as a team. The leopard hunts alone."

"Maybe that's why leopards are the endangered species," I said.

Mike straightened up. "Pearson's a leopard, not a lion. That's her 'method.' But the Hope Pearson method is not working. Know what I think? We may end up solving this case ourselves."

Ω

I dropped into the Moskva Mini Mart on Friday afternoon as I returned to Bayside Towers.

Vlad greeted me cheerfully in his heavy Russian accent. "Hey, Addie. How many today?"

"I'm out, I think. Three, or four?" I replied.

"As many you want," Vlad said, handing me four G Zero Berry bottles from under the counter. "You know we order just for you."

"I appreciate the service, Vlad," I said, handing him my credit card.

As I slowly put the energy drink bottles one by one into a plastic bag, I casually asked Vlad, "You and Sergei don't live around here, do you?"

"No, no. San Geronimo. Many Russians there."

"So how did you guys find this shop, here at Bayside?"

"Simple. Sergei sister husband—how you say? Brother-in-law. Big Russian businessman, very successful. He own buildings. Rent us Mini Mart."

"Interesting. I had thought Andy Freel owned Bayside."

"Don't know no Andy. Sergei brother-in-law, name is Alex."

"Cool. Thanks Vlad," I said, and departed.

Ω

Later that evening, Carly and I relaxed on our balcony with a bottle of La Marca.

"Not seeing Cal tonight?" I asked.

"Nope, we're spending the day tomorrow. Since Tyler ditched, Cal's not going shooting. I'll take him to the Flea Market instead. Try to civilize him."

"Good luck with that." I laughed.

"You seeing Danny tomorrow?"

"Yes," I said. "The weekends seem to be good for us." I took a long sip. "Carly, I want to bounce something off you."

"What is it?"

"I know it's very fast. It's only been, what? Two weeks. But I'm thinking...I'm thinking of asking Danny about moving in."

Carly coughed. "Moving in?"

"Yes. I had to tell you, before I ask him. I don't know if he'll want it. But I just want you to know I'm thinking about it. Because that would affect you too."

"Wow," Carly said, setting down her plastic cup. "Wow." She fixed her eyes over the balcony's railing into the distance.

"Upset at me?" I asked.

"No, no. I mean, I'm happy for you. Danny's a great guy."

"I'm not marrying him or anything. He may not even agree."

Just then my phone rang. "Hey, Elyse," I said.

Elyse was screaming.

Ω

"It's Tiffany! Get over here to Tiffany's!" Elyse had shrieked into the phone.

I burst through the doorway to Tiffany's apartment. Tiffany lay motionless on the floor, and Elyse was applying CPR.

"Did you call 911?" I yelled frantically. Elyse nodded, tears streaming down her face as she worked. Moments later, sirens sounded outside and shortly two paramedics rushed into the apartment. One immediately pushed past me and squatted next to Tiffany's body as Elyse stood up shakily. I held Elyse, who tried to catch her breath as she spoke to the standing EMT.

"It...must be her allergies...I couldn't find her EpiPen anywhere...we...we were supposed to get together tonight...I called...and called...she didn't answer. So, I...came down and knocked, no answer...let myself in, I always let myself in...and there..." she pointed to Tiffany's body, and burst into uncontrollable, heaving sobs.

I held Elyse tight, tearing up as well. I scanned the room. There was an open box of chocolates on the buffet.

The crouching medic stood up slowly, shaking his head. "Nothing, she's been gone for a while. I'm sorry."

A Sheriff's deputy was in the doorway now, telling the building residents who had gathered in the hallway to stay back. Elyse collapsed into a chair as the officer began to question her and one of the paramedics.

I picked up the chocolate box. The label on the package read:

Allergy Advice
Recipe: No nuts or gluten
Ingredients: No nuts
Factory: Product made in nut free area

Next to it was a printed note.

Tiffany-
Congrats on your Work Anniversary. Doug Mallory.

I called Mike, and then Pearson, and told them to get to Bayside immediately.

Ω

For the third time, I watched as the body of a former classmate was wheeled away on a gurney.

"She was a good girl," I said softly to Mike.

Mike had arrived within minutes, while Pearson only got to Bayside after Tiffany's body had been removed from the apartment. The three of us stood in Tiffany's dining area, next to the buffet. The box of chocolates was now in a ziplocked evidence bag on the buffet. Pearson lifted the box to inspect it through the transparent plastic.

Mike reported to Pearson what he had discovered in the past twenty minutes. "The EMTs had a rapid allergy test kit in the bus—in the ambulance, I mean. Those chocolates contained peanut butter, even though the label said they didn't. I already called the store, their name's on the box. They said no way, can't be, send us a picture. I sent the lady a picture of the chocolates on my phone, and she starts yelling, that's not what ours look like, those look like they're homemade!"

"What is a Work Anniversary?" asked Pearson.

"It's this stupid LinkedIn thing," I said. "They know when you started working somewhere, so they post to your contacts when you've been at that job one year, two years and so on. Nobody takes it seriously."

"Would Mallory?" Pearson asked.

"He cared about peoples' jobs, for sure. But he didn't even help Tiffany get hers, I don't see why she'd think he would care enough to leave her chocolates. I can't believe she fell for that."

"Well she checked the label, and it said no nuts," said Mike.

"And where was her EpiPen?" I asked, looking around.

Mike said, "The EMT told me sometimes the anaphylactic response happens so fast, if you don't have the EpiPen right by your side, it can be too late, you collapse and can't get to it."

"And she always checked the food in her apartment, so she didn't need to keep the EpiPen handy at home," I added. Turning to Pearson, I said, "Everyone knew Tiffany had a terrible peanut allergy. She almost died at Mallory's end of semester party. Everyone saw it. Even Andy Freel was there."

"I also called Mallory, just now" said Mike, and Pearson's head snapped up. "I mean, I hope that's OK. I thought we needed to get his take. He was totally shocked. He said of course he didn't drop off any chocolates, he never does anything like that."

"He wouldn't put his name on it if he gave her poisoned chocolates," I said.

Mike responded, "Unless it would seem so obvious that someone was framing him, that nobody would actually suspect him."

My eyes fixed on the spot on the floor where Tiffany's body had fallen.

"She was so sweet," I said, shaking my head glumly. "She was very intelligent. But too trusting."

I turned to Mike, "There goes your color theory, by the way."

Pearson put down the plastic bag, and said to me, "Not just the color theory. If I recall your whiteboard correctly, Tiffany Chen doesn't match any of the seven powers, either."

Suddenly, my chest felt hollow.

Pearson's forehead was dramatically creased, and she wore a deep frown as she stared past us through Tiffany's kitchen window.

CHAPTER 23

THE MEDICS, POLICE, PEARSON AND Mike had left Bayside Towers. I remained with Elyse in her apartment, and we cried together late into the night. After a few shots of whatever alcoholic beverage Elyse had in her cabinet, she drafted a short note to the TBT group telling everyone about Tiffany's tragic death.

The following morning, Saturday, found me too emotionally drained for my weekly long run, and too unsteady to prepare for an extended stay at Danny's. While I organized my overnight bag, I received my fifth email from UnluckySevenFP:

> *From: unluckysevenfp@gmail.com*
> *To: Addison Morita*
> *Subject: Re: Investigate this*
> *Which "Power" is Tiffany? I'll shed some light*

The answer's in the book, in black and white

My head throbbed with pulsating pressure. *Tiffany was one of the seven? Which one?* I raced to Danny's apartment on my Mantis, and rang his doorbell urgently.

When Danny opened the door I threw myself into his chest. He held me firmly.

"I heard about Tiffany. I'm so sorry, Addie."

"I don't feel safe, Danny," I said, looking over my shoulder instinctively. I collapsed on Danny's couch, clutching my bag by my side. I told Danny about the doctored chocolates and the note from Mallory.

"Oh, come on," he said. "It's obviously someone trying to frame Doug."

"You're probably right," I replied. "But we can't rule anything out. In fact, Tiffany messes everything up. I don't see how she matches any of the seven powers. My whole damn chart is wrong, and anyone could be a target. Me, or you even..." I plunged my head into my hands.

Danny massaged my shoulders. "Calm down. Remind me, where did Tiffany work?"

"Elektryk, it's just a marketing consulting firm," I said, rubbing my eyes. "It doesn't meet any of Helmer's criteria, not even close, I'm sure of it. And the killer obviously targeted Tiffany. The note, the box at her door, the peanut allergy."

"Let's think," said Danny, pacing.

"Pearson basically ridiculed me last night," I said. "'Tiffany's not even on your seven powers chart.' Like, 'I can't figure this out, but you're not doing any better yourself.' It's not enough the killer is taunting me, Pearson's got to get in on it too."

Danny stopped pacing. "You got another email? Let me see."

I showed him my phone screen.

"'*The answer's in the book, in black and white.*' Hmm, there's a mention of colors again," Danny said, resuming his pacing.

"Black and white aren't in the rainbow, and Tiffany Chen doesn't have anything to do with *7 Powers.*"

Danny suddenly clapped his hands loudly. "The *answer's in the book* in black and white! *In the book*! That's it!"

He rushed over to a shelf and hurriedly ran his finger along a row of volumes, yanking out his worn, coverless copy of *7 Powers* and flipping through it as if he knew the content and page numbers by heart. He slapped the open book on the dining room table, holding its spine open, and jabbed vigorously at the open page.

"There. Right there."

I rose from the couch and bent over to see where he was pointing.

"Helmer's chapter on Branding. What's his example?" Danny said excitedly.

I scanned the page quickly, just as I recalled the answer.

"*Tiffany's,*" I said, straightening up. "You think—"

Danny slapped the table. "Addie, I told you before. This person—this psycho—is not trying to get an 'A' in Mallory's Business Strategy seminar. He's teasing you. He's playing with associations to the seven powers. *You're* the one who decided it was the employers. And in most cases you were right. But it could be any connection. Tiffany, Tiffany's, *boom*, you've got Branding."

"You really think so?"

Danny bent over imploringly, clenching his fists. "It's a *game*, Addie. It's a sick game. Play his game. Think like him. You've got five. There are just two left."

I slumped into a chair at the table, and held my forehead.

"Danny, I'm cracking up. It's too much. Pearson, now Tiffany. I just wanted to get away from it today. To be with you. I didn't want to be working on the stupid case today. Pearson won't listen to me anyway."

Danny grasped my shoulders again. "Addie, this is your chance. And it's life and death. I'm here for you. I'm here to help you. Let's see if we can figure out who the last two targets are."

"I didn't even bring my chart."

"We'll make a new one," Danny said enthusiastically, grabbing a pen and tearing a clean sheet of paper from a notebook on his shelf. He slapped them on the tabletop. "Let's go."

Ω

Two hours later, Danny pushed his chair back from the table.

I said, "So, the only local match for Cornered Resource is Perry. And the last one is either Malcolm as Process Power, or Victor as Counter-positioning."

"There it is. Clear as day. Pearson won't be able to argue with it," Danny said. "You've solved the *7 Powers* puzzle. Addison Morita, Ace Detective. You should be able to convince Pearson to focus just on these three people, and then you have a good chance to catch the killer."

"*Ha*, convince Pearson," I said. "Easier said than done. But I'll give it a shot. Monday morning. Meanwhile..."

I rose from my chair, grabbed a fistful of Danny's T-shirt, and led him into the bedroom.

Ω

I awoke on Monday morning and clutched my bedsheets around me, for what I hoped might be the last time at Bayside Towers.

I had slept at home Sunday night, after spending a blissfully romantic weekend at Danny's. *Today's the day*, I thought. *Later today, I'll ask Danny about moving in.*

Pearson arrived at the D.A.'s office at around 10:30 and summoned us into the conference room. Mike and I settled into our usual seats but Pearson remained standing.

Mike spoke first. "I think we have to put Mallory at the top of our list," he said, rocking in his chair. "That note on the chocolates could be a classic red herring. Nobody's going to suspect the guy whose name is on the note. It looks obvious that someone else is trying to set him up. Just like we thought about him and the bitcoin blackmail scheme. Classic misdirection. And Mallory has plenty of motive."

"Multiple motives," I added. Turning to Pearson I said, "Danny says it's very possible Mallory said 'Cindy,' not 'Andy,' on that phone call. Just as you suspected. So Mallory's got Andy trying to keep him at First Principles. He's got Cindy blackmailing him to get him to move to New York. If there's a serial killer at the college, Andy has much less leverage over Mallory. And if Mallory gets rid of Cindy along the way, he solves that problem too. And maybe the *7 Powers* connection is to show that *he* has all the power."

"Enough," ordered Pearson, who had been standing motionless but now came to life. "These are all...just...theories. No evidence. The facts lead to the motives, not the motives to the facts."

Pearson paced back and forth at the head of the conference table, frowning.

"I am not happy," she proclaimed angrily, as she leaned over with both fists planted on the table. "We have five dead bodies. In four of those murders, we have virtually no physical evidence. We have no idea when the killer was even on the premises. The only one we have anything on is Rocky. I keep coming back to that. But we're stuck on that."

"Like a broken record," I blurted.

"Excuse me?" Pearson's eyes popped open wide.

This was not how I had planned to petition Pearson, but I had committed. "You keep coming back to Rocky. I get that. But only a few suspects are unaccounted for that night, including Tyler. So how about an all-out manhunt for Tyler, instead of Mike chasing his shadow? And why are you so opposed to triaging motives? Go after Mallory, Jimmy, put them through the wringer, really interrogate them, instead of just dancing around? And how about finally looking at the remaining *7 Powers* targets? I have them down to three people." I pointed toward the whiteboard. "Just three, remaining, likely targets. Perry, Malcolm and Victor. I can explain how I got to them. Let's monitor them, use them as bait, work with them to catch this guy. Why not? We're running out of time."

Mike's mouth had dropped open. Pearson glowered at me like a wild cat about to devour its prey.

"Are you telling me, Morita," she roared, "how to do my job?"

My blood pressure was spiking. "I am not *telling* you anything. I am suggesting that you consider other ways of approaching what we know, and what we don't know. For example, I'm saying we know the first five targets have all been local. We believe there are seven targets, and the killer has repeatedly told us that he's following *7 Powers*. Tiffany *was* one of the seven, she was Branding, because Helmer uses Tiffany's, the company, as his example for Branding in the book."

"Did your boyfriend give you that idea, too?" Pearson snapped.

I plowed through her remark, exasperated. "And I've matched the other four of the seven powers, for Rocky, Indigo, Peter and Cindy. So there are only three local people left who could fit the remaining two powers: just Malcolm, Perry and Victor. Why don't we put them under surveillance, or maybe even get them on board for some kind of sting operation?"

Pearson emitted a sinister laugh. "Surveillance? A sting? Well, someone has been reading a lot of crime novels lately. In the real world, Addie, I cannot get resources for twenty-four seven surveillance of three potential murder targets just because some junior computer crime researcher says so, based on an Economics book. And I cannot set up three simultaneous stings when I have no way to predict when the killer acts. The first three murders were within ten days of each other, then the next two over what, three weeks? How do you propose to pull off such an operation?" Pearson's fiery gaze burned through me. *Those eyes.*

Pearson collapsed into a chair. "I should throw you out of here, right now, for insubordination. Or stupidity. Take your pick."

She paused, then proceeded. "But then the D.A. will be on my back. *What's the status, why aren't things progressing, why can't you people just get along...*I have lost all control. This investigation is completely out of control." Pearson was talking to herself now.

Mike's eyes met mine again, bearing a look of horror, a joint witness to Pearson's meltdown.

I know it's hard for you, Hope, I telegraphed. *Just give in. Give in to the truth. You're stuck. Be a lion, not a leopard. Let me in. I can help you. We can work together, and solve this case.*

Pearson, staring at the table, said softly, "Morita."

"Yes?"

"Please excuse yourself. I need to speak with Detective Bromley."

Ω

I slumped at my desk, drowning in melancholy, while Pearson and Mike remained ensconced in the conference room for hours.

At one point, Marvin's dawdling footsteps padded behind me. Before he could deposit himself on my desk's corner, I snarled over my shoulder, "Go away, Marvin."

"But Morita—" he started.

I whirled around. "If you value your life, Marvin, get away from me."

Marvin backpedaled slowly, and I resumed my morose meditation.

Sometime in the mid-afternoon, the conference room door *clicked* open. Pearson and Mike paraded straight to the elevator without looking in my direction.

I called Danny.

"Hey, Addie, what's up?"

"I can't take this anymore. My head's going to explode."

"What? Someone else?" Danny gasped.

"No, no. Not that," I said. "I confronted Pearson with our ideas. I guess I got a bit carried away. She basically threw me out."

"You're off the case?"

"I was never *on* the case, Danny. But now...She tossed me out of the room, Danny!"

"You sure you're not overreacting, Addie?"

"I'm sure. I need to get out of here."

"I'm here for you. What can I do?" Danny asked.

"I just need to see you."

"OK, hang in there. Let's go on a drive. We can go to Lagoon Park, do something to clear your head."

"That's it. I need to clear my head. I need to go on a run. I don't want to go out alone. Go on a run with me."

"Now?"

"Now."

Danny paused. "Well, I have Happy Hour at four. I can get out after that."

"Meet me downstairs at Bayside at 5:15," I said and hung up.

Ω

Danny approached me from the Bayside Towers parking lot as I stretched in the traffic circle.

"How far are we going?" he asked cheerily.

"Until my head clears up."

"That bad, huh?"

"Yes, that bad," I said.

"Well I hope I can keep up," he said.

"We'll go slow," I said. "Ready?"

"So what happened?" Danny asked over the *thwack-thwack*ing of my rucksack, as we jogged in the direction of the bay. I recounted the entire conference room confrontation.

"You're right, definitely sounds bad," Danny said.

We ran on. We were out along the bay. The sinking sun cast a burnishing glow over the marsh as a light breeze fanned us.

"I think you're right," Danny said. "Pearson's lost control of the case, and she lashed out at you. Sounds like she has a lot of personal pride at stake."

I agreed.

"I wonder if she'll quit," Danny said.

"Quit?" I asked.

"Quit the case. If she can't stand losing. She cares so much about her pride. Her reputation. If she steps off the case, she's not accountable. At least in her own mind. For her record." He was struggling to run and talk at the same time.

"She'll pull a McClanahan," I said.

"A what?"

"One of the lawyers at the D.A.'s office, said he worked with a public defender named McClanahan, and all the guy cared about was his record. If he didn't think he could win a trial, he'd find an excuse to quit. They called it 'pulling a McClanahan.'"

"Exactly." Danny wheezed.

"And then what?" I asked.

"Who knows? Maybe they ask you to take over," he said, panting. "You know the most about the case at this point."

Danny stopped short, gripping his side and wincing. "How far have we gone?" he asked through clenched teeth.

I checked my watch. "Two miles."

"How far do you usually go?"

"On my long runs? About eight miles, give or take. We don't have to go that far though, if you can't."

Danny gasped. "No, can't do that today." He held his side again, grimaced and stretched. "Must've been the punch."

"Want to head back?" I asked.

"Yeah...yeah, sorry. Let's go slow," Danny said, reversing direction. He jogged with a noticeable hitch in his stride.

As we returned to Bayside Danny was still trying to smile, though he was clearly suffering, and perspiring heavily.

"You really don't look good," I said, as Danny slumped against the wall of the Mini Mart. I reached into my pack and handed him my energy drink.

"Thanks." He emptied the bottle in a few gulps, then wiped his face with his shirt. "I don't know what's wrong with me. I should be fine on a run like that." He shook his head.

Danny gazed up at the twin apartment buildings rising over our heads. "How long have you been living here, Addie?"

"Six years," I said. "Hard to believe."

Danny ran his hand through his hair. "Listen, I've been thinking..." he started.

Say it. Say it, I thought.

He put the empty energy drink bottle on a low ledge beside him, and placed his hands behind his back as he leaned on them against the wall, bathed in sweat.

"You...you keep coming over, with your little overnight bag, then you go home again."

Say it.

"I mean, I get it, it's only been a few weeks. But I'm...I'm really enjoying the time we spend together. I haven't felt this way in a long time. Ever, maybe. So I was thinking, if you want to..."

Say it. My heart pounded.

"I was wondering, if you wanted to...you know, move in."

Ignoring his sweat-covered body, I threw myself into him, and we kissed.

"Not tonight, though," I said. "You look awful. I'm sorry I pushed you. You'd better get some rest. Want to come up?" I asked.

"No, it's OK," Danny said. "Gotta get up early. Mallory's picking me up first thing. Recruiting. Probably just need a hot shower, is all. Must've been the stupid punch."

"Go home, take a shower and get into bed. I'll check in with you later," I said.

We embraced, and I watched Danny as he hobbled toward the parking lot.

"Danny?" I called spontaneously.

Danny turned around in the middle of the traffic circle.

"I think I love you," I heard myself say.

"I think...I think I love you, too."

I watched Danny limp farther into the Bayside Towers parking lot until he disappeared.

Neither of us could have imagined how our lives were about to change.

CHAPTER 24

WHEN DANNY HAD TURNED AROUND and said those beautiful words, *I think I love you*, those words I thought I might never hear, certainly not from a man like Danny Armstrong, he had been standing on the spot outside Bayside Towers where Rocky's body had crashed to earth exactly one month earlier. My euphoria over our mutual proclamations of love momentarily dissolved into a macabre flashback. I suddenly could see Rocky's body, still covered in plastic, lying on the ground.

I violently shook my head to erase the memory, and picked up the empty bottle that Danny had left on the ledge beside me. *Everything is disposable*, I thought. *Even the people around me have become disposable.* How quickly misery turns to exhilaration and triumph, then back to nightmarish dread. Was the weight of the case, of my classmates' deaths, so great? Why was I allowing these negative thoughts to cloud my happiness? Life must go on.

I entered the lobby and noticed my reflection in the mirrored wall. The lithe, pony-tailed runner staring back at me should have been jumping for joy, floating, yet she seemed pensive.

So work is falling apart. There's a serial killer on the loose. But Danny Armstrong just told you he loves you. Smile, Addie, things are looking up, I said to her.

Everything is Saiou's horse, the girl in the mirror replied, and smiled.

I pushed open the lobby's back door, heading toward the recycling bin with Danny's empty bottle. Suddenly, a shadow flashed in the corner of my eye and running footsteps pounded on the pavement. As the fleeing man turned the corner around the back wall of the Mini Mart, all I glimpsed was his black jacket and dark hair. A lit cigarette smoldered where the man had stood, just behind the rear lobby exit.

You're emotional, you're jittery, you're imagining, I told myself. *Pull yourself together.*

I discarded the bottle and took the elevator upstairs.

Carly immediately sensed something brewing when I entered our apartment. "What's with you?" she inquired. "You went on a run?"

"Carly, I had the worst day ever, then the best day ever. I think I got thrown off the case I'm working on, and then...Danny asked me to move in!" I exclaimed.

Carly's mouth opened wide. "You asked him?"

"No, you won't believe it. I was going to ask him, yesterday, but I didn't have the guts. And then today, we went on a run, and at the end—just now, downstairs—he asked me! Just like that."

Carly covered her mouth, and uttered, "Wow."

"Carly, Danny might be the one, and I don't want to lose him. I've got to see this through."

Carly regained her composure and turned back to the kitchen sink. "Well, this is hard for me to say, but I'm happy for you. You deserve something good to happen, with all the craziness around here."

"I appreciate it. You're the best. I'm going to shower, and then I'll tell you all about it."

"Oh, by the way," Carly called. "Jimmy was here before, looking for you."

I backtracked from the doorway of my room. "Jimmy? Jimmy Tresko? He came here?"

"Yeah, just knocked on the door. Asked if you were here. Didn't say what he wanted."

"Do you remember what he was wearing? A black jacket maybe?"

"Lemme think," Carly said. "No, I don't think so. Just a T-shirt, I think, and he was holding a motorcycle helmet. That's all I remember. Why?"

"I saw someone downstairs," I said. "But it sounds like it wasn't him. Strange. I wonder what he wanted."

I returned toward my room.

"I'll miss you," Carly called from the kitchen.

$$\Omega$$

I got Danny's voice mail. "Hi, it's Danny. Sorry I can't take your call. Please leave a message and I'll get back to you as soon as I can."

"Hey, it's me," I spoke into my phone. "Sent you a couple messages last night, haven't heard back from you. You looked terrible yesterday, sorry I dragged you out on that run. Just wanted to make sure you're OK. Anyway, packing up. I'll try you later."

My bedroom in the apartment I would soon no longer be sharing with Carly Mendez was as uninteresting as my lifestyle had been for the past two years. The neutral gray walls featured few decorations. Above my bed, I had nailed a macrame wall hanging, one of Carly's latest finds from the Richmond flea market. A framed lithograph of Van Gogh's *Portrait of Dr. Gachet* watched me from the far wall. Some of the plastic knobs had fallen off my standard-issue Ikea dresser. A desk, which other girls might use for makeup but I used for late-night writing, had two large drawers which held my manuscripts. My old Dell laptop, its battery shot, remained permanently plugged in on the desk next to a laser printer that also barely clung to life. I reclined on my bed, arranging a few small piles of clothing.

"Need any help packing?" Carly peeked through my doorway to monitor my progress. We had stayed up late the night before, as I recounted to her the short history of my relationship with Danny and my hopes and plans for our possible future.

"No, thanks, I'm only taking the most important things, just clothing. Anyway, I only have one duffel. I'll be back, don't worry. I'm leaving plenty of stuff. Don't rent the room just yet."

Carly laughed. "So long as you're still paying your half, no problem." She consulted her watch. "Not going in today? It's almost eleven."

"I'll go in soon," I said. "Nothing burning for me over there, anyway."

Sometime after lunch I rode to the office. As I climbed the stairway to the second floor, the sting of the prior day's conference room expulsion supplanted my thoughts of newfound romance and hope.

I walked morosely to my desk. Mike was not in view, though the conference room appeared to be occupied. Marvin, noticing my arrival, began to gather papers on his desk.

The conference room door opened with its now-familiar *click*. From the corner of my eye I saw Mike emerge, then Pearson. They approached my desk slowly, with Mike leading.

Mike rolled his chair so that it faced me. Pearson lowered herself into the seat between our desks. Pearson's face was expressionless. Mike's was ashen.

"Addie," Mike said, clasping his hands on his lap. "I'm guessing you haven't heard."

Pearson's stone-cold eyes bore into mine.

"It's Danny," Mike said. "Danny Armstrong. He was found dead this morning, at home. I'm so sorry." He glanced nervously at Pearson.

Mike and Pearson blurred as my eyes welled with tears. In an instant, I was back in the hallway outside ninth grade Chemistry class at Roosevelt High. Ms. Kingsley had her arms around my shoulders. *There's been an accident, Addie. It's your mother.*

"No. Nooooo...it can't be..." I moaned, and put my head down hard on my desk.

Mike's voice, right next to me, sounded so distant. "Mallory found him...coroner...same symptoms as Peter...poison..."

I groaned again. "Why...why Danny...What does he have to do with all this...?"

Pearson placed her hand gently on my knee and asked softly, "Addie, it is possible Danny was not the actual target."

Mike said, "It's possible the poison was intended for someone else. We need to know, when was the last time you saw him?"

"Yesterday. Nooooo..." I sobbed, banging my head on the desk.

"All right, Addie, all right," said Pearson. "Tell us what you remember."

I lifted my head, my face twisted in anguish. "Yesterday...we went on a run, after work. After Happy Hour. He looked terrible...complained about his stomach...he couldn't breathe well." I paused to regain some composure.

"He was really struggling to run. It was a short run, should have been easy for him. He said it wasn't normal. He kept holding his side. He said 'it must have been the punch.' They have punch, in big bowls, at the Happy Hour..." I tailed off.

Pearson gently rubbed my knee, and Mike slouched with folded arms. "When was the last time you heard from Danny?" Pearson asked me, softly again.

"We—oh, god," I said. "I was going to move in with him tonight..." I sobbed.

"Addie, I know how hard it is," said Pearson.

"I sent him home from Bayside. We finished the run at Bayside...I sent him home, he looked terrible. I said, I'll check in with you later. I messaged him a few times last night but I didn't hear back. I figured he went to bed early, and then Mallory picked him up first thing to go recruiting."

"He never responded to you?" asked Mike.

"No," I said. I lifted my phone from the desk. There was a new email:

From: unluckysevenfp@gmail.com
To: Addison Morita
Subject: Re: Investigate this
A fly in the ointment, not a student
Looking only at classmates wasn't so prudent

"Oh, god..." I moaned again. I held my forehead with my right palm and showed the screen to Mike with my other hand. He read the email out loud to Pearson.

Pearson's guise had shown small cracks over the past week. But in an instant her entire facade fractured. Something about this sixth email, the evidence that Danny had been targeted, caused her to snap.

"Let me see that!" she hollered at Mike, and snatched my phone from him. With wild eyes, she read the email out loud to herself, then again, slowly.

Pearson covered her face with her hands and shook her head. "Danny was a target. Danny was a target. Dammit, dammit, dammit. You screwed this up, Pearson. You screwed the whole. Thing. Up."

Her mood change was so striking, her sorrow so deep, that it almost mirrored mine. "This changes everything...Back to square one...," she said.

She stared at my phone's screen again, mouthing the words of the email for a third time, and placed the device back down on my desk. She pulled her own phone out of her pocket, and typed a brief message.

She grabbed my arm and stood up, pulling me from my chair. "Addie, I need you now. I have been terribly mistaken, from the beginning. Come with me."

CHAPTER 25

"MIKE, CALL THE NUMBER I just sent you, tell them I will not make the meeting," Pearson ordered as she passed Mike's desk, towing me behind her.

Pearson's grace and fluidity were gone. She collided awkwardly with the conference room door as it opened, and she dropped into a chair, banging it into the conference table. The RMS Pearson had struck an iceberg and was sinking fast.

Her phone vibrated. Was her hand shaking? "OK. Thank you. I will be meeting with Addie now. Make certain we are not disturbed."

Pearson's straining efforts to maintain composure could not alter the deathlike pallor of her face. She spoke in a forced, measured tone.

"I was wrong about everything. I am crushed. I have never been so wrong about a case before."

"You had a theory," I said.

"Yes, a theory. I made the mistake I swore I would never make. I assumed. I never assume. But this, with Danny, this throws everything back to square one for me."

The spectacle of my idol, Special Agent Hope Pearson, unraveling in the same room where we had first met a month earlier was jarring.

"I have been worthless," she said, more to herself than to me. "Worthless. Innocent people have died." She wiped at her eyes. *Tears!* Those eyes, those terrifying eyes, were shedding tears.

"Perhaps if I had listened to you, Addie, more closely, from the beginning..."

My mouth was agape, and I quickly closed it.

My ears rang in the eerie silence, as Pearson, sagging in her chair, stared down at the table.

"Addie, I know losing Danny is very traumatic. Sometimes this work requires us to achieve a level of equanimity that can seem superhuman." She paused.

"I have lost friends, colleagues, partners. This is an unforgiving line of work. I recognize that every situation is different. But I need to know if you are up to the task, Addie."

"I...I think so, I...don't know what you have in mind," I stuttered. *Was she quitting?*

"I am lost, Addie. I have completely lost my bearings on this one. We have run out of time. We need a Hail Mary pass. You have been looking at this case from a different perspective from the outset. I need your direction, since mine has gotten us nowhere."

My voice shaking, I asked, "What do you mean by 'my direction'?"

Pearson folded her twitching fingers together on the table and leaned forward. "If you are correct, and I believe you are, then there is one more target. Only one more victim. And then we will lose the killer forever, or at least, the ability to catch him before he acts."

"I agree," I said.

"My method has not worked. We have no more time for methodology. We need to play the odds, make our best guesses. Pursue those options, and focus only on those options. So I need to know, from you, right now, who the top three suspects are. In your opinion, based on their possible motives and what we know so far. We will go after them, only them. We will each focus on one, and we will hope that we are right about one of them. So who would you say are your top three suspects?"

"Tyler, obviously," I said. "Given that he disappeared as soon as we started to take an interest in him. Mallory. And then...I'd say Jimmy."

Pearson drummed her fingers on the table, her brow crumpled. She tapped a few times on her phone. "Jake. Are you free tomorrow? OK, call you back."

She turned to me. "OK. This is what we are going to do. Jimmy said he was down in Salinas with Heidi on the night Rocky died, but Mike said the alibi was suspect. You will go down to Salinas tomorrow to talk to Heidi. Leverage your friendship, camaraderie, to see if you can get the truth out of her. Do not tell her in advance that you are coming, so Jimmy has no opportunity to meddle. Jake will pick you up tomorrow morning and he will stay with you all day. You will need to be protected as much as possible. Jake is a former policeman, does a lot of work for me. He will keep an eye on you."

I cocked my head.

"Addie," Pearson explained, "if Danny was a target, you could be as well."

Pearson continued her instructions. "I will have Mike put out an APB on Tyler immediately, and he will focus on that. And I will go to talk to Mallory again. We will meet up back here tomorrow afternoon. I will be in regular phone contact meanwhile."

"Got it," I said.

"Are you sure you are all right?" Pearson asked.

"I will be."

Pearson stood up. "Mike will drive you home."

"I'm OK," I protested, but Pearson held up her hand.

"Mike will drive you home. Take the rest of the day to reset. We need to have you as sharp as possible, and you have been through a lot just now. You have my number if you need anything. Keep your eyes open. I will send you Jake's number. He will let you know what time to be ready in the morning. Are you sure you are OK?" she asked.

"I think so. I'll be OK," I said.

Ω

On Wednesday morning, June 12, promptly at nine o'clock, a graphite gray Buick sedan pulled into the traffic circle at Bayside Towers. A towering, bald black man wearing a paisley golf shirt and tan pleated slacks, bearing a broad smile and a prominent belt holster, stepped out.

"Addie?"

I waved. The man stood at the open driver's door, facing me over the roof of the car.

"Morning! Jake Patterson. Your chaperone for today. *Ha-ha-ha.*" Jake had a deep belly laugh. "Yes ma'am, me and Lucille, we'll be taking care of you today."

There was nobody else inside the car. "Lucille?" I asked.

"B.B. King named his guitar Lucille. This here, she's my Lucille." He patted his holster. "Me'n Lucille, we've been lookin' after Hope Pearson for a long time. Front or back?" He motioned toward the passenger door.

"Where does Agent Pearson usually sit?"

"In back. Always in the back. She likes to ride in style, know I'm sayin'? *Ha-ha-ha.*"

"OK, then I'll sit in the back." I slid into the rear seat of the Buick with a surging sense of intrepidity.

"Have you known Ms. Pearson for a long time?" I asked Jake, as we pulled away from Bayside Towers.

"*Known* her? Hell, we're family. *Ha-ha-ha,*" said Jake. "On her daddy's side. He's from the Chicago kin, we're from the 'Nawlins kin, originally. But I've been out here for about thirty years. Only family Hope had when she got out here for school. We looked after her then. She was different back in the day, a wild sort, know I'm sayin'? She turned out all right, of course, as you can see. I think me'n the old lady get some credit for that, know I'm sayin'?"

"Were you a cop too?"

"Yeah, semi-retired now. Family business, I guess. *Ha-ha-ha.*"

"So you say she used to be different?" I asked.

"Well, you know, Hope is so serious now. Always with that face. *Ha-ha-ha.*" He wrinkled his mouth into an exaggerated scowl. "Know I'm sayin'?"

"Oh yes, I know it well," I said.

"But when she first got out here, she was a wild child. Had to bail her out of some jams now and again, know I'm sayin'? Back in the day. Bless her soul. But she turned out just fine."

I tried unsuccessfully to imagine Pearson as a 'wild child.'

"Tell you what, though, I don't know what this case is about, she didn't say. But I ain't never heard her this way. Stressed, know I'm sayin'? She tells me, Jake, I ain't gonna be on this case much longer. And she says to me, she says Jake, you keep a close eye on Addie. Don't let nothin' happen to her. Not on my watch. She must really be looking out for you, know I'm sayin'?"

"She said that?"

"Yes, ma'am."

"Do you speak to her often? Regularly, I mean?" I asked.

"Oh yes, of course, all the time. Few times a week, for sure. We check in with one or the other."

"So she's sounded different lately?"

"Yes, ma'am, that's what I'm sayin'." Jake glanced over his right shoulder. "Stressed-like."

"Interesting," I said. "You know, I don't know her well, of course, but I feel like she's started to act strange. I mean, last week, we had this meeting, and then afterward she took me to this shady bar, and knocked down a bunch of beers."

"The Last Dance? *Ha-ha-ha.* She took you there? That ain't strange at all, no ma'am. That's her *place.* Drank Stellas, am I right? She don't take nobody there. Only girlfriends and the like. That means you *rate,* know I'm sayin'?, if Hope Pearson takes you there."

"Not sure you're right," I said, catching Jake's eyes in the rearview mirror. "After those beers, she basically threw me off the case. Though now I'm back, I guess. Can't figure her out."

"Well, she is a moody sort, know I'm sayin'? *Ha-ha-ha.* But if she took you to The Last Dance, that's special, all I'm sayin'. And now? She's sure concerned about you now."

Jake paused. "Hey, if I'm jabberin' too much, you just tell old Jake to stop talkin'. Sometimes Hope, she says, that's enough now Jake, I gotta work, *Ha-ha-ha.*"

"It's OK, Jake," I said, laughing.

"Salinas, right? I'll shut up 'til we get to Salinas," Jake said.

Not going to be on the case much longer? She might do it, I thought. *She might quit, and hand the case off to me.*

We drove in silence for a while. My thoughts drifted back to Danny. In all the confusion, the turmoil, at the office yesterday with Pearson and Mike, it made sense that we had not considered why Danny had been targeted.

My shabby lambskin wallet held the folded yellow paper with my handwritten table of students, employers and *7 Powers* possibilities. I unfolded it on the Buick's back seat and reviewed the list again for a few minutes.

Danny had to be Process Power. Nobody knew *7 Powers*—Helmer's *process*—better than Danny. Not even Mallory.

Rocky and Cindy would then be Scale Economies and Counterpositioning, and that left only Cornered Resource. The only local on the chart who matched Cornered Resource was Perry.

I called Mike, who answered with unusual gravity.

"How are you holding up, Addie?"

"Thanks, I'll be OK."

"You on your way to Salinas?"

"Yeah. Listen, things were so crazy—we didn't discuss which of the seven powers Danny is, and who's the last one left."

"Right, I was just thinking about that."

"So, I'm certain that Danny is Process Power, and that leaves only Cornered Resource. And the only person in the San Rafael area that matches that one is Perry Greenberg. I think we should start keeping an eye on Perry, as soon as possible. Before it's too late."

CHAPTER 26

WE ENTERED SALINAS A LITTLE after eleven o'clock. Now was the time to surprise Heidi.

"Heidi, it's Addie," I said, on the phone, in the back seat of the Buick.

"Hey, Addie, what's—what's going on? Why are you calling?"

"I'm sure you're following what's happening up at school. And now Danny," I said.

"Yeah, I heard. Crazy."

"Well, I'm in Salinas. I need to talk with you. It's important."

"You're—you're in Salinas? Now?"

"Yes, I'm here. I'll meet you anywhere. Just need to talk."

"Um...all right," Heidi said nervously. "I'm at work, but I can step out. Is Starbucks OK?"

"Sure, just tell me where."

"Let's meet at the Starbucks on North Davis Road, it's right off 101. I can be there by twelve."

I hugged Heidi warmly when she entered the coffee shop. "Wow, haven't seen you in a long, long time," she said. "How are things? The D.A., right?"

"Right," I said. "Let's order."

We collected our beverages and found an empty table near the entrance. I spoke with grave intensity.

"Heidi, I'm helping out with the investigation of the murders. We have some ideas about who might be behind them."

Heidi, biting her lip, kept her unblinking gaze on mine.

I continued. "We're looking closely at the night Rocky died. I know Detective Bromley spoke with you, and you told him Jimmy was with you that evening."

Taking a deep breath, I gambled. "Heidi, I know Jimmy wasn't with you that evening."

Bingo. Heidi's eyes moistened and she trembled. "Jimmy didn't do it, Addie."

I reached across the table and grasped Heidi's hand. "It's very important that you tell me the truth. About where Jimmy was that night. If he wasn't with Rocky, or with you, I need to know where he was."

Heidi did not speak. She glanced nervously to her right and left, as if someone was watching her.

"Jimmy came to Bayside Towers looking for me the other day," I continued.

"I swore to him," Heidi broke in, wiping her eyes. "I swore to him, I gave him my word."

"What did you swear to him? What is it, Heidi?" I said, in as soothing a tone as I could manage.

"Jimmy made me promise I would back him up. He panicked, Addie. He didn't kill anyone. He just panicked. I don't want him to get into any trouble...but...murder is much worse," she stammered.

"Worse than what? Tell me, Heidi. Tell me what he did."

She inhaled deeply. "I'm only telling you this if it won't hurt him. He didn't have anything to do with any murders."

"I'm listening."

"So, Jimmy trades stocks, you know that. He has a bunch of investors, in his account, however that works. Other people's money, not just his own. He made some bad trades that first year, lost a lot of money right away. He needed to make up the losses. So he started talking to people."

"Inside information," I said.

"I guess. When we went public—my company, I mean, on the Nasdaq, Jimmy started to take an interest in my work. He'd call me, and we'd chat. I figured he was probably using what I was telling him to trade, but I didn't think it was such a big deal. We had been pretty friendly at school. I felt bad for him. I didn't realize the extent of what he was doing until very recently. Until he told me."

"Told you what?"

"So Jimmy had been down here, in Salinas, actually, the week before Rocky died. He said he was passing through, and wanted to catch up."

"But he was really just pumping you for confidential information," I said.

"Yes. And apparently, he was doing the same thing with Vineet, in Palo Alto, but it was much more serious."

"Cybergetic is also publicly traded," I said.

"Right," said Heidi. "And as opposed to me, Vineet had been in on it from the beginning. He had given Jimmy some money, so they could both profit on the tipped trades."

"So?"

"So Vineet gets cold feet. He doesn't want to play along anymore. But Jimmy needs more information. So..." Heidi paused, and took a long sip of her coffee, considering what to say next.

"So," she continued, "the night Rocky died, Jimmy was actually with Vineet, in Palo Alto. Strong-arming him."

"Strong-arming?"

"Jimmy went down to Palo Alto, and told Vineet that if he didn't keep giving Jimmy tips, Jimmy would anonymously rat on him. Inform Cybergetic's management that Vineet was profiting from company secrets." She sipped again.

"So what happened was," Heidi continued, "when your detective called him, Jimmy was caught off guard. He didn't want anyone to know he had been at Vineet's that night. He could've made up anything, I guess, but he just panicked, in the moment. He knee-jerked and said he'd been with me, since that had been true the week before, and he figured I could credibly vouch for him, instead of him just saying he was at home. It was the first excuse he thought of. Then he called me and Vineet to back up his story. I felt bad for him, I guess."

"You swear to me that's the truth?"

"I swear, Addie," said Heidi, laying her palm on her chest. "Jimmy didn't kill anyone."

Her imploring eyes fixed on mine for a prolonged moment. I stirred my latte.

"There's something else I need to tell you, though," Heidi said. She fidgeted with her phone nervously.

"Tyler came by yesterday," she said.

My hand shot to cover my mouth momentarily. "Tyler? You saw him? We've been looking all over for him."

"I know, that's why I'm telling you."

"Where did you see him?" I asked.

"Yesterday, out of the blue, Tyler called me. It was a number I didn't recognize. He sounded bad. He said he's in Salinas, he's on the run, he's laying low. Somebody's following him, he's not sure if it's the police, or whoever's going after people from our class. He sounded crazed, scared. He needed cash. I felt bad. I guess that's a recurring theme."

"You met him? You weren't afraid?"

"No, not afraid. Confused, I guess. He sounded so sincere. Helpless, almost." She held her cheek, shaking her head. "But I'm still here, right? It just didn't sound like he was dangerous. To be safe, though, I agreed to meet him in a public place, the big Walmart here in Salinas. And I gave him some cash, five hundred bucks. He was so grateful."

I pulled out the folded yellow paper from my wallet.

Briller, Heidi. DripLogix. Cornered Resource.

"He was right next to you. You're Cornered Resource," I said in a subdued voice.

"I don't understand what you're saying, Addie."

"Listen, Heidi, I don't want to frighten you. But you may be in danger. I need you to be extremely careful. And if Tyler contacts you again, call me immediately. OK?"

"Well, that's the thing," Heidi said slowly. "He wants to talk to *you.*"

"What?" I sat forward so clumsily that I rattled our table, startling the customers nearby.

"Tyler said he needs to see you. I messaged him, just before. I told him you were coming to see me. He told me to give you his new number. He wants to see you."

I stared at Heidi, with a mixture of anger and sympathy. *How could someone be so dumb?*

Heidi must have sensed my disbelief. "I'm sorry Addie," she pleaded. "I didn't know what you wanted to ask me. I don't know what's going on. I don't know who to trust or believe anymore."

"I'm not upset. This could actually be very helpful. I'm just telling you, please be careful."

"I will," Heidi said, and tilted her watch. "Oh, I've got to get back. I'm sending you Tyler's new number. I'll call you if I hear anything else."

Heidi picked up her phone and left the Starbucks, passing in front of Jake's parked car.

Ω

The Buick idled at the Starbucks entrance. Jake had parked facing the front window where I had been sitting with Heidi.

I hopped into the back seat, my skin tingling.

"How we doin'?" Jake greeted me. "All good?"

My phone buzzed. It was a message from Heidi, with a phone number, and the word *Tyler.*

"All good," I replied to Jake, smiling.

I had two missed calls from Pearson. I dialed her number.

"Just finished with Heidi," I said.

"Anything? Anything on Jimmy?" Pearson's voice was charged, frantic.

"Mike was right, Heidi was covering for Jimmy," I said. "Jimmy was with Vineet, not in Salinas, the night Rocky died. He was squeezing Vineet for inside information on Vineet's company. Didn't want anyone to find out, so Heidi covered for him. She'd been giving Jimmy tips about DripLogix as well."

"Dammit. Not what I was hoping for."

"Anything from Mallory?" I asked from Pearson's seat in the rear of the Buick.

"Nothing to work with," Pearson said. "He admitted to the affair with Cindy. She was trying to blackmail him. Wanted him to leave First Principles, move back to New York. But he maintained his innocence. Actually afraid he might be the next victim."

I re-examined Heidi's message. "Mike have any leads on Tyler?"

"No leads. Nothing."

Our conversation stalled.

"Dammit. Dammit, dammit," said Pearson. "I am running in circles. Dammit."

I did not say anything more.

"I have to go," said Pearson, and hung up.

She's lost it. She's going to pull a McClanahan, I told myself.

That was the last phone call I ever had with Special Agent Hope Pearson.

CHAPTER 27

"HEY, JAKE," I CALLED FROM the Buick's back seat.

"What's up? Too quiet? You want me to start talkin' again? *Ha-ha-ha.*"

"Sorry, I need a bio break. I should've gone, back at the Starbucks. Coffee's kicking in."

"No worries, no worries," Jake said, waving his hand. "Jake'll find you a little girl's room, straightaway."

He left 101 at the next exit and in a few minutes we were in front of another Starbucks.

"I'll be right out," I said, pocketing my phone.

"Take your time, take your time," Jake said.

I locked myself in the Starbucks' restroom. I breathed deeply and dialed the number Heidi had sent me.

After five rings, a hesitant voice answered.

"Hullo...?"

"Tyler?"

"That you, Addie?"

"Yes, it's me. Heidi gave me your number. Where are you?"

Tyler paused, for too long. "I can't tell you. I don't want to talk on the phone. I want to talk face to face. Just me and you."

"What's going on, Tyler?"

"I don't...can't talk right now, OK?" Muffled, unidentifiable noises echoed behind Tyler and he lowered his voice. "I'm not safe, OK? I know people are after me. I know you're...you're connected to the cops. I have...I have things I need to tell you."

"Tyler, is this your new number? Can I reach you on this number?"

"No. I don't know. I'm getting a new one. Listen, I need to go. I'm going to come up to San Rafael to see you. Only you. Only if you don't tell anyone else."

"Tyler, I can't promise."

"You need to promise me, Addie. Nobody else. Saturday. Just me and you. If you can't guarantee we'll be alone, I cancel. I'll message you with a time and place. Probably from a different number. I gotta go."

Our call cut off.

My heart was pounding. So was a fist on the door of the bathroom.

My thoughts raced.

Am I the seventh target? Cornered Resource? The police, the justice system? Derives power from a legal "monopoly" on enforcement? Could fit.

We could stage a sting, on Saturday. Mike and his guys would be positioned nearby. I would be the bait for Tyler. I could wear a recording device, or a buzzer to call for help. If the killer was Tyler. And if not, whatever he could tell me would likely be critically important.

My thoughts swirled and jelled into the skeleton of a plan, to protect myself for my meeting with Tyler and arrange for appropriate backup nearby.

More pounding. "Somebody drowning in there?" a voice shouted.

Jake would be getting suspicious. I unbolted the door and pushed past an angry cluster of cross-legged coffee drinkers.

Ω

"Everything OK?" Jake asked as I re-entered the Buick.

"Sorry about that. Long wait."

"Thought I might have to come in there and rescue you, know I'm sayin'? *Ha-ha-ha.*"

"You and Lucille would've made quite a scene, Jake." I laughed.

"Well anyhow, Addie, we got a slight change of plans. Your boss called."

She won't be my boss for much longer, I thought.

"What change?"

"She sounded real upset, I'm tellin' you. Known her for over twenty years, never heard her like this, know I'm sayin'? She says we're goin' to First Principles College. Some kinda gathering or something."

"A gathering? At First Principles? Are you sure?" I asked, sitting forward.

"As sure as sure can be. First Principles College. Euclid Hall?"

I called Mike.

"Mike, what's going on?"

"Can't talk, Addie, I gotta make all these calls for Pearson."

"Just tell me what's going on," I insisted.

"Don't know. All I know is, she's getting everyone together at First Principles. She's making an announcement. She sounds like crap."

"Who's 'everyone'?"

"I don't know. That's just what she said, 'everyone.' I'm calling the class list. The Mallory class."

I glanced at Jake's face in the rearview. He was glaring at a lineup of brake lights ahead.

"Pulling a McClanahan?" I asked Mike.

"Could be," he said. "I guess we'll find out soon enough. Gotta go and make these calls." He hung up.

"Traffic," announced Jake, as we slowed to a crawl on 101. "Hate this road."

Ω

Danny. Danny, bless your soul. You were right.

Pearson was going to step down. She would do it with her me-first attitude. Always about her. Her reputation. Her record. That's what it was.

Failing to solve the case would tarnish her pristine reputation. Hurt book sales. *The Detective Who Couldn't Solve the First Principles Case.* So she would abandon ship, just before it was too late, before the killer finished his work.

And she would hand that mess off, publicly. To me. The thorn in her side. To the annoying little snot, who thought she could show up the mighty Hope Pearson. *You think you know how to do this job? You take it. And you take the blame.*

Hope Pearson's cool, solemn exterior merely hid the wild child, the insecure misfit desperate for the fatherly adoration she would never receive. What drove her was not justice, was not service of the public. What drove her was a ravenous desire to transcend her ineradicable insecurity.

Everyone would forget that Special Agent Hope Pearson had been involved. They would just remember that when the curtain closed, it had closed on Addison Morita.

But Pearson did not know what I knew. She did not know that I had found Tyler Lukela, finally. And I sure as hell was not going to tell her now.

Ω

We inched north along 101. "What time do we have to be at First Principles?" I asked Jake over his shoulder.

"She said five. We got time, still. We're good. You want the radio?" He reached for the dial.

"No, that's OK," I said.

I jotted notes on the back of the folded yellow paper from my wallet.

Cornered Resource
- *Perry*
- *Addie*
- *Heidi*
Thursday - Mike & Sheriff Davis
      - sting op for Saturday
      - surveillance plan for Perry & Addie @ Bayside

Bayside, I thought. *I shouldn't be living at Bayside Towers anymore. I should have moved in with Danny.*

I began to weep. Jake noticed.

"Hey, everything OK back there?"

I wiped my nose with my hand.

"I'm...I'm sorry, Jake. Don't mind me. Just this...this stupid case. I've lost people close to me. Takes its toll."

"Don't need to tell me." He waved his hand. "Been there. Lost a few friends, back in the day. Warriors. One right by my side. Yup, you never forget, know I'm sayin'? Hope's been there too, don't know if she told you, she's been there too. Part of the business, know I'm sayin'? Part of the business." He shook his head sadly.

"I know, I know," I said. "I need to focus. Not dwell on the past. Just focus. Don't mean to bring you down with me, Jake."

"Ain't nothin' gonna bring old Jake down. Part of the business, know I'm sayin'? You focus. That's right. It's what you gotta do."

I gazed out the window for what seemed like hours, from Pearson's seat in the back of the Buick. Twenty-five years old, and about to take over a major homicide case, the case even Hope Pearson couldn't solve. For the rest of the ride to First Principles, I concentrated my thoughts on plans for the coming days, chasing away the creeping anxiety.

Ω

"Euclid Hall? She said you'd know where that is," Jake said, as we pulled into the First Principles parking lot.

"It's in the main building. I'll show you."

My heart sagged as we passed Danny's empty parking spot. *Reserved - Chief of Staff.* I stifled a groan.

We got out of the Buick and I directed Jake toward the Descartes Building. I hurried to keep pace with his long, lumbering gait to the main doors.

Descartes' lobby was empty, guarded by the ring of giant palm trees. "Wednesday evening in June, nobody around," I commented to Jake.

I pressed the elevator button, and Jake bent down to my altitude. "Now, don't get lost, hear? I'm not gonna sit on top of you, but stay close. Strict orders."

"Got it," I said, and we ascended to the sixth floor.

A number of my former classmates were already spread out along the elevated corridor. Some bunched together in small groups, while others stood alone. The stillness of the building caused even the quietest conversational echoes to reverberate throughout the atrium.

Another elevator door opened and Mike stepped out. I waved to catch his attention and he strolled over to where Jake and I stood.

"Jake Patterson, this is Detective Bromley," I said.

"Call me Mike." Mike extended his arm to Jake, who enveloped Mike's hand in his.

Mike surveyed the scattered clusters lining the curved parapet, and checked his watch. "Good, almost everybody's here."

"Are you thinking what I'm thinking?" I asked Mike softly, trying to hide my intention from Jake.

"Don't know. I really don't know," said Mike.

CHAPTER 28

DOUG MALLORY, BUSINESS STRATEGY SEMINAR, Lecture 15 –
Counter-positioning

"...Think of Counter-positioning as a corollary of Switching Cost. In Switching Cost, your customer has developed an addiction to your product, which makes it hard for them to switch to your competitor's product. In Counter-positioning, your competitor, the incumbent, is addicted to a business model, which prevents them from switching gears and doing things your new way. It's very, very rare for an incumbent to kick the addiction of an entrenched habit or method..."

Ω

I stood next to Mike and Jake, rather than joining my former classmates. For four years we had mingled in these hallways. I had studied with them, partied with them, and competed against them. But now, they stood on the other side of an invisible divider. They gathered like a flock of sheep, like bewildered extras mixed up in someone else's drama.

They had all but forgotten about me since graduation. *You still at the D.A.?* It was almost a pejorative. Soon, they would be rooting for me, hoping that I could rescue them from the hell of the past few weeks. How fortunes turn.

Everything is Saiou's horse.

"Where's Pearson?" I asked Mike.

He was leaning against the balcony railing, his back to the open atrium below, arms folded. Jake stood about ten feet away, giving us privacy.

"No clue. Haven't seen her all day," Mike said.

"Did you have any idea, when we first met at the D.A.'s office a few weeks ago, that things would turn out like this?" I asked him.

"Definitely not. Never seen anything like this. A lot stranger than chasing kids for breaking windows, tell you that." He exhaled loudly, then his eyes lit up. "Hey, I got into social work school. M.S.W. program. Just found out this morning."

"No way," I said.

"*Yup*, San Jose State."

"Pearson's alma mater," I said.

To my right, Jake put his phone to his ear. He listened intently, then strode a few giant paces to the doorway to Euclid Hall.

"Ladies and gentlemen!" Jake's booming voice bounced throughout the cavernous building, and all the chatter suddenly ceased. "May I have your attention, please. Special Agent Pearson will be here in a few minutes. Can y'all please line up in an orderly fashion for a brief security check, and then proceed into the hall."

Jake stepped to the side of the open door into Euclid Hall, and motioned for the people standing closest to him to approach.

"That's right, line up here. Just a quick security check. That's right, one after the other."

Mike and I approached and stood at Jake's side. The first people in line were Perry, Victor and Elyse.

Jake spoke loudly as he checked Perry, then Victor. "That's right, just a quick pat-down. Nothing to worry about. That's right. Arms up, thank you."

Jake ran his hands over the arms, torso and thighs of Perry and Victor.

"Sorry ma'am. No female assist today," Jake said to a horrified Elyse. "I'll be gentle, don't worry, happily married with five kids. *Ha-ha-ha.*"

Jake ran his palms as lightly as possible over Elyse's limbs as she held her mouth agape, staring at me. The mood among the dozen or so still in the hallway had shifted dramatically. As they fell into line outside the Euclid Hall door, nobody uttered a word.

Brian and Malcolm passed through Jake's quick pat-down, and there was a brief gap in the line. I ducked past Jake toward the open doorway.

"*Whup*, one sec, honey," said Jake, holding his arm across the doorway. "Arms out."

I raised my eyebrows, and Jake winked. "Everybody. No exceptions," he said, and patted my arms and pockets quickly. "Go ahead, *hon,*" he said.

The intimate amphitheater seated about fifty people. Though the hall was over six years old, it was as pristine as when we had been students at the college. A stage and podium faced four ascending semi-circular rows of plush purple upholstered seating. Varnished light-brown parquet flooring matched the desktops and paneled walls.

Those already inside had spread out, and I chose a seat in the highest of the four rows, at the edge closest to the front wall. As the others entered, nobody sat too close to me. It seemed they implicitly understood that I belonged to a different team.

On the far end of my row, across the room, sat Andy Freel, next to Alex Andreyev. *Interesting that she wanted both of them here,* I thought. Caroline and Janet had come over from Union City. The Amazon girls had not traveled from Seattle on such short notice, and neither had Heidi or Shanice. And, of course, Tyler was absent. But at a quick glance, all the other Californians appeared to be present.

And Doug Mallory, accustomed to commanding the podium, sat in the first row. It was the closest he could get, as he was for the first time not in charge of a session in Euclid Hall.

The room was eerily still. Everyone present seemed to sense that something significant was about to happen, but nobody other than me, and perhaps Mike, had any premonition of what might follow. People shifted nervously in their seats, and exchanged furtive glances. Jimmy muttered something inaudible and laughed sarcastically at his own remark.

Jake, standing in the doorway, cleared his throat loudly. At once, everyone whirled around. And Special Agent Hope Pearson, in her trademark black cardigan, black slacks, and a lavender top, entered the room. Slowly, methodically, her eyelids lowered, she descended the stairs toward the podium.

CHAPTER 29

DOUG MALLORY, BUSINESS STRATEGY SEMINAR — Final Lecture

"...*As we conclude our study of 7* Powers, *and as you prepare for your careers in the innovation economy, it's critical that I stress one final, fundamental point that Helmer makes, but I think requires greater emphasis. These powers, these seven fundamental strategies for ensuring long-term dominance, only work if the company has already created something unique. Innovation, creativity, that's what gets you into the game. These seven powers can only help you win if you have innovated your way into the race, if you have started off with a strong, creative foundation, some unique perspective or insight into what's broken in the world, and how to fix it. Everything starts with creativity and innovation, only then do the seven powers become relevant."*

Ω

Sometimes, there are moments like these, when your life's trajectory changes in an instant.

Pearson reached the bottom-most step at the amphitheater's base, then angled to her left rather than stepping up to the podium, as if in a trance. Almost everyone had reflexively stood when she entered, the way a courtroom gallery stands for the judge, and they now rustled back into their seats.

Pearson held a folio in one hand. She stood directly in front of the barrier separating her from the first row of seats. Mallory, immediately opposite her, shuffled one seat to his right with magnetic repulsion.

Pearson slouched, with spent shoulders and sunken eyes. From my elevated vantage point in the fourth row she appeared destroyed, like an old fishing boat battered by a tempest sea and wrecked with shattered hull and scattered nets onto a rocky shore. A whiff of miasma whispered to me from within the ionized air, a faint hum of decay, and defeat.

Pearson forced words from her mouth in a low monotone. "For those of you who do not know me, I am Special Agent Hope Pearson, of the California Department of Justice. Until today, I have been leading the investigation of the deaths of Robert Violetto, Indigo Murray, Peter Greene, Cindy Caldwell, Tiffany Chen and Danny Armstrong."

Until today. There it is.

"Everything began here, in this room, and at least for me, will end here. You learned here that in your world, failure is normal. Only those who harness at least one of a handful of elemental strategies, survive.

"In my world, however, failure is not normal. I do not accept failure. My method, my strategy, has worked for me, up to now. This time, I chose the wrong strategy. I relied on assumptions that were incorrect."

Say it, say it.

"I have never had a case like this one. From the day I took over the investigation, one month ago, until today, it has been a battle, at times with unseen forces, and at times with myself, and I have lost these battles."

So you're stepping down. Say it.

I rubbed my thighs as if warming up for a run.

Like a weary, failed prophet unable to stave off a wrathful plague, Pearson continued. "Innocent people have died on my watch, and while that comes with the territory, their ghosts will haunt me."

Elyse sniffled loudly, and dabbed a tissue at her eyes.

"Some of the deceased were at one time suspects. At first it seemed Peter Greene might have pushed Rocky from the balcony. Cindy Caldwell had her share of troubles." Pearson glowered at Mallory, who studied his shoes.

"I regret that I suspected those who became innocent victims themselves. And a number of you here today have been suspects, given your behavior. Everybody hid something, which made this investigation impossibly difficult."

Jimmy suddenly called out. "Where's Tyler? That would help."

All eyes were on Jimmy as he smirked. My pulse quickened.

Ignoring Jimmy's outburst, Pearson continued.

"I am always focused on evidence. Facts. But the killer has been incredibly devious. In almost all of the deaths, there was virtually no usable physical evidence. In most instances we could not even pinpoint the specific time when the killer had made contact with the victim. I kept coming back to Rocky, where at least we had a time of contact. But even then we were stonewalled by false alibis, obfuscation, and lack of other clues."

Alex Andreyev leaned over and whispered something to Andy Freel, who nodded.

"As some of you may know," Pearson said, "the killer has made references to a book you studied, here in this room with Professor Mallory. Hamilton Helmer's *7 Powers.*" Pearson stepped back and withdrew a copy of *7 Powers* from the folio she held.

"I quote to you from Helmer's introduction:

The arc of any celebrated business is underpinned by decisive strategy choices, that are few and typically made amidst the profound uncertainty of rapid change. Get these crux choices wrong, and you face a future of persistent pain, or even outright failure."

Pearson raised her eyes from the folded page. "Amidst the profound uncertainty of rapid change, I got certain crux choices very wrong. Helmer continues,

...you must constantly attune your strategy to unfolding circumstances."

She snapped the book shut. "So I have to publicly admit, that as the leader of this investigation, until today my approach was unsuccessful. I fell prey to my assumptions. I did not adjust my strategy to the changing circumstances, to the absence of factual evidence. Perhaps I should have focused earlier on motive, or potential targets. But now, unfortunately, it is too late to change what is already done."

Say it. Say it. From today, Addison Morita will be leading the investigation. I leaned forward.

"So, I have gathered you here, to announce..."

Say it, say it.

"That I have discovered the identity of the murderer."

A collective gasp rose from the assemblage. My body tremored as if someone had jammed my fingers into an electrical socket.

There had been no change in Pearson's countenance, no jubilation, no fist raised in victory, not even the hint of a smile. Just the same, solemn, mournful, frozen stare.

Andy, his arms folded, sneered, "You're bluffing." A murmur reverberated through the room.

Pearson lifted her hand. "Settle down, please. I can assure you that I know who the killer is. Do not doubt me."

She raised her copy of *7 Powers* again. "Pasteur's famous line, 'Chance only favors the prepared mind.' Helmer quotes that, in his introduction. Just as I was about to give up, just as I had lost all hope, a piece of information came to light that turned the case around. I was fortunate enough, or prepared enough, to identify it."

Andy cupped his hand and covered his mouth as he leaned toward Andreyev. Jimmy chortled. Mallory's face was pale.

"In fact," Pearson said, addressing Andy, "not only do I know who the murderer is, but the murderer is right here. In this room."

Euclid Hall erupted into a melee of shouts and shrieks, people springing up, or slumping, or stiffened in abject horror.

"Silence." Pearson raised her hands, and her voice rose as she addressed the room like Moses at Sinai. "Listen to me carefully. Here is what is going to happen. At nine o'clock tomorrow morning, a file with all of the evidence, which I assure you is conclusive, will be handed to District Attorney Schmidt. The perpetrator of these crimes will be arrested shortly afterward. You will note that the District Attorney is not here this evening. If the person who committed the crimes would like to step forward now and admit their guilt, they may do so."

A chilly silence descended over the room. Eyes darted right and left.

Pearson softened her tone and scanned the room. "I would like to take this opportunity to thank all of you for coming this evening. I would also like to recognize Detective Bromley and Investigator Morita, who played important roles in this investigation. I can assure you that there is no more danger. You are all free to go. Good night, and Godspeed."

Nobody moved at first. Then Jimmy stood up and proclaimed, "What a fucking circus." He brushed past Elyse and Perry on his way out of their row, toward the door where Jake stepped aside to let him pass. Gradually, and without much conversation, Mallory, Andy Freel, Alex Andreyev, and the former members of Mallory's senior seminar filtered out of Euclid Hall. Mike, at the rear, glanced back at me and Pearson as he stepped through the threshold, toward a career in social work.

Ω

Pearson slowly climbed the steps toward me. She seemed beaten, rather than buoyant.

"I have so many questions, Agent Pearson."

She stood in the aisle, next to where I had remained. "I'm sure you do, Addie. I thought I told you to call me Hope."

"OK, Hope. Explain to me, how is it possible? How could things turn around so fast? Just yesterday, you were ready to give up."

"Well, Addie, you thought you knew something I did not know. I found out something you do not know, obviously. We play our games, right?"

I laughed. "Oh, games, exactly. Surely you're bluffing. Tyler's not even here."

"That is because Tyler is not the murderer."

Those eyes. Those goddamn eyes.

Pearson blinked at me. "May I sit?" She perched on the lower row of seats, swiveling back to face me. She motioned to Jake who still stood in the doorway. *One minute*, she mouthed to him.

"Sorry, I'm not buying it," I said. "Andy was right, you're bluffing. It's a last-minute ploy. To try to scare the killer into coming forward on his own."

"I am not bluffing."

"Then if you know who the killer is, why not arrest him here, now? He might get away. Why wait?"

Pearson smiled for the first time. "I have my reasons. One, I need a new manicure. I assume there will be lots of TV time tomorrow, and I did not have time to get one today. Things were too hectic. I have an appointment at my salon, tomorrow at eight." She examined her nails. "I am thinking...ivory. Or perhaps red."

"Not a time for joking, is it?"

"Oh, not joking. I will need to look my best for the cameras. But yes, there are other reasons to wait until tomorrow."

"I think the least you could do is tell me who it was. I mean, I know you don't like me very much, but at least the courtesy, you know. For the work I did."

Pearson nodded. "Yes, of course. That would be the least I could do."

Pearson glanced at Jake again, and shifted into a more comfortable position. "I kept focusing on facts, but there were so few facts. You kept harping on motive. Focus on motive, not just facts, you said." Pearson's smile widened slightly. "We were both right. Even the smallest piece of evidence can turn a case. And you reminded me that even the slightest motive can turn someone into a monster. Sometimes the killer is the damn gardener. Either way, I always say, the key is usually hiding in plain sight, right in front of you. So there it was, right in front of me, the whole time."

I rolled my eyes. "Don't keep me in suspense, Hope. Who is it?"

Pearson's wide smile gleamed.

"Why, Addie. Of course, it's you."

CHAPTER 30

"THAT SOUNDS HILARIOUS," I CHUCKLED. "But I don't get the joke."

"I am not joking," Pearson deadpanned.

"Seriously," I said with a dismissive laugh.

"Deadly serious."

My eyebrows rose. "Well then," I snorted, "you'd better have some strong evidence to back up such a preposterous claim."

Pearson tilted to her right and crossed her legs. "Leave evidence aside for a moment. You liked to tell me to focus on motive. So let us look at motive, first.

"As I said, even the slightest motive can turn someone into a monster. We have a young woman who is the product of a troubled and traumatic childhood. A very frustrated social servant. Dead-end job. Going nowhere while all of her friends are rocketing forward, each in his or her wonderful career. A career that she could have easily had.

"She has received bad advice. Her flimsy ideals, cultivated over four years, have survived about a half hour in the real world. But all is not lost. Perhaps she can become a successful writer. That does not work out either. Her first novel gets rejected. She needs a great story, something that can carry her next book, and turn her life around."

"*Ha*, I see where you're going with this. It's completely ridiculous," I said.

"Allow me to continue, please? I have had to sit through a number of your lectures, have I not? So, our heroine decides to kill two birds with one stone. Or, seven birds, if you wish. The greatest murder mystery in California history meets one of the most important business strategy books of all time. People will buy her novel in droves, place Helmer's *7 Powers* beside it, cross-reference, discuss, analyze, surmise. A guaranteed best-seller.

"And then, an unexpected gift. Hope Pearson herself is assigned to the case. The story becomes even more compelling. The mystery even Stella Westcott could not solve."

Pearson paused briefly. "I wonder, in fact, who was victim number seven meant to be? What's left — Cornered Resource? I first thought it might be Mallory. That would have been elegant. Five students, then the T.A., then the master himself. Or, could it have been me, once I entered the picture? Am I Cornered Resource? The personal embodiment of an inimitable skill, a unique capability? Not only does Stella Westcott fail to solve the case, she becomes the final victim. A true *coup de grace*. A must-read."

"This is all...total speculation!" I spat out the words.

"I am not speculating, Addie. It is an excellent book. I have already read it."

"I don't know what you mean," I said.

"Of course you know what I mean. Your manuscript. About this investigation. Very well done, so far. And helpful."

I could not find my voice. Finally I stammered, "Where'd you get my manuscript?"

"Why, the drawer. In your desk, at Bayside Towers. With all the other manuscripts." She blinked again.

"You have no right to go through my belongings," I snarled.

"Judge said otherwise," said Pearson. "Once we presented her with the evidence. Shall I tell you about that?"

My mouth was suddenly dry.

"The truth is," Pearson continued, "I was absolutely baffled. I really was. Even up to yesterday, when we were at your desk and told you about Danny. That was not an act. I had no handle on this case. Until you slipped. After that, it was definitely an act, since yesterday. A good one, if I may say so myself."

I wanted to speak, but could not.

"The turning point was the sixth email, about Danny. The one about the fly in the ointment? Two things. First, all the other emails were sent to you after the TBT group found out the victim had died. But you got sloppy. When Mike and I came to your desk to tell you about Danny, we had just received the call from Mallory. Only we, and Mallory, knew. And you already had received the email on your phone.

"So OK, perhaps the killer anticipated Danny's death, and jumped the gun. Or, maybe it was Mallory. But then you held up your phone to Mike, to show him the email on the screen."

Pearson licked her lips.

"I notice everything, Addie. Allow me to pause for a moment, and go back to The Last Dance. I cannot say that I suspected you then. But I have very sharp instincts. Something was not right about you. I needed to get to know you better."

She chortled. "Though I fed that dead geranium two more beers while you were in the restroom, I did not find anything from our conversation useful, at the time."

Pearson tapped her temple. "But everything goes in here. Into the files. I noticed we had matching iPhones. Yours had that nice turquoise case."

"So?" I gulped.

"So, the phone you showed Mike, at your desk, with the sixth email. It was shiny, thin...and black. I grabbed it from him. I turned it over in my hand. It was a cheap Samsung. That was odd."

Pearson pantomimed a thinking motion. "Was it possible you had two phones? A burner phone? That you had sent the emails all along, not some anonymous murderer?"

I glowered at Pearson with a quivering frown.

"So I moved quickly," she continued. "Sent a message to Mike, to inspect the phone as soon as we got up. Placed the phone on your desk and grabbed your hand, and pulled you into the conference room. While I pretended to be upset and confused about the investigation, Mike messaged back. The killer's Gmail account, and your personal account, were both on the Samsung. Well, I *was* still upset. Just not confused anymore."

Pearson uncrossed her legs. "After that it was fairly simple. We needed to get you out of town and get into your apartment, so I sent you down to Salinas with an armed escort. Just to be on the safe side." She motioned to Jake again, with one finger raised.

"We found plenty of goodies in your apartment. Your duffel bag for Danny's still packed. Nice touch. More important was the half-empty jug of antifreeze. Why does a girl who rides an electric scooter have a half-empty jug of antifreeze, in the middle of the summer in California? Oh, plus the vials of fentanyl in your closet. And the manuscript of course."

The blood drained from my face.

"The manuscript actually helped complete the puzzle. Quite well-written. See, I was sincere when I told you that I would be willing to review your work. Spent most of this afternoon reading it. Your roommate is right, your style lacks some sentiment but I find that understandable under the circumstances. Your attention to detail, however, was extremely beneficial.

"Go back to that first night, Rocky's death. You wrote that Elyse was asleep from the wine you had given her. You were only one floor below Rocky's apartment. Rocky liked pretty girls, knew you well, had been drinking with Peter. Not hard to get in quickly, sweet-talk him onto the balcony, and take him by surprise. An orange belt in judo could get enough leverage. Get back down to Elyse's, legs a bit sore from the sudden effort, and wake her when the police cars come.

"There were other details. The BYOB to Peter's house for the memorial, a great way to plant a drink laced with antifreeze into his fridge. Cindy's backyard was just off your Saturday running route along the bay. Your *butterkuchen* baking skills came in handy when you needed to pass Tiffany's chocolates off as professional quality.

"And then Danny. Poor Danny. I bet he really did love you, or at least his false image of you. Did you love him? Are you capable of love? We will never know. But we know that when you tossed him the energy drink after your run, you knew you would never see him again."

Pearson exhaled. "Never, never seen anything like it."

My calm in the face of Pearson's allegations surprised me. As she had been speaking, my heart rate had slowed and moisture had returned to my mouth.

"So then why not just arrest me now. If you're so sure?"

Pearson grinned. "First of all, professional courtesy, perhaps. The manuscript. A good story. Take the next few hours, fix it up, finish it. You are almost done."

Pearson studied her nails. "Yes, definitely going with the red. I have the perfect top to match."

Pearson stood up. "Also, Addie, you have no way out. In fact, you could say that you are a Cornered Resource, could you not? Funny how things work out."

She stepped away from me, then turned back.

Her eyes locked with mine, for the last time. That chameleon face. Those estranged, amber eyes.

"Jake will take you home. Carly has been moved to a safe location. You will be under tight surveillance until tomorrow morning. The District Attorney will not be interested in a deal after the nightmare you put us through. The trial will be a spectacle, and costly, and embarrassing, not just for you but for others.

"So, I have given you a few more hours. My suggestion? Save yourself, and the State of California, the trouble. Finish the manuscript tonight, print it out. Pour a tall glass of antifreeze and watch the sunrise. Then, drink down the glass, and at the end of the manuscript, in big block letters, write: I DID IT."

Pearson turned, and trudged past Jake through the Euclid Hall doorway.

I sat completely still in the emptied auditorium, like an insect trapped in amber resin. Solitary. Alone. Once again, as always, the one left behind.

At least the story would live on.

The more I considered it, Pearson's suggestion seemed the logical thing to do.

So—

I DID IT.

Acknowledgements

"No one who achieves success does so without the help of others. The wise and confident acknowledge this help with gratitude." - Alfred North Whitehead

I am extremely grateful for the inspiration, encouragement and assistance I've received in creating this book.

Hamilton Helmer gave the business world a great gift with *7 Powers*, and I believe his significant insights into business strategy warrant wider exposure. Hamilton neither assisted in this book's writing nor endorsed its content. But I am very grateful to him for his good wishes when I told him about my plans to publish this book, and for helping me become a smarter investor through his work. I hope my book will cause many new readers to pick up Helmer's *7 Powers*.

I am thankful to my wife, Shafrira, for first tolerating then encouraging my foray into writing. Any creative process has moments of uncertainty and self-doubt, and she has always been there to support me.

My children and now grandchildren inspire and delight me. And no, just because there are a few profanities in this book, doesn't mean you guys can now say them around the house. To paraphrase Kurt Vonnegut, a few bad characters ended up in my books, and they use bad words.

I am my parents' son, and they deserve much of the credit (or blame?) for my creative drive, sense of humor, and general love of books.

Novel writing requires knowledge of both structure and technique. I have collected insights and guidance from countless sources, but I primarily gleaned whatever technical skill I have from the following important books: *Stein on Writing* by Sol Stein, *Consider This* by Chuck Palahniuk, *On Writing* by Stephen King, *Pity the Reader* by Kurt Vonnegut and Suzanne McConnell, *The Hero With a Thousand Faces* by Joseph Campbell, *Save the Cat!* by Blake Snyder, and *The Science of Storytelling* by Will Storr. I am grateful to these authors for sharing their knowledge and wisdom.

Huge thanks to those who helped me turn a rickety first draft into this book. Thanks to Rina Sussman and Michelle Krueger who reviewed earlier drafts, and to Tom Howey for the clever cover design. And I am deeply indebted to my editor, Ann Bridges, a kindred business fiction author herself, who not only skillfully edited the manuscript but guided me through the entire publication process.

Diversity is a significant problem in the tech world. I am proud to have invested in many startups led by amazing, dynamic women. Proceeds from the sale of this book will support FemForward, a multicultural nonprofit initiative that supports and promotes women in tech. I am honored to be an advisor and supporter and I wish to acknowledge their important work.

Finally, dear reader, thank you for dedicating some of your valuable time to reading this book. I hope you found it enlightening and entertaining. If you enjoyed *Murder at First Principles*, please recommend it to a friend and take a moment to review it on your favorite online platform. I will be forever grateful.

BEN WIENER

About the Author

Ben Wiener is the founder and Managing Partner of Jumpspeed Ventures, an early-stage venture capital fund. In addition to *Murder at First Principles,* Ben has published a number of short fictional stories and essays, and his second full-length novel, *Fever Pitch,* will be published in late 2021.

Ben graduated with honors from Columbia Law School and he clerked on Israel's Supreme Court before embarking on a career in startup entrepreneurship and investment. He grew up in Allentown, Pennsylvania, and currently lives, invests, runs, reads and writes in Jerusalem, Israel.

Ben Wiener's forthcoming thriller, *Fever Pitch,* explores the secret to the "perfect pitch" as one startup founder struggles to save his company, his family...and his life. For pre-ordering, and to learn more about Ben Wiener's books and writing, visit:

www.benwiener.net

Made in the USA
Middletown, DE
26 June 2021

43169443R00168